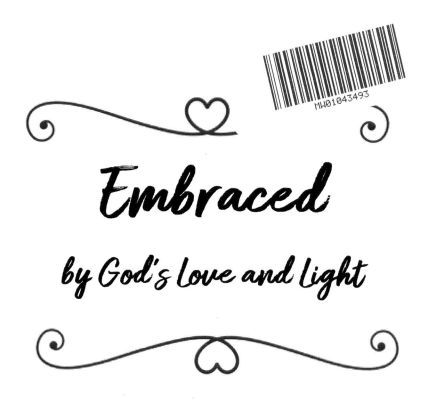

Embraced

by God's Love and Light

Read many surprising stories,
of those who have shared
how they found God's love and light
through their unique experiences with Him!

Suzanne Wilkinson

Embraced by God's Love and Light – Unique Personal Experiences with God

Ebook ISBN: 978-1-964451-65-7
Paperback ISBN: 978-1-964451-66-4
Hardback ISBN: 978-1-964451-67-1

Printed in the U.S. and Canada

First Edition – 2024

(1). Inspirational – Religious aspect - Christianity, (2). Devotional, (3) Christian life, (4). Christian literature, - Christian Authors (English) (5) Collaborator/Author – Rev. Suzanne Wilkinson

Cover design and interior layout by Rev. Suzanne Wilkinson.

Table of Contents

This book is dedicated to my family,

near and far.

May their souls grow heartily,

And their spirits soar with fruitful joy,

and may they find true hope in the

living God through His Son Jesus Christ.

Life is so tender, so fragile, so precious.
We can hold fast to Him! May
He bless you & yours always.

Give thanks to the Lord for he is good. His love endures forever.
(Psalm 136:1 NIV)

Acknowledgement and Dedication

Embraced by God's: Love and Light would not have come into being without the combined effort of a team of willing volunteers who have written about their experiences with our awesome, almighty God – the great "I Am."

The following personal true-life experiences are from people who have willingly told me of or submitted their experiences to me. With their permission, these stories have become part of this book. It can be challenging to get behind a project that deals with the unexplained, often personal experiences and unique coincidences of life.

In humility, I have asked for these remarkable stories from many people, and this book is their response. Each story written here is printed with the permission and blessing of the storyteller.

To all who have shared their God whispers, sensed God's presence, answers to their prayers for healing or protection, and have experienced unique coincidences or spiritual encounters with God, I genuinely thank you. I applaud you and send each one of you my heartfelt gratitude.

The goal of this book is to acknowledge and thank our Triune God for His presence in our daily lives. The writings of those who have shared their walk with God flow with hope, inspiration, encouragement, gratitude, joy, peace, and praise.

I especially and sincerely thank Scott Wilkinson for his prayer support and editing skills, which have been a genuine help and encouragement. Words are inadequate to express my thanks to him and to all the contributors who have sent me their stories.

I dedicate this book to my family and those willing to share their God encounters, answers to prayers, and the sensing of God's holy presence.

God is not dead but continues to work through His followers to heal, provide, protect, comfort, and offer divine guidance and hope in many unique and diverse ways. Each story is a precious treasure, as through it, you will be *Embraced by God's Love and Light.*

Take Time to Hear the Good Shepherd's Voice

May we be careful as we listen for Jesus' voice and avoid foolishly dismissing it, for the fundamental truth remains: The Shepherd speaks clearly, and His sheep hear His voice. Perhaps His words come through a verse of Scripture, the words of a believing friend, or the nudge of the Holy Spirit. Our triune God speaks today! Many have heard or known Him through experiences. Some of their stories are recorded here.

"My sheep hear my voice, and I know them, and they follow me: And I give unto them eternal life; and they shall never perish, neither shall any man. **(John 10:27-28 KJV).**

"But if we walk in the light, as he is in the light, we have fellowship with one another, and the blood of Jesus his Son cleanses us from all sin." **(1 John 1:7 NIV)**

The LORD is my shepherd, I lack nothing.
He makes me lie down in green pastures,
He leads me beside quiet waters, he refreshes my soul.
He guides me along the right path for his name's sake.
Even though I walk through the darkest valley,
I will fear no evil, for you are with me;
your rod and your staff, they comfort me.
You prepare a table before me, in the presence of my enemies.
You anoint my head with oil; my cup overflows.
Surely your goodness and love will follow me all the days of my life, and I will dwell in the house of the LORD forever.
Psalm 23 - A psalm of David. (NRSV)

Psalm 71:15-18 conveys the importance of communicating the wonderful ways God works. Embraced by God's Love and Light attempts to do this through the lives of many who. I celebrate them and thank them, for without their contributions, this book could not exist.

Contributors

"Therefore, since we are surrounded by such a great cloud of witnesses, let us throw off everything that hinders and the sin that so easily entangles." **(Hebrews 12:1a, NIV).** When the writer of Hebrews talks about "a great cloud of witnesses," he is likely referring to all those who lived by faith and died in their faith. Having "a great cloud of witnesses" means we have many examples of people past and present who have lived by faith. Their faith inspires and encourages us and deepens our faith. By the telling of these encounters may we be encouraged and moulded more into the likeness of Christ.

Within this treasured edition, many contributors have written their stories. I have received what they shared and have tried to capture the importance and spirit of their story. In doing so, I have endeavoured to assist with writing their encounters. I consider this involvement an incredible privilege and am deeply grateful to each storyteller.

Andrea Kidd	Janey Bordihn
Anna Reesor	Janine Maxwell
Barbara Ribble	Jennifer Chapin
Brandon Kong	Jim and Charlene Mason
Carole Clyne	Jim Paterson
Carol Ford	Jim Thomas
Christine Kenel Peters	Jonanne Fenton
David Branon	Judith Alexander
Donna Smith	Kathy Ailles
Dr. Melissa Isada	Karen Pascal
Dr. Maria Kon	Lorraine Beech
Esther Barnes	Magda Wills
Esther Phillips	Margaret Russell
Gary and Janie Brooks,	Marianne Still
Grant Moller	Mary George
Heather Mackey	Mary Johnson
James Peters	Mary McMullen

Maureen Coles   Rev. John Torrance – *194*
Milton Fletcher   Rev. Suzanne Wilkinson
Muriel Rosenberger   Rev. Neil Miller
Nancy Parratt   Richard Doust
Ochelle Baller *(190)*   Roslyn Farmer
Rachel Bernard   Ruth Adams *(67; 196)*
Rev. Barbara Fuller   Ruth Vallis
Rev. Dr. James Clubine   Sarah Miller
Rev. Freda MacDonald   Scott Wilkinson
Rev. Joan Masterton   Wilma Medley

Introduction

The words "*handiwork,*" "workmanship," or "masterpiece" are what we are in the hands of God. "***For we are God's handiwork, created in Christ Jesus to do good works, which God prepared in advance for us to do.***" **(Ephesians 2:10, NIV)**. God is the Divine Master Artist over His creation. He has created us as works of His creation. The art [of us] is already there in the eyes of God. He alone knows our potential. The job of the Divine Artist (sculptor or potter) is to bring out the beauty, the goodness, and the joy of His creation in us. "***Yet you, Lord, are our Father. We are the clay; you are the potter; we are all the work of your hand.***" **(Isaiah 64:8, NIV)**.

God is actively creating, transforming, and restoring us into His unique masterpieces: "***God, who is rich in mercy, made us alive***" **(Ephesians 2:.4-5)**. As we experience the 'ups and downs' of life, we find joy in knowing the Divine Artist is at work, actively shaping our lives as we yield to Him: "***for it is God who works in you to will and to act in order to fulfill his good purpose***" **(Philippians 2:13)**

In John 10:27, we read, "***My sheep listen to my voice; I know them, and they follow me.***" As we take the time to listen to our Shepherd's voice, we will become what our Heavenly Creator wishes us to be. Listen and discern the voice of God, whether by a nudge, a whisper, through a coincidence, a call, or a life challenge, and know that God is at work, creating you into His image and as His masterpiece.

What does one see when looking at a large piece of marble before a sculptor? Does one only see the marble or the masterpiece yet to be created? The Divine Artist's job is to reveal the potential art hidden in the marble." As we go through our life experiences, be reassured that the Divine Artist is still at work today.

Embraced by God's Love and Light contains many stories of how God reveals Himself in a myriad of ways as He extends His grace to all. The contributors of their experiences have found directions, heard a call, experienced protection or healing, and God's transforming power. Our Good Shepherd's love and presence in our lives is real. We must express gratitude for His love and guidance as He seeks to interact and transform us to our fullest potential.

The stories within this book are written by discerning people who witness God's presence, hear His call, or experience Almighty God's intervention in their lives. The power of their stories is transformative, bringing to life deeper faith such that they are willing to share their experiences. May this book bless all who read of their unique encounters with their Heavenly Father. I thank these wise writers who have sensed and willingly shared their story of the Divine Sculptor at work.

We're adrift in an endless, often turbulent, never satisfying sea apart from God. Through Jesus, God's Son, we're reconciled to God and discover our meaning, value, and purpose. I hope these stories of encounters with God will bless all who read them, and each reader will sense God's presence and transform power into the masterpiece God desires for each of us.

May God bless you always,

Suzanne Wilkinson

"The LORD is good, a refuge in times of trouble. He cares for those who trust in him." (Nahum 1:7 NIV).

A Flash of Light Awoke Me

When I was in my early 20s, I was quite successful in the corporate world, both in magazine publishing and in sales and marketing for a well-known luxury hotel. I was living in Calgary at that time.

And yet, below the surface of my groomed persona, with its designer suits and coiffed hair, I was seething with anxiety, driven by internal demons that I could not fully understand. I had been driven all my life until that point, faster and faster, until I could see that wall looming ahead.

My anxiety threatened to engulf me. On a business trip from Calgary to Toronto, I started to get chest pains and a shortness of breath on the plane. When I got into my hotel room, my anxiety grew as the walls of the room narrowed and seemed to suffocate me. Everything seemed menacing and dark. I told an associate I could not continue the trip and asked him to cover for me. Then I flew home.

Up until then, I would say that I was utterly irreligious. I did not attend church; I did not pray or meditate. I did not think of God. But I always felt at home in the solace of nature and my mother. Whenever I felt great anxiety, I would retreat into her arms for solace.

So, when I got home from this aborted trip, I went into the Rockies with my father to see old childhood friends. They were "back to the landers". Their land was surrounded by dense forest, impenetrable and wild, and because I always loved trees, I appreciated they encircled me for the few days we were there and embraced me in their silence.

I brought *Atlas Shrugged* by Ayn Rand, a book that almost fell off the shelves a few days earlier. I felt that there was something profoundly prophetic about the book, and I couldn't put it down. It talked about how the world that we had created, our industrial world, would falter under the thumb of authoritarianism, where our freedoms would be eroded. As I started to read this book, I also began to get flashes of insight into a world beyond, as though a veil had parted. I had fleeting.

glimpses of figures moving in a foreign land, and I saw a central figure in these brief visions that I somehow knew very well. The name "Jesus" started to come to me, but there was nothing I could hold onto, and because I didn't put much thought into anything spiritual at that time, I brushed these thoughts and images away.

One night, I pleaded with my father and our friends and went to bed early. It was pitch black outside, and the only sound you could hear was the wind soring in the trees. I read for a while and eventually drifted off to sleep.

A flash of light awoke me, accompanied by a metallic "whooshing" sound. It originated just outside my window, a bit to the left beyond my periphery, so I couldn't see the source of this phenomenon. I only saw the light swoop by my window at regular intervals. I feel not fear but only bewilderment, as I knew nothing could land in that space. I got up to investigate, but a great force, gentle in nature, pushed me back onto the bed, and I fell into a deep sleep. When I awoke to a stunning and crisp fall day, I asked my father and friends if they had heard or seen anything like this at night. They had not.

It was after that night that my dreams and visions of Jesus began. I walked with him, and I talked with him, and the lucid dreams became so intense that at one point, I crossed through time to find myself with a small group of women who were wailing with anguish as they took him from the cross. I tried to rub life back into his hands and brushed away the tears from his face. He had been crying. My spiritual pilgrimage began from that point.

Jennifer Chapin

"We write this to make our joy complete. This is the message we have heard from him and declare to you: God is light; in him there is no darkness at all." (1 John 1:4-5 NIV)

A Glimpse of Heaven

"And I shall see Him face to face, and tell the story saved by Grace"[1]

The dead leaves swirled around my feet as I approached the car. The bare trees were bracing themselves for the cold death of winter. Cold death, that's what was on my mind. My father's death. The image of him lying in a cold grave haunted me.

The sound of a Salvation Army Brass Band drifted over the hospital grounds. They were playing "The Old Rugged Cross," one of Dad's favourite hymns. I looked back to see if the band was near his window, but he'd probably drifted into a drugged sleep as soon as I left.

Dad had been diagnosed with liver cancer just a few months prior. On the day of his diagnosis, I was attending a BBQ with choir members from my church. I came home in high spirits to find my parents grappling with the sobering news.

Reflecting on my adoptive dad's life, I realized we focused little on his family background. Our attention was mostly on my mother's relatives and her heritage.

Dad was one of eight children. His parents, Charlie, and Annie were both born in Ireland. These two immigrants married in 1897 in Fredericton, New Brunswick. A historic census lists Charlie as a labourer and Annie as a homemaker. A baby arrived one year after their marriage, and one more came every two years after that. Annie was 41 when she gave birth to their last son.

On our annual trips back to the Maritimes, we visited the small rooms above the local taxi office where Dad's elderly mother lived. I never met his father because he died before my adoption.

My dad was the middle child of six. He had two older sisters and one older brother. I like to think the older girls mothered and cared for him. I was told my dad had only attained a grade three or four education. He needed a job to contribute to the household.

Dad met and married Anna while working in the Marysville Cotton Mill. They moved to Toronto, only a short time after they were married.

I still have a small pin recognizing my dad's perfect attendance record as a milkman for Silverwood's Dairy. He delivered milk in Toronto using a horse-drawn carriage. Later, they purchased a fish and chip shop at Bloor and Dovercourt. They survived the Great Depression with this business. Fish cost fifteen cents and chips ten cents. They sold it shortly after adopting me. My adoptive mother took the lead regarding documents and financial matters. Dad was a dreamer and tried to find a way to make fast money. My Mother tried to find a way to save money, and I tried to stay out of the tug-of-war. Dad sold used cars, opened more restaurants, and managed a motel and restaurant, none producing a great income. But we managed.

Because of dad's propensity for making a deal, mother worried about what we might find when he died. He liked buying cars at auctions and trying to sell them for a profit. He parked them somewhere other than home, so we wouldn't know about the transactions. Fortunately, after he passed away, there were no outstanding cars to sell.

When we arrived at the hospital the day dad died, he was experiencing insulin shock. He needed an immediate sugar intake. I ran to the nurses' station and asked for orange juice. A few minutes after he drank the liquid, he seemed to rally. The disease and chemo had ravaged his body, but as we talked to him, his face brightened with a radiant smile. He wasn't focused on us. He lifted his eyes towards the ceiling and uttered his last words.

"I feel wonderful." Impossible, or was it?

We were asked to step out into the hall. Within minutes, the nurse came and told us he had just passed.

The Bible tells us, *"Fear not, I (Christ) am the first and the last and the living one. I died, and behold, I am alive forevermore, and I have the keys to Death and Hades."* **(Revelation 1:17b-18 ESV).**

4

Over the final months before this last hospital stay, dad had read through his Bible two or three times. He loved the Lord and was preparing for his move to glory. He often blessed others when they came to visit him. I glimpsed heaven in my dad, who modelled Jesus as best he could. I will always believe Christ revealed himself in those last few seconds. What a blessing to witness this. In the end, my dad gained much. https://www.hymnal.net/en/hymn/h/316 [1]

Carol Ford

A God Given Miracle

Many years ago, as a registered nurse in a busy city hospital, I worked in the premature baby nursery. I have seen many miracles in my nursing career, but this was life changing. An infant was born two weeks shy of six months, a very early delivery. I had the privilege of seeing a yet unnamed tiny baby girl, less than an hour old. The doctors had directly attached more than half a dozen tubes into her little body, one in her nose, mouth, brain, lungs, kidneys, and wrist, for an I.V. tube to provide highly controlled miniature drops of nourishment. The baby was delivered early because the mother was very ill and fighting for her life. It was a matter of one or both dying. This little girl weighed one pound, seven ounces.

I was looking at the smallest human being I had ever seen. As I looked on, I felt I had fallen to my knees in His presence before the true and awesome GOD. At that moment, even though I was in a busy hospital nursery, it felt like it was only me and my heavenly Father, my Abba. The silence was deafening. I was unaware of any other distraction; it was only me, a very little baby girl, and God. In the silence, it was only to Almighty God that I cried. Who else is there to call out to in a moment so profound?

The answers came in the form of a psalm. It was the words of Psalms 46:10, **"*Be still and know that I Am GOD*"** and **"*Fear not: I AM, is with you*" (NIV)**. I sensed God's presence in that moment. Then and to this day, I believe God was there and was our source of help and peace. At that moment, I knew this unnamed baby would live.

This little one was named Laura. I came to know her when she turned three. She was a healthy, vibrant, attractive little girl who was a joy to both her parents and filled with energy and potential. Thanks be to God.

Suzanne Wilkinson

A Legacy to Celebrate

Recently, Karen Pascal, a long-time friend, spoke at her retirement from the Henry Nouwen Society. I knew Betty Madsen, Karen's mother, a very strong Christian, and lovely Danish lady. Karen is the middle child and has a younger sister, Anne-Lis Morris, a noted potter, artisan, sculptor, and skilled maker of beautiful jewellery. Karen's older sister, Janet Britta, was a painter. Our world is a better place because of this family and their unique gifting, contributions to the arts, and Christian witness in many different realms.

Formerly, Karen was well-known as the founder and president of *Windborne Productions*. She brought to her role as Executive Director of the Henri Nouwen Society her dynamism, extensive background in the arts, strong business acumen, and success as a film and television producer.

These are the words spoken at her retirement. Karen said, "The reason we called this event, "Called to be Fruitful" was because of a life-changing encounter I had over 50 years ago.

I was at a point of real desperation. Though I had already experienced some success as an artist, and I had a beautiful young family, I had such a deep sense of emptiness.

In my desperation, I cried out to God and simply said, if you are there, you must know how awful I feel. And I added, if Jesus has anything to do with you, please make it real to me because it was never real before.

I found a Bible. I flipped it open and put my finger on a verse, challenging God to talk to me. This is the verse my finger landed on.

"You did not choose me, but I chose you and appointed you so that you might go and bear fruit—fruit that will last—and so that whatever you ask in my name the Father will give you." **(John 15:16, NIV).** It was then Karen sensed God's call to be fruitful. It gave Karen's life a purpose and her calling.

"On this evening when we are celebrating my retirement, I want to share that the fruitfulness of this time with the Henri Nouwen Society was such an unexpected and wonderful blessing in my life. I jumped in nine years ago because we needed someone to help pull together the 20th Anniversary Conference. I did not expect to stay, but I thank God that I could play a small part in bringing the rich and life-changing words and teachings of Henri Nouwen to audiences right around the world.

I remember when I started, I asked if the world still needs what Henri Nouwen has to offer. Today, I am convinced it needs Henri's wisdom, authenticity, and vulnerability more than ever.

I want to tell you a bit about the vision and work of the Henri Nauman Society. I hope that as you hear about the exciting thing we are planning, you will want to help put 'legs' on our vision and support the things the Henri Nouwen Society has to offer to the world today."

Karen Pascal concluded her brief retirement address by reading a prayer that Henri wrote four months before his unexpected death.

"I do not know where you will lead me. I do not know where I will be two, five or ten years from now. I do not know the road ahead of me, but I know now that you are with me to guide me and that wherever you lead me, even where I would rather not go, you will bring me closer to my true home. Thank you, Lord, for my life, for my vocation, and for the hope that you have planted in my heart. Amen." Karen Pascal

A Miracle at Christmas

With great trepidation, my sisters and I entered the ICU at St. Michael's Hospital in Toronto on Christmas morning, not knowing if our mother would still be alive. Three days before that, surgery took place to remove a piece of her skull to release some of the swelling in her brain, resulting from cancer surgery three days earlier. At that time, the surgeon told us that she would either live or die within those three days.

Her cancer journey began the previous spring when pain appeared on the left side of her face. Visits with her family doctor resulted in being told that her problem was only her nerves, as she was a worrier. She should go home and relax. She wanted to believe that diagnosis and tried to manage at home as long as she could. When the pain became too severe, I took her to my doctor, who immediately realized her need and made an appointment with a neurologist while we sat in his office. The neurologist treated my mother with kindness, admitted her to the hospital and ran tests but could find no cause for her pain.

As the pain increased, the doctors ordered her to be transferred to St. Michael's for a consultation with a neurosurgeon. This highly qualified doctor also could not identify the reason for my mother's pain and eventually decided that exploratory neurosurgery would be necessary. However, it was a very uncommon practice in those days. Interestingly, her doctors could not – or would not – give her morphine for the excruciating pain because it was "addicting." She was a case study for neurology students, so unusual was her case.

Following the surgery, the surgeon told us that cancer had been found beneath the brain and that he could not get all the tumours out without affecting her brain functions. The doctors considered her case to be terminal. The surgery caused the brain to swell, resulting in the second surgery to release some of the swelling and pressure. Hence, the three days of waiting as she hung between life and death.

After the second surgery, she had been unconscious and unresponsive. We were anxiously apprehensive as we quietly approached her bed in the ICU. While we stood waiting, silently gazing down at her, she slowly opened her eyes, recognized my sister's skirt, and said, "Before I saw your skirt, I had no hope. I thought I was dying." It was as if God had given her a new lease on life. Then, on that Christmas morning in 1972, we witnessed a Christmas miracle and knew our mother would live.

Before leaving Mom's room, I gave her a handmade card from my ten-year-old son Ron. On the front, he had copied Psalm 46:1, NIV- *"God is our refuge and strength, a very present help in trouble."* She cherished that card and eventually stored it away with her other treasures. After her passing, I returned the card to Ron, and it is now among his treasures.

Our family Christmas waited until my mother was allowed to return home and had gained a little strength. To make the day a little more festive, my husband cut down a small cedar tree and set it up in my parents' home. We decorated this "Charlie Brown" tree with lights, bobbles, and an angel at the top, and we knew we had the most beautiful tree in the world. Yes, Christmas had been delayed, but it was a most beautiful celebration as our mother was home again, having skirted death.

My mother underwent chemo treatments and slowly regained her health, relieved to be finally free of pain, and we were cautiously optimistic that perhaps God had completely healed her. She enjoyed spending time with family and friends, tending her beloved roses and camping with my father in their trailer at the lake. However, complete healing was not to be, as cancer reared its ugly head once more during the summer, and mother entered the hospital again in the fall. As before, although her pain was excruciating and she was dying, the medical people would not give her morphine. Thankfully, a heart attack mercifully ended her suffering on November 13th, my oldest sister's birthday.

Throughout her ordeal, she never once blamed God for her cancer or for not healing her, and her faith never wavered. Our mother had enjoyed another year of life. As my father and I sat nearby, she slipped from this life into the next, to her heavenly home with the God whom she so loved. Is not that transition God's greatest miracle?

Anonymous

A Silent Night

It was early Christmas Eve, and I was driving home from visiting my elderly aunt in a retirement home in Brampton. We had a good visit, and I stayed longer than anticipated. I needed to get home, quickly have something to eat and then go on to a candlelight service as planned.

I wasn't sure I had made the right decision when I turned down my sister's invitation to join her for their traditional Christmas Eve with friends and relatives. I had gone the previous year, my first Christmas in my new home in Newmarket, but it had felt strange to have a bustling evening with a crowd of people when our family tradition had been to spend a quiet evening at home after the early Christmas Eve service at church. Traditions are so firmly ingrained in our being, and to deviate from them can leave us feeling empty. I had decided I would rather be alone than in a crowd and was seeking a new tradition of my own that would meet my needs.

As I drove north on the 400, the car felt like a cozy cocoon in the dark night. There was very little traffic on the road, and once I got north of the city limits, I could see a multitude of stars in the sky. After driving in silence for the first part of the journey, I turned on the radio. It was around 7 p.m., and a special program on children's Christmas around the world had just begun. The music and narration by children were moving and transported me back to the first Christmas evening 2000 years ago. My isolation in the car gave me a sense of the aloneness that Mary and Joseph must have felt that evening. I'm sure they also longed to be with family for the special event that would be their first Christmas.

As I came over the crest of the hill before the Highway 9 exit, I looked down at the beautiful sight of the lights in the community of Holland Marsh. The children on the radio were singing *Silent Night*, and it all seemed so fitting. The quiet setting, the music, and the scene below reminded me of what the town of Bethlehem must have looked like to the shepherds up on the hills. I sensed God's Presence in a way I had never experienced before in all the years of celebrating Christmas. This awareness of His Presence continued for the rest of the journey.

When I stepped inside the house, I lit a few candles and turned on the radio, the Christmas tree lights and the fireplace. I sat in silence until the program had ended. After deciding to cancel my plans to attend the candlelight service, I spent a long time sitting quietly, savouring the evening's experience. I felt God had given me the incredible gift of a deep consciousness of His Presence, and I knew I would never have to be lonely on Christmas Eve again. I can relate to author Ruth Haley Barton when she states: *"The only time when I am not lonely and my longing for union is satisfied is when I am in solitude."* This was the message of Christmas when a Child was born, and He was named *Immanuel, God with us.*

Anonymous - Magda

"Let the redeemed of the Lord say so, whom he hath redeemed from the hand of the enemy;" (Psalm 107:2-8 KJV)

A Stream in the Wilderness

The many Voices of God. Used to encourage. Used to teach. Used to bring hope. To admonish. To guide. To heal. The list is endless. As I spent many long weeks, long months, and long years healing from a childhood of pain and suffering, Jesus often spoke to me intimately. Through Scripture. Through prayer. Through impressions on my heart. There were times when He would hold me close. Times when He would dance with me, the child self, or the adult self, twirling me as He showed me His great love. There were even times when He was so close His Voice was audible. These moments brought healing. These moments brought peace. These moments encouraged me to carry on in what had become a difficult journey of unearthing the roots of my pain. After a particularly difficult session with my prayer counsellor, Jesus impressed upon me to take a side trip as I travelled towards home. It was quite a side trip. Close to an hour out of my way. But a side trip that brought

11

healing. A side trip that brought peace. A side trip that brought new perspective and hope to the life that lay ahead.

There is a retreat centre an hour from my home. Over the years, I spent many days worshipping there. Seeking the Lord through powerful teaching. Singing His praises. Wandering the beautiful hills and following the babbling brook through the property. A restful place. A place of peace. That is where Jesus led me that day. But the healing did not take place on the property. Yes, I wandered the beloved hills. I meandered beside the cascading creek. But it was as I drove down the steep roadway towards the entrance and crossed the bridge over the beautiful river that the true healing took place. I felt the Lord tell me to pull over to the side of the road. Park my vehicle. Walk to the bridge. As I emerged from my car on that bright spring day, the sun was warm on my face. The trees along the riverbank were tall and stately, a mixture of evergreen, birch, and maple. The birds were chirping. The frogs were peeping. A squirrel scurried by, an acorn grasped in his mouth. The musky scent of decaying undergrowth mixed with the aroma of newly blooming spring flowers heightened my senses.

As I looked upstream, watching the tumbling of the waters over the rocks, I wondered what these waters had seen. Where they had been. What joys they had witnessed. What pain. You see, I love water. There is nothing more pleasant to me than to sit by a lake and watch the ripples as the breeze blows by. At times, the sunlight bouncing off the water's surface looks like shimmering diamonds. There is nothing I love more than watching the pounding waves of the ocean as the water meets the beach. I grew up near a great lake. Summers were spent camping or cottaging on lovely lakes and rivers. Now, as adults, my husband and I spend our summers on our boat amongst the rugged rocks and windswept trees of a different great lake or boating through the canal system in our area. Water brings me joy and peace. It always has. But that Friday, as I took the detour home and continued to watch the tumbling waters flowing towards me, Jesus encouraged me to go to the other side of the bridge. My perspective changed as I gazed downstream.

The turbulence in the water was not as evident. Instead of the frothy bubbles, the water gracefully flowed over anything in its path. The sharp and ragged rocks were now covered by the velvety blues and greens of the river. Satiny moss could be seen on the stones. The hazards were softened. Less threatening. More inviting to join in the journey that lay ahead. I once again crossed to the other side of the bridge, marvelling at the fast flow of the spring runoff. It seemed fraught with danger. Slippery stones. Broken tree branches caught in the current. Fallen leaves caught in the eddies at the edge of the river looked like small boats having a leisurely cruise before being caught once again in the swirling waters. The sound was not thunderous but nonetheless daunting. It was then I heard the Voice of God in my heart. "My child, stop looking upstream. Stop looking at the turbulence of your past. Stop feeling the pain. I have healed you. Looking upstream, you are looking at what was. Where you have been. That was necessary for a time, necessary to uncover the root of your pain, but necessary no more. It's time to look ahead. Look where you are going. Cross the bridge. Look downstream. Look towards your future. A future full of possibilities. There will still be storms at times, but you are strong. You can deal with whatever comes your way because I am with you. You are prepared for what life will bring. Stop looking upstream at the past. Start looking downstream, towards your future."

Just as rivers carve out alternate routes in the silty sand as they meander through a valley, Jesus can give us a new perspective on our life's circumstances. After He spoke to me, I felt such peace. Such joy. Such a healing balm coming from my Lord.

Hope. Strength. An inconceivable Love, An unbelievable Peace.

Would life be easy? No. It rarely is. Would life be without rapids? No. But through Jesus, we are healed. Through Jesus, we are strengthened. Through Jesus, we have the knowledge of how to navigate through the tumultuous waters of our lives. And just as a river has rapids and gushing waterfalls, it also has gentle meanders and quiet pools. Just as my childhood had times of pain, there were also many, many times of joy. In life, there will be times of turmoil.

Times of stress. Times of peace. Times of calm. And for each stage of life, Jesus is with us, giving us hope, strength, and joy in the chaos. Yes, Jesus has many, many Voices. Through these, I have been encouraged. This is just one of the multitudes of ways He has spoken to me. But I am thankful. He truly is our Personal Saviour. He knows our comings and our goings (Psalm 139:3 paraphrased).He knows our thoughts and our fears. And He can reach down to us and bring us peace. He can sit beside us and hold us as we weep. He can lead us beside still (or turbulent) waters and restore our souls (Psalm 23:2 paraphrased).

Kathy Ailles is the author of Untarnished (Word Alive Press, 2022). kathyailles.ca, kathy@kathyailles.ca

A Time-Sensitive Prayer Was Answered

Our daughter Deborah wanted me to look after her baby girl Michaela starting September 1st so she could return to her teaching position. I was willing to do this, but it was a long drive to her home.

We immediately put our two-story, four-bedroom home up for sale. Meanwhile, I drove daily to our daughter's home and prayed that the Lord would find us a bungalow in my daughter's community close to her home.

We had sold our home, and we had only six weeks to find the bungalow we needed and make the move while I was always caring for a small baby. We put our furniture in storage and moved into our daughter's home. We used a sofa in the basement as a bed until we found our new home.

Our realtor called and said that just three minutes away, there was a bungalow for sale. Did we want to see it? We went immediately. We were sadly disappointed. The house needed a lot of renovations. The big room in the basement had no walls. That house was not suitable for us.

Fortunately, the very next day, our realtor called us to say that the realtor of the house we had seen yesterday overheard us say that we wanted a bungalow in this neighbourhood. A home was going up for sale, just doors from the unsuitable house we had seen the day before. Yes, we would love to see it.

That house was perfect, and we could put an offer in before it was to go on the market. We met their owner's price and were able to move in just in time for Christmas. Our new house was three minutes from our daughter Deborah's home. The owner of our new home worked for the same company as Alex, my husband's employer. I don't know if that helped us get that home, but it certainly didn't hurt. Our God heard our frantic prayers, and we trusted Him to provide. He did, and beautifully so. Life has had lots of challenges, but God has never disappointed us.

Donna Smith

A Tribute to a Life of Suffering, Faith, and Purpose

I can think of nothing more uplifting than meeting a remarkable woman like Dr. Helen Roseveare. I had the privilege of hosting this committed, faithful missionary doctor. We need examples of faithfulness; hers is a story of a woman whose life became transformed over time into the image of Christ. She made a profound and lasting impact on me.

Dr Helen Roseveare was born in 1925. She grew up in a Christian household and in an Anglican church environment. Her conversion experience included an encounter with Philippians 3:10, NIV- *"I want to know Christ—yes, to know the power of his resurrection and participation in his sufferings, becoming like him in his death."* She ensured that all hospital patients heard the gospel through the ministry of hospital chaplains. God used her witness to call me into a chaplaincy role, serving in the community and hospital after my nursing career.

Helen earned her medical degree from Cambridge University. While studying there, she attended a missionary conference where God spoke to her, and she committed her life to missions. She remembered declaring that she would go where God wanted her to, whatever cost. And so, she remained when most missionaries had fled the Congo. Her suffering came at the hands of the Simba rebellion, a regional uprising which took place in the Democratic Republic of the Congo between 1963 and 1965. The national army of the Congo eventually liberated her.

Perhaps Dr. Roseveare is best known for the tragic fact that she was kidnapped, savagely beaten, and raped twice. She chose to live a missionary life in the Congo as a medical missionary from England. When the Congo declared independence from Belgium, in protest over white rule, she was captured by rebels who held her prisoner for five months and brutalized her. She responded that it was not right to ask whether her sacrifice for the gospel was worth it. For her, the real question was whether the sacrifice of Jesus was worth it.

But even though Dr. Roseveare's testimony to those who tormented her reflected the love and grace of Christ, what grabbed my attention most about her was not the events of that brutal period. Before these events, she had built a 100-bed hospital and maternity complex without which many thousands would have otherwise died. She oversaw the training of hundreds of young men and women trained in various medical fields and ensured that all heard the gospel through the ministry of hospital chaplains.

After the brutal events of the revolution and after a time of healing in her native England, she returned once more. This time, she established a 250-bed hospital with a maternity complex and leprosy centre. She also founded a training college for paramedical workers throughout the country, many regional hospitals, a "doctor fly-in service" the list goes on and on. Her accomplishments almost seem superhuman.

But in the end, when the government started budgeting subsidies for hospital students, she was accused of misdirecting those subsidies. It was through wrongful slander over these subsidies that she submitted her resignation. No one thanked her for her service, and she left a lifetime of world-changing ministry with dishonour.

When she struggled with the injustice of not even having a plaque in her honour, she came to a fantastic conclusion. In her struggle, she said that she heard Jesus say to her, "Either it will be Jesus only, or you'll have no Jesus." She realized that all these sufferings had come to her so that she might be content in Jesus only and not in fame, reputation, or honour. Her reward was Jesus.

Thank you, Dr. Helen Roseveare. When I think of you, I can't see you; I see only Jesus in you. I see the truth that "*everything a loss because of the surpassing worth of knowing Christ Jesus my Lord, for whose sake I have lost all things. I consider them garbage, that I may gain Christ*" (Philippians 3:8, NIV). For Helen, Christ was more than enough.

I personally met Dr. Roseveare in the mid-eighties and remember one story she told at a conference I attended. There were no incubators in the Congo for newborn babies since the climate is generally hot, and funds were scarce for equipment, especially for providing a heater. This was the first time anyone there had heard of an incubator.

Dr. Roseveare told the true story of what happened one evening when a premature baby was born. This precious baby girl needed special care and protection from cool wind drafts to keep her warm. The electricity in the missionary hospital was intermittent, and this fragile life hung in the balance. The nurses and doctor prayed for divine help to warm this baby girl. This was an impossible prayer, as who would think of sending a heater or an incubator to the tropics?

Back in Scotland, a lady's prayer and knitting group of faithful missionary supporters had packed a box and sent it to the Congo four months before this tiny baby was born. That box arrived at the hospital at just the right time and found its way to Dr. Roseveare's attention. Upon opening it, she discovered that it contained knitted items: a little knitted doll, a small, knitted blanket, hospital supplies, including bandages and medicines, and a hot water bottle.

Right away, Dr. Roseveare filled the hot water bottle with warm water, wrapped it in the knitted blanket, and took it and the little doll to where the caregivers were attending the makeshift cradle containing the premature baby. It was carefully placed beside the swaddled baby, who was snugly wrapped in the knitted blanket.

That knitted blanket and the hot water bottle had been sent months earlier from Scotland, packed by faithful missionary supporters to answer a prayer that saved a little life in the Congo.

With joy, the doctor gave the baby's little sister the knitted doll and the other supplies were put away to replenish essential hospital needs.

Forty years later, I still marvelled at this true story of our amazing God, who loves us enough to send a hot water bottle thousands of miles, by land and sea, over rugged country roads to arrive in the Congo at just the right time to save a little premature baby's life. Thanks be to God for the faithful life of Dr. Helen Roseveare and the love and mercy of our awesome prayer-answering God.

One of my favorite quotes is, "Can you thank Me (God) for trusting you with this (difficult) experience, even if you never know the reason why?"

Helen Roseveare/Rev. Suzanne Wilkinson - Written with biographical information on Dr Roseveare by Dr John Neufeld, https://www.backtothebible.ca/blog/drhelenroseveare/

Do not be anxious about anything, but in every situation, by prayer and petition, with thanksgiving, present your requests to God. (Philippians 4: 6 NIV)

"Therefore, do not cast away your confidence, which has great reward. For you have need of endurance, so that after you have done the will of God, you may receive the promise."
(Hebrews 10: 35-36, NKJV)

A Voice Message of Reassurance

Rev. Neil Miller is a Canadian who has worked in South Asia for over two decades. You may reach out to him through the "Contact Us" page on the link: https://listeningtogod.net/. This article was originally published in http://lightmagazine.ca. This article is reprinted from *Light Magazine* and here with permission.

Some readers know that I am starting a business in South Asia. At the beginning of October, I thought everything was good to go, and I would soon have all the registration documents I needed. Then, at the last minute, I encountered a substantial financial obstacle. Three days later, I was still trying to figure out what to do when Oni, a woman from South Asia, sent me the following voice message:

I was praying at midnight, as I often do. The Lord spoke to me about my life, but today, He spoke to me very little. You know, when you have a conversation with a friend, you can't force them to talk. Today, he spoke only one or two words. Then I asked him if he wanted to tell me something more. He said, "No, that's it." I laughed.

Then suddenly, you came to mind. I said, "Lord, you know the situation Brother Neil is in. Tell me something related to his life that will surprise him. Lord, give me something profound for him." You know what the Lord said? He said just this:

"Trust in the LORD with all your heart and lean not on your own understanding; in all your ways submit to him, and he will make your paths straight." (Proverbs. 3:5,6).

Oni didn't know about the financial obstacle I was facing. I can't even remember if Oni ever gave me a word from the Lord before. But the Lord spoke through her to give me a word of encouragement. Two days later, my huge financial obstacle disappeared. It wasn't that someone gave me a lot of money—the requirement for the funds ceased to exist.

Rev. Neil Miller

A Walk with God

We climbed ever higher on the narrow path, two silent souls connected by heart as well as hands. The rays of sunlight shimmering through the golden trees could not compete with the radiance that shone from inside. The source of that light was love.

Our journey together began in the valley, where I had just finished preparing a meal for a large crowd. People were seated at picnic tables in a park next to a road closed for construction. The road was being widened to accommodate more traffic flow in and out of the city where these folks had come from for a time of fellowship and food. After spending hours on my feet, I was about to sit down to rest my weary legs when I noticed a mother trying to lift her young son onto a chair beside a picnic table of men. While I struggled to help the mother, a young physician walking along the road scrambled over the bank of loose gravel to come to our aid. He lifted the young boy with ease onto the chair and then held out his hand, inviting me to walk with him. I noted that his hands were grazed from climbing over the high gravel embankment that separated the road from the group, and I felt badly that the knees of his trousers were dirty and torn.

As we walked silently for the longest time, I felt the ache in my legs and back slowly fade. The beauty of the scenery on this warm autumn day erased all pain and discomfort from my mind, and I sensed a strength flow from my companion's hand into mine. After a while, as the path started to get rougher and steeper, he broke the silence to declare his love for me. His words confirmed what I had been feeling, but then his face was saddened as he told me I had never expressed how I felt about him. His eyes gazed directly into mine as he asked, "Do you love me?" Grief and guilt overcame me, and words failed as I concentrated on the path that was becoming increasingly more difficult and steeper. His hand continued to guide and support me as I pondered what to say. When we reached the hill crest, we stopped to catch our breath while taking in the beauty of the panoramic view before us.

Still, in silence, we started to descend, and just as I was about to share my love for him, a friend appeared on the path before us. She said she wanted to talk to me about something that was troubling her, and I wasn't sure what I should do. My companion leaned over and whispered into my ear that he would like some more time alone with me, so I took my friend aside and told her I would get together with her a bit later. She replied that she was jealous of the love that was evident between us and walked away with stooped shoulders and head bent low.

The young physician and I continued our journey together on a path that was now taking us to the city of Toronto. We ended up in a historic home at Yonge and St Clair that had been converted into a museum. We wandered together from room to room, studying old furniture and relics that spoke of the traditions of the people who had lived there in the past. My troubled friend appeared on the scene once more, and this time, my companion led her to one of the rooms, where he sat down on the floor with her and shared his personal story. I heard him explain that he was a physician who had failed his professional exams because his method of practice was not in keeping with the scientific approach of medical school. He believed that care and compassion is the key to healing those who are wounded and diseased. As he continued to speak with a gentle voice, I woke up from my dream and realized that I had been on a walk with the God of love.

Reflection:

Later, while reflecting on this dream from September 2012, I was reminded of a sermon by our youth pastor just the month before when he spoke about images we have of God. He used overheads to show us various traditional images in art that reflect how God has been viewed over the ages. He then asked us to reflect briefly on the image we have of God in our minds. The picture that came to me was that of a loving man walking hand in hand with me. This is a far cry from the image I grew up with as a child, of an angry God in the sky looking down on us to make sure we behave. My healing has come from a transformation in my mind from a fearful God of judgment to a gentle God of love.

A misconception common to Christians is that we need to earn God's love by working hard for Him. In the dream, the scene takes place on the front lawn of a church. I was tired from hours of preparing and serving a meal for a crowd. In a recent program, Joyce Meyer related that in response to a questionnaire in which Christians were asked to name one question they could ask God, the most frequent reply was, "How do I know when I've done enough?' We can get so caught up in the works of our God that we neglect the God of our works. The danger is that we can become bitter and resentful in the process, like the older brother in the parable of the prodigal son. We lose our ability to be a light reflecting God's love to the world, like the church in Ephesus:

"I know your deeds, your hard work and your perseverance…. Yet I hold this against you: You have forsaken your first love you had at first. …. if you do not repent, I will come to you and remove your lampstand from its place."
(Revelation 2:2, 4, 5b, NIV)

Anonymous ~ Magda

A Waste of Time?

"I'm depressed," Jim said.

"How long have you been feeling that way?" I asked.

"Ever since I moved to this country."

Jim, Steve, and I shared and prayed during the small group time at our international worker's conference in South Asia. The day before, Steve had shared deeply, setting the tone for today's meeting.

Hearing Jim talk, I suspected there might be some buried issues in his heart, leading to his sense of depression. I asked Jim if he would like me to lead him in an inner healing prayer session. Jim was interested, so I explained a simple inner healing model that I have found to be effective.

The prayer model was this: First, connect with Jesus in an emotionally positive way. Then, ask Jesus if there is any lie embedded in your thinking. Lies we believe are frequently the source of our unhelpful thinking and behaviour. After the lie is identified, ask Jesus what truth he wants to give in place of the lie.

Jim was keen to give this a try, so we plunged in. I suggested that Jim start by picturing Jesus sitting at the table with the three of us. After a few moments of silence, I invited Jim to share his thoughts and feelings.

Jim said, "Jesus is behind me."

"What is his emotion toward you?" I asked. "Joyful and playful."

"How do you feel in response to Jesus's emotions?"

"Irked that Jesus is so joyful."

I suspected that maybe I had just stumbled upon a buried lie. I advised Jim to ask Jesus what lie he was believing.

Jim responded, "That a relationship with Jesus is a waste of time because I am not doing anything. If I am not doing something, I am not up to par." I noticed a smile playing on Jim's face. He told us that he just saw himself falling back into Jesus's lap.

I continued my questions. "When did you start believing this lie?"

"I was trying to be number one in high school and college. This was pleasing to others. Well, maybe it was pleasing to me. I never took a sabbath."

Knowing that much of our dysfunction stems from a warped sense of identity, I prompted another question. "Who does Jesus say that you are?" He says, "You are mine."

Clarifying what I had heard so far, I said, "I think the issue here, the lie that you are believing, is that your value depends on your performance. Ask Jesus what the truth is."

"Grace." "What does grace look like?"

"Walking at Jesus's speed." "What does this look like in practice?"

"Leaning back and resting in him and talking with him whenever I need to, like I am doing right now."

Trying to get a handle on the encounter he had just had with Jesus, Jim kept asking, "What just happened?"

What happened was Jim had an experience with Jesus, an experience where he heard Jesus speaking into his heart, addressing issues that were impacting his life. The good news is this kind of experience is not hard to replicate. All you need is a quiet place, a listening ear, faith to focus on Jesus, and some gentle questions.

Rev. Neil Miller

Allowing God's Spirit to Live in Me

I became a Christian at age sixteen, at a Billy Graham crusade in Toronto, Ontario, Canada. A high-school friend, a Christian, encouraged me to go on the bus trip with a church youth group. I went forward at that crusade. On returning to my church, I became actively involved in the youth group and faithfully attended the Sunday School classes. I lacked the opportunity to receive one-to-one discipleship. It wasn't until I was in my 30s that I had the opportunity to take classes at a Bible College. It was there I was disciplined and grew in my faith.

Even before that, one might have considered me a 'good girl' although I struggled with various temptations. On becoming a Christian, I unfortunately did not change overnight. The desired transformation has taken a lifetime and continues. I find hope in these words, *"See what great love the Father has lavished on us, that we should be called children of God! And that is what we are! The reason the world does not know us is that it did not know him. Dear friends, now we are children of God, and what we will be has not yet been made known. But we know that when Christ appears, we shall be like him, for we shall see him as he is. All who have this hope in him purify themselves, just as he is pure."* (1 John 3:1-3, NIV).

Now, I can see that, over time, my character, motives, ambitions, ideologies, and desires are being transformed. The Spirit of God is in me - changing my old self into a new creation. **"Therefore, if any man be in Christ, he is a new creature: old things are passed away; behold, all things have become new." (2 Corinthians 5:17, KJV).**

Anyone who believes and belongs to Christ and seeks to follow Him will become a new person. This process is called sanctification and continues for the child of God right to the end of life. These changes are nothing short of miraculous!

Before becoming Christians, none of us had the Spirit of Christ; we didn't truly sense the working of the Holy Spirit. We don't recognize His nudging, protection, or the encounters that come along. Christ may be unknown and perhaps foreign to us. I grew up in a Christian home, yet I did not fully understand what Jesus had done for me.

Spiritually speaking, we all fall short of the perfection of Christ. God is rich in mercy and brings life to us through the working of the Holy Spirit that comes through faith in God's son, Jesus.

Once we believe Jesus is the Redeemer Saviour, we become God's adopted children, and God gives us His Spirit. We begin to see how we fall short and are grateful to be seen by God in the robes of Christ's righteousness.

"I delight greatly in the Lord; my soul rejoices in my God.
For he has clothed me with garments of salvation and
arrayed me in a robe of his righteousness" **(Isaiah 61:10a, NIV).**

Once we accept Christ, a transformation begins. Out of gratitude, the Christian follower wants to change, be transformed, and have a heart inclined to please their Heavenly Father. Then, God is heard and seen in various ways in our ordinary lives, and we become aware of how God speaks and guides us. When we trust in the finished work of Jesus Christ, we want to change and become more like Him.

Life brings with it many challenges. When I become doubtful, have to feel inadequate, or become discouraged, I must remember the miraculous work of God's grace (see Romans 8:1-11). I must remember that God sees me complete in His Son, Jesus Christ. He is patient with me as a mother is with her child. We may be inclined to flounder in our sins and forget about God's love and forgiveness, which are made possible through faith in Jesus' work on the cross. Christ died to pay the penalty for our sinful debt and set us free. I am delivered from sin's bondage and seen in Christ's perfection (though I have not arrived nearly to that perfection, yet I endeavour and move forward). If we let a negative and rebellious attitude linger and discourage us, we may drift from our faith.

It's essential to be aware of the peril that our sins can be to our faith's health and, ultimately, our eternal life. If we ask for forgiveness, God will forgive and lead us back to obediently walking forward with the guidance and empowerment of the Holy Spirit.

Realizing how far we fall short of God's holiness, we will, with God's help, turn towards Jesus and focus our lives on Him. The Holy Spirit produces a grateful and willing spirit to seek Him and move toward love for others, patience, goodness, and disciplined lives and actions. Our sin should never let us forget that we are in Christ and have God's Spirit indwelling us. As we are willing, we will indeed become a new creation. The flesh may be dead because of sin, but the Spirit is alive because of Christ's righteousness.

My Christian journey has been one of deepening awareness and turning towards the truth of the Saviour, Jesus Christ. He has always been present, calling me towards Himself in deepening measure from early childhood onward. My salvation was assured in my teens, but the sanctifying process of becoming a new creation in Christ has taken many years and continues with its ups and downs. I have not always been faithful to Him, but He has always been faithful to me. He is my true love, joy, support, hope and salvation.

Knowing this has given me purpose in life and has brought me comfort and assurance amid life's challenges. Having and raising children has been a significant pleasure and a highlight in my life. My sons and family have immensely blessed me. I continue to pray Paul's prayer in Ephesians 1:15-23 over my family members. My favorite verse is Psalm 27:4, NIV- ***"One thing I asked of the LORD, that will I seek after: to live in the house of the LORD all the days of my life, to behold the beauty of the LORD, and to inquire in his temple."*** I wish I could have pursued my nursing career more fully, but I do not regret being home with our sons in their formative years. I loved and found meaning in my career as a Registered Nurse and later as an Ordained Minister and Chaplain. When COVID-19 came, I retired from my chaplaincy position. Now, I continue to minister on an on-call basis, lead 'Life Groups,' and often volunteer.

In the movie "Chariots of Fire," I know what Eric Liddell meant when he said, "When I run, I feel His pleasure". I have felt God's pleasure when I have offered messages, especially as an officiant at a funeral/memorial service or listening and encouraging another as a Chaplain. I see God in unique and various ways. I feel His presence, sense His nudging, and hear His voice (not audibly), but through circumstances. I am and will ever be grateful to be a part of the family of God and a child of the King of kings and Lord of lords, Jesus Christ.

"You, however, are not in the realm of the flesh but are in the realm of the Spirit, if indeed the Spirit of God lives in you. And if anyone does not have the Spirit of Christ, they do not belong to Christ. But if Christ is in you, then even though your body is subject to death because of sin, the Spirit gives life because of righteousness." **(Romans 8: 9-10, NIV)**

Suzanne Wilkinson

An Angel Unaware

It was about twenty years ago, early in my ministry, when this fantastic coincidence happened. I had been invited to speak before a group of women at a church in Ancaster, Ontario, Canada. This required me to travel to Ancaster, approximately an hour and a half drive from Toronto, where I lived. The scheduled meeting was to start at 10 a.m. on a weekday.

I was well dressed for this occasion as I made my way out of Toronto on the Queen Elizabeth Highway on a beautiful fall morning. Travelling at about 100 miles an hour, I suddenly experienced a blowout of the rear passenger tire, causing that tire to deflate abruptly and the car to swerve. Fortunately, I was in the curb lane and could rapidly pull off the highway onto the shoulder next to a service road.

Appropriately dressed to speak before an audience, yet needing to get going, I quickly got the jack and small doughnut tire out of my trunk. I left the trunk lid up so drivers passing by would see that my car and I were experiencing a challenge. I was within sight of Bronte Road, about two-thirds along the way, heading out of Toronto.

Unexpectedly, I heard a young man say, "Don't touch that. I'll help." I looked behind me, and there, along the service road, was this stranger climbing the fence and coming my way. Without any introduction or small talk, he said. "Ma'am, I'll change that tire for you." Without a word, he had the doughnut tire on and was putting the tools away in my trunk. I offered to pay him, but he dusted off his hands and said, "Follow me."

As quickly as he had come, he was back over the service road fence and into his car, leading me to the next exit and into a plaza with a Canadian Tire Store. He pulled up in front of the big garage service doors and paused. As I pulled up parallel to his car, I rolled down my passenger window to speak to him. No sooner had I done that when he said, "Have a great day," and off the young stranger went, travelling toward Toronto. He must have seen me across five lanes of traffic travelling eastbound when he noticed my car on the opposite westbound side of a six-lane divided highway. This unnamed young man had spotted me and decided to help.

This ordinary-looking fellow sprang into action. I could not pay or thank him before he was gone. I arranged for a new tire to replace the damaged one. The service was prompt since it was only shortly after nine in the morning. It struck me as unusual to notice that no other cars were in the different service bays. With a new tire installed, I was quickly on my way, heading west towards Ancaster. This whole episode took less than half an hour. Believe it or not, I was not dirty. I didn't even have a run in my nylons and was on time for the meeting to start at ten.

For me, this was a true-life miraculous illustration I could use to start my message that morning. The given text that day was 2 Corinthians 5:17, *"Therefore if any man be in Christ, he is a new creature: old things are passed away; behold, all things have become new."* **(KJV)**.

My honorarium for speaking that morning was enough to cover the cost of a new tire and its installation, for which I was most grateful.

For me, this young man was an angel in disguise. I will never forget this incident. That experience was God's way of helping me, and I will call it more than a coincidence. It was a gift of God at a moment of need. I have marvelled at God's timing each time I remember that morning and His gift of a caring, capable angel who came unaware to me that beautiful fall morning. That young man's actions were a gift from someone who exemplified my message from 2 Corinthians 5:17.

Suzanne Wilkinson

"He who overcomes shall be clothed in white garments, and I will not blot out his name from the Book of Life; but I will confess his name before My Father and before His angels."
(Revelation 3:5, NKJV)

An Immediate Answer to Prayer

Throughout the 1980s, '90s, and early 2000s, I was blessed to be a part of a movement called Women Alive. Each May, we held a conference at the University of Waterloo where notable Christian speakers, like Helen Honeywell, Jill Briscoe, Kay Arthur, Joni Eareckson Tada, Dr. Helen Roseveare, Corrie Ten Boom, and others were invited to speak.

Their messages were always inspiring and often transformative to those who had the opportunity to attend and listen. For many of those years, I was one of those privileged people.

I was on the leadership team at one of these conferences. I had a more intimate view of the behind-the-scenes happenings. I heard this incredibly true story of how God immediately answered a small but needed prayer. Corrie Ten Boom was the keynote speaker that year.

Cornelia "Corrie" ten Boom was a Dutch watchmaker who, along with her family, harboured hundreds of Jews amid the Nazi Holocaust to protect them from arrest during World War II. It's believed their efforts saved nearly 800 lives. Eventually, betrayed by a fellow Dutch citizen, the entire family was imprisoned in Auschwitz-Birkenau internment camp and suffered greatly. It was there in that lice-infested camp that her sister Betsy died.

However, Corrie survived and told her story in her moving autobiographical 1971 memoir, *The Hiding Place.* Having grown up in a devoutly religious family, Corrie ten Boom started a worldwide ministry and travelled extensively as a public speaker. She died on her 91st birthday. I was told this story by someone who was there and saw this prayer answered first-hand. I know it is a true story of how God answers a little prayer for an elderly giant of the faith.

Corrie Ten Boom was staying in the residence, where she had a room for her stay at the conference. A representative from the Women Alive executive was to bring her from the student residence to the large auditorium, where she was to speak to the assembled audience, mainly women, at that gathering of about three thousand.

As they started down the long hall leading to the assembly, in her 80s, Corrie told her hostess she was tired and would like a glass of milk and a cookie to give her some energy for the evening. However, dinner time had passed, and all the food distributors were closed, so there was no place for Corrie to get even a small snack. Moreover, going outside the university to obtain food would take time, and Corrie was due to speak shortly.

A person from the executive accompanying Corrie heard this elderly lady's quietly spoken but heartfelt prayer for a little snack. She thought her request was an impossible one. She wondered how God would bring a little refreshment for Corrie before they arrived at the auditorium, which was just a moment down the corridor.

As they walked along that hall heading for the assembly, a student living in residence and waiting for the start of summer courses approached them, carrying a food tray. As this student passed them, she paused and offered the untouched food on her tray to the elderly Corrie. On the student's tray was an unopened carton of milk with a straw and a wrapped, untouched cookie.

God heard the prayer of one of his precious adopted children and answered it just at the right time. Corrie paused, and together, they stood in the hallway as she enjoyed the miraculously offered milk and cookie. This passing student knew nothing of the prayer, but Corrie knew, and it was enough to appreciate that God heard and answered her little prayer. One of Corrie's well-known quotes is, "Never be afraid to trust an unknown future to a known God."

Jesus said, "Love each other as I have loved you. Greater love has no one than this: to lay down one's life for one's friends. You are my friends if you do what I command." **John 15:12-14 (NIV)**

Suzanne Wilkinson

Before the King of Kings

I'm trying to experience all moments as God's moments and to increasingly pay attention to His whispers and nudges. I have a lot of moments that I could share, but I do not have a grand story to share, although the moments are all part of a grand story!

One of the most recent moments is one I can share of my husband, John's, passing. It was the morning of the Coronation. I woke up at five am to watch the celebrations in my bedroom. (John was in a hospital bed in the living room as he had been physically declining for the last few years, having experienced much pain and mobility limitations).

I heard John moan and thought I heard him say something. I came into the living room, where we had placed his hospital bed. I attempted to make John more comfortable by fluffing his pillow, covering him well and giving him some morphine (he was on a morphine pump). John was unresponsive. I decided it was too early for him to have the T.V. on and returned to the bedroom, where I planned to watch the crowning of King Charles.

At 7 am, I felt a strong, compelling nudge to return to the living room and watch the Coronation with John there. When I approached the bed, I was startled to see that John's breathing had changed. As a Reg. N., I knew he was dying (John had not roused, remained unresponsive, and his colour was different). I took the bed's side rail down and quietly turned on the television to watch as I sat beside John in those final intimate moments.

John loved the monarchy and the beautiful hymns and music of pageantry, especially the way the Brits do it. I knew he would want to see it if he could awaken. I pulled a chair beside the bed, held his hand, and sat quietly with him for an hour and a half. As I did so, I became aware that his breathing became more laboured, and it was not long after that John breathed his last breath.

Months have passed, but I still smile when I think that John was escorted into glory by the prayers, gorgeous choral music, and hymns that day in the abbey. We were together, which is how John would have wanted his passing into his future eternal home to be. I will always be grateful to God for allowing me to awaken early that memorable morning.

John was an adopted child of the true King of Kings and Lord of Lords, Jesus. Together, we marked my dear husband's passing into the eternal kingdom as we watched a king crowned in the presence of that King of Kings and Prince of Peace.

Anonymous

Broken Circle – A Story of Redemption

This story sheds some much-needed insight into the life of James M. Peters. It is representative of many of our native people across Canada. I applaud James for his willingness to share his life story so we can learn about his struggles as one of Canada's first people. James writes his life story in his recent publication, Broken Circle, how God has walked with him from his early life in more than a dozen foster homes and detention centres, bringing him hope and the promise of salvation. His book tells how the oil of gladness, deliverance and healing took the form of the loving patience of Christians, whom God sent as street workers, shelter workers, pastors, chaplains, and friends. To top it off, a loving and determined wife, Christine, came into James's life in answer to the fervent prayers of righteous servants of the Lord.

This story of James inspires us never to give up hope. In James's case, even in the face of violent reactions by those who mistreated him. Yet, at the same time, many ministered to James over an extended time and prayed without ceasing.

James Peters, originally from the Coldwell Band of Pelee Island, was taken away from his family and community when he was only four and placed in its series of foster homes until he was sixteen. He often ran away from these homes, and when released from their care, he found himself homeless and on the streets of

London and later Toronto, Ontario. James found some solace through alcohol consumption that blocked the pain and kept him warm on winter nights.

Peters shares his lifelong search for the lost connection to his family and home community. I met James when he and his wife became members of a life group I was leading. James had a hilarious sense of humour and wisdom often beyond his years. He did not hesitate to comment on his challenge with alcoholism and his struggle to find his identity.

James wrote, "I don't know if or how my story will help others because I mostly see all my failures, but I guess if you look at the "bigger picture.," you start seeing how a seemingly hopeless life became a life filled with much goodness. All I know is that I gave God the enormous mass that was my life, and he's somehow brought me through.

I want my people to know that there is hope. Our Great Creator loves us very much. He created us to be First Nations. He loves how we worshipped Him on the big drums and the flute - and how we continue to do so. He loves the way we dance. Our Creator grieves when we grieve. He wants us to know how special and unique we are. He created us for a purpose, and he wants to walk the path of our lives alongside us. Our Creator wants to see us laugh. He wants to heal our broken hearts.

If I have learned anything in my life, it is OK to run. It was OK to run from the things that were meant to harm me and cause me pain, but there was also the right time to stop running so that I could see and receive the good things on my path of life. I did not cause the brokenness between My People and those who came to this great land. But it was not good to hide behind my struggles with addiction, as this just caused more problems as I walked my path. I need to learn to forgive myself and those who brought me harm and caused the broken circle.

Most importantly, I've come to know the Great One, the Great I Am. In the circle of life, He is the one to whom we can find wholeness. He is the beginning and the end. He can bring complete healing to our broken circle."

I had the privilege of attending James's funeral service in the late summer of 2023. I continue to be a friend of Christine, his wife, a courageous Christian woman. I thank her for sharing James's story and wish the best for her and their children, Naomi (an accomplished artist) and Jonah (a lover of the land and an accomplished gardener). Through their many challenges, their lives continue to show us love, light, hope and faith through Jesus Christ.

Peters, James M., *Broken Circle*: *The Life of James M. Peters,* published in Canada by Goldrock Press www.goldrockpress.com, 2021, page 87. With Permission from Christine Peters.

By God's Grace

I am now in my middle years, having lived an active life with two artificial legs from childhood onward. Let me tell you my story as I give God the credit for my life. I was only two when a baby brother joined the other seven family members. We lived in a century-old farmhouse, where I have lived my entire life. It was late September, and the cornfields were at full height and ready for harvest. Apparently, it was a beautiful fall day with a gentle, warm autumn breeze when I was placed in a playpen in the backyard, where my older siblings were to tend me. My mother was busy in the farmhouse nearby, looking after our new baby brother.

Suddenly, the free-range hens were squawking and scattering, running everywhere. Startled by this commotion, my siblings ran off to find out what was disturbing the chickens. As a sturdy child, I hoisted myself over the playpen's side and was free to roam around. My favorite toy was an old army bugle made of strong metal. Apparently, I carried it with me everywhere I went. I could see my father on the tractor in the cornfield, so I went off, likely hoping to get a ride with my dad on the tractor. I was too young to anticipate the danger, so I went to the cornfield.

With the full-grown corn well over my head, my father didn't see me. The tractor had stopped momentarily, and my father's attention was on something ahead, so I climbed onto the back of the corn binder. Before long, the tractor was going again, pulling the corn binder behind it. Unnoticed and precariously sitting on the lip of the corn binder, I was swiftly swept into the grinder. Before I knew it, the grinder pulled my little body downward into the blades, which cut into both my legs. It would have pulled me out through the back end of the grinder except for the fact that I was carrying that old army bugle which jammed the gears. Fortunately, I carried that old bugle everywhere. It was a toy to me as I had no interest in dolls at that stage in my life.

Well, by God's grace, that horn saved my life as it jammed the gears of the corn binder. My father jumped down from the tractor to find out what had jammed the gears. What a fright it must have been to discover me with blood spurting everywhere.

Dad had always fainted at the sight of blood, and there was lots of blood that day, but he scooped me up along with my two legs, which were fragile, hanging only by the skin. He ran for all his life as he carried me back to the farmhouse.

Immediately, a call was made for medical assistance. Fortunately, my parents installed a phone in our old farmhouse that summer, only a month before. The local doctor packed up my legs and cut off the bleeding with tourniquets, and off we went to the highly acclaimed Sick Children's Hospital in Toronto.

The doctors were able to sow my legs back on, but over time, gangrene set in on my right leg, and it had to be amputated. I still use my left leg and marvel at the grafts that have held for so many years of active and fulfilling life while still living and working on that same farm where I was born.

While I was recovering at Toronto Sick Children's Hospital, where I was learning to walk again, I managed to get out of the crib I was in and, despite my limitations, managed to elude the nurses. When the nurses discovered that I had disappeared, they called security and were about to call the police and my parents, but despite a search, they could not find me anywhere.

Later, a security man found me several floors below in an area with a playroom. I was riding a rocking horse, which I liked, oblivious to all the chaos I had caused. You could say I was an adventuresome, determined child. This is only one of the many miraculous adventures I have experienced. But I will always be grateful to God for the amazing grace he showed me and for the life I have experienced.

Years later, I accepted Jesus as my Lord and Savior. I am no longer such a rebel or quite so adventurous. I know God is always with me as my protector and guide. I rely on Him as I journey through life. In life, we will have many trials, which hopefully teach us and mature us into more Christlike people. It is always my hope to encourage others in their trial. I also hope my true story will encourage you in your trial. I say glory to God and thank Him for this life and the eternal one yet to come.

Nancy Parratt/Suzanne Wilkinson

Cancer is a Terrorist

At first, my husband, Graham, and I thought his back pain, indigestion, growing paunch, and decreasing energy were just symptoms of malevolent middle age. We didn't know that terrorist cells had infiltrated his body and were building tumours in the nooks and crannies of his abdomen.

Last November, an oncologist gave the cells a name: non-Hodgkin's lymphoma. Cancer. Inoperable but treatable. Nine months of chemotherapy stemmed, for a time, the tumours' growth. They allowed Graham to continue his work as executive director of The Scott Mission in Toronto. But the missile drugs zapped his energy and strength. They caused a great deal of collateral damage to his healthy cells—hair, skin, blood, digestive system. The tumours, however, developed a resistance to the drugs. They

37

plundered nutrients from Graham's food pressed against his vital organs and dared doctors to shoot other weapons from their medical arsenal into Graham's bloodstream.

As I write this, Graham has just begun his third chemo regimen. He can hardly walk, eat, or breathe. His doctor was not optimistic. Humanly speaking, it would appear that the terrorist cells have won.

Even as Graham's private war loomed large within our home, terrorist cells of a different sort lurked in the nooks and crannies of our planet, plotting to disrupt and destroy the comfort of the "Christian" West. When the planes slammed into the World Trade Centre on September 11, the televised experts tried to place the blame and explain the evil that changed the world at that moment. They diagnosed terrorism. I felt as if my world had been invaded by a cancer that would produce all the worst-case scenarios of end-times prophecy.

Cancer is a terrorist. Terrorism is a cancer.

Both cause pain, fear, uncertainty, suffering of innocent people, and hardship to a degree no one can predict. Both sap energy and test the limits of human love, endurance, and trust. Both strikes unpredictably. Both defy reasonable explanations.

Both cause us to cry to God in prayer that can't be put into words.

As the world embarked on a war that would beat terrorism into remission, I turned for comfort to the same eternal truths that have sustained Graham and me through his war with cancer.

I remembered a quotation from a sermon two summers ago: "For the Christian, the bad news is not the final news."

Throughout his illness, Graham and I had accepted that it would end in one of three outcomes: God would heal him through chemicals, God would heal him in response to prayer, or God would heal him by welcoming him to a place where there is no cancer. Each is a hope-filled prospect. We do not believe we have the right to demand or choose Graham's mode of healing—only the right to trust in God's perfect love, accept each day as a gift from God, and live to God's honour and glory.

"Not only are God's ways higher than our ways, but also he is good, merciful, gentle, loving, faithful, kind, and perfect," Graham wrote in his first of many email updates on his condition. "These things—and ALL the things God is, all of WHO God is—are true and will always be true, regardless of how I or anyone else happens to experience him at any given time."

Nothing in Scripture tells us our days will be free of pain or suffering. God did not promise to spare his people from the scourge of cancer or terrorism. Instead, he gave us the testimony of Job 13:15a-16a, KJV: ***Though he slay me, yet I will trust in him…. He also shall be my salvation.*** God also gave us the promise of Jesus: ***Here on earth you will have many trials and sorrows. But take heart, because I have overcome the world*** **(John 16:33b, New Living Translation).**

And so, amid the shadows of adversity, my heart resounds with the hymns of faith and Easter hope that have strengthened God's people for generations: "Great is thy faithfulness," "How firm a foundation," and especially "Thine be the glory, risen, conquering Son, / Endless is the victory thou o'er death hast won."

As I live with the horrible uncertainty of Graham's cancer and the war on terrorism, familiar passages of Scripture speak with fresh clarity and relevance.

"Yea, though I walk through the valley of the shadow of death, I will fear no evil, for thou art with me" **(Psalm 23:4, KJV).** God is with me—not on my side waving my country's flag in this present conflict, but by my side as the merciful, good, and strong companion in whose house I will dwell forever.

"Who shall separate us from the love of Christ? Shall trouble or hardship or persecution or famine or nakedness or danger or sword?... No, in all these things, we are more than conquerors through him who loved us. For I am convinced that [nothing]… will be able to separate us from the love of God in Christ Jesus our Lord." That's Romans 8:35, 37-39, NIV, but the whole chapter is precious.

"You will keep in perfect peace all who trust in you, whose thoughts are fixed on you! Trust in the Lord always, for the Lord God is the eternal Rock" **(Isaiah 26:3-4, NLT).** This verse came to Graham during one of his many sleepless nights. He noticed that it doesn't say what we're to trust God for or about.

"It doesn't say we're to trust him to do something. It just says that we're to trust him!" Graham wrote. "To me, that has to do with trusting his character, trusting his nature, his plans, his intent, his ways—which are far higher than ours. As God said in Isaiah 55:8-9, NLT, *"'My thoughts are nothing like your thoughts,' says the Lord. 'And my ways are far beyond anything you could imagine.'"*

In an email last March, Graham cited the first 4 verses of Psalm 11. They seem strangely pertinent to our troubled times. ***"I trust in the Lord for protection,"*** David tells his advisors. ***"So why do you say to me, 'Fly to the mountains for safety! The wicked are stringing their bows and setting their arrows in the bowstrings. They shoot from the shadows at those who do right. The foundations of law and order have collapsed. What can the righteous do?'"*** **(NLT).**

If that is our question today, let us also affirm David's answer: "But the Lord is in his holy Temple; the Lord still rules from heaven."

"When things are beyond our control, faith says, 'But they're not beyond God's control,'" Graham commented. "I praise God that he's allowed me that measure of faith. Not that I compare it with David's. But I do believe that the Lord still rules from heaven. And if I believe that the whole universe will one day conform to his purpose for it, then I MUST believe that he still rules from heaven. And if I believe that—well, nothing else matters as much as that." (Graham died on November 5, 2001).

The terrorist cells may destroy, but they won't win. Not in the end.

Esther Barnes - Barnes, Esther, published in The Canadian

Christ Was Tugging at His Heart

It was a natural step for Brett to attend a Christian college and study the Bible. After all, he'd been around people who knew Jesus his whole life - at home, school, and church. He was even gearing his college studies toward a career in "Christian work."

But at age twenty-one, he made a startling discovery as he sat with the small congregation in an old country church and listened to a pastor preach from 1 John. He realized that he depended on knowledge and the trappings of religion and that he'd never received salvation in Jesus. He felt Christ was tugging at his heart that day with a sobering message: "You don't know Me!"

The apostle John's message is clear: **_"Everyone who believes that Jesus is the Christ is born of God"_ (1 John 5:1, NRSV).** We can "overcome the world," as John puts it (v. 4), only by belief in Jesus. It is not knowledge about Him but deep, sincere faith in Jesus, demonstrated by our belief in what Jesus did for us on the cross. The Scriptures told him that Christian jargon, the trappings of religion, and head knowledge were not enough. That day, Brett placed his faith in Christ alone.

Today, Brett's deep passion for Jesus and His salvation is no secret. It comes through loud and clear every time he steps behind the pulpit and preaches as a pastor - my pastor.

"God has given us eternal life, and this life is in his Son. Whoever has the Son has life..." (vv. 11-12, NIV). For all who have found life in Jesus, this is a comforting reminder! God still speaks. In this case, a tug at Brett's heart changed the direction of his life.

David Branon - [1] _Branon, Dave, The Daily Bread, Grand Rapids, Michigan, U.S. A., October 4, 2023 (_This excerpt of Dave Branon[1] devotional addresses the need that _"Everyone who believes that Jesus is the Christ is born of God."_ 1 John 5:1-5, NIV_)._

Deconstruction and Reconstruction

Being a part of InterVarsity when I was a student was where I learned how to properly study the Bible for the first time – reading the text in community and not a book about the Bible, listening to someone's interpretation of the Bible or simply trying to understand the Bible by reading it myself. Sharing this way was also when I started to see inconsistencies between how I saw Jesus interact with people, namely the oppressed and outcasts in that society, and how I saw my church interact with its members and those outside the church.

I gained a reputation at my church for being an angry, loud, and opinionated person for trying to encourage our church to reach out to our lower-income neighbours or to become more concerned with prominent issues that were being talked about in the news, such as houselessness, reconciliation with Indigenous peoples and racism in North America.

A common refrain you hear everywhere in Christian spaces is that young people are leaving the church, and one of the reasons that people will say this is happening is because of deconstruction.

Deconstruction has become this big, scary, ambiguous word associated with a lack of faith or hope. Instead of what I think it is, people asking questions about the faith they grew up with and rejecting aspects of Christian culture that are sadly linked with abuse (spiritual, racial, sexual, etc.), inconsistencies with Scripture's depiction of Jesus or narrow or limited understandings of what it means to follow Jesus.

Christians who look down on deconstruction discredit the many ways that young people are trying to see how the practices of Christianity can be consistent with the character of Jesus. Deconstruction is the same process many of the early followers of Jesus went through when trying to figure out whether Jesus was the Messiah. Jesus was excellent at deconstructing. The Sermon on the Mount (Matthew 5-7) is one massive deconstruction of Jewish law. Jesus breaks down the common understanding of the law for His

42

listeners and tells them their knowledge is limited and insufficient. Jesus upended everyone's ideas of what they thought the Kingdom was like, who the Messiah was and what that Messiah came to do. He reoriented their lives to a newer understanding of how God interacts with His world. He reconstructed the law to be about the heart rather than strict legalism. As Jesus said about himself: "*Do not think that I have come to abolish the law or the prophets; I have come not to abolish but to fulfil it.*" (Matthew 5:17, NIV).

In my deconstruction, Intervarsity was a community that loved me and went through my questions with me, not because they knew the answers, but because they were willing to sit with me in the tension of figuring out if Christ had any merit considering these inconsistencies. I had mentors and friends within InterVarsity who guided me through the thick of my questions and never told me what the 'right' answer was but allowed me to discover what it could be.

Through this vital ministry, I have felt the nudge of God in my life. His guidance through the mentoring I have received has opened doors and directed me along a new path. In this sense, I am now on a faith-building track, having encountered the triune God previously unknown to me.

Students need people who are willing to go through their questions with them. By deciding to volunteer or even join staff with InterVarsity (even if it's just part-time), you are helping students healthily deconstruct to reconstruct their faith into something that can be good. Saying yes to mentoring young people, being invested in their lives, and rebuilding their trust in Jesus is a yes to humility in recognizing where the previous generations of Christian leaders may have got it wrong and hurt people.

Will you help us raise an age of kind, healed and whole believers who reflect the love of Christ?

Kong, Brandon / InterVarsity Communications, May 2, 2023

Deep Water Dreams

"He reached down from on high and took hold of me; He drew me out of deep waters." **2 Samuel 22:17 (NIV)**

"He reached down from Heaven and rescued me." **Psalm 18:16 (NLT)**

"When you go through deep waters, I will be with you. When you go through rivers of difficulty, you will not drown." **Isaiah 43:2 (NLT)**

The Bible (Old and New Testament) relates many instances where God spoke to people in dreams and visions. There is much debate about whether God still speaks to people in dreams and visions today. Speaking from personal experience, my answer is a resounding YES! God indeed continues to use prophetic dreams and visions to warn, guide and encourage His children.

"Like an open book, you watched me grow from conception to birth; all the stages of my life were spread out before you, the days of my life all prepared before I'd even lived one day." (Psalm 139:15-15)

My dear mother told me that as a frightened pregnant teenager, she fervently prayed. God answered in miraculous ways. My mother would often remind me that God's hand was in my life and encouraged me to never forget to whom my life belonged. I have kept a daily prayer and dream journal for several decades. I find that the more I pay attention to my dream life, the more God reveals to me. For the most part, my life's journey seems to have been a steady stream of one fierce storm after another. I believe that God, in His Wisdom, knew that in those tumultuous times, I'd be more receptive to Heavenly messages in my dream life when I was not neck deep and distracted in my waking life.

Upon reflection, I now understand that God knew what my life experiences would be even before I was born– trauma, danger, heartache, loss, and illness. I was born into a Catholic family that had a great deal of brokenness. Addiction, mental illness, and physical/emotional violence were just some of the visible symptoms of invisible wounds. I had recurring dreams of frantically trying to escape death by drowning. I believe that these dreams, although terrifying, contained prophetic reassuring messages of the Lord's promise to rescue and protect, to never leave or forsake me, no matter how scary life's storms got.

Initial Deep-Water Dream

The scene was Jerusalem on the day that Jesus was to be crucified. The streets were crowded with people screaming and running in all directions—total chaos. While clutching the hand of a small boy, I desperately searched for a place to hide. We were stopped by a Roman guard, and I was questioned about the cross hanging on the chain around my neck. I was so scared—I knew that if I said I was a believer, it meant a certain death for me and this young child. I lied and said that the chain/cross was just a gift from someone else and meant nothing to me. The guard did not accept my answer and kept interrogating me. I denied that I was a follower of Jesus three times. I remember feeling so much guilt and shame around this cowardly denial. Me and the young child were arrested anyway and put into a holding tank. The door was slammed shut and locked. Water began to flow into the tank from below. To my horror, I realized this was our execution chamber. When the water rose to hip level, I picked up the child and put him on my shoulders to keep his head above water. I tried to remain calm so that the child would not be frightened; I reassured the child that everything would be okay. Eventually, the water rose to my nostrils. I stood on my tippy toes to delay the inevitable drowning. I was terrified and felt helpless to save the child or myself. In my mind, there was no turning back— our lives were over. As my nostrils became submerged in the water, I looked up and saw floating above the water line a man in a flowing white gown. He reached down into the water with a nail-pierced hand and grabbed my outstretched hand, and he pulled me and the child to safety.

Subsequent Recurring Deep-Water Dreams

The setting is on a beach. It is apparent that a tsunami or tidal wave is about to crash onto shore. I felt a terrible foreboding that these waves would rise so high as to swallow up everyone and everything in their path. I desperately ran to get onto higher ground.

I climb up hills, trees, or staircases in tall buildings—whatever will take me to a higher elevation. Eventually, enormous tidal waves reach landfall. All around me, there is death and destruction. In my mind, it is just a matter of time until I meet death. Suddenly, I see a man in a flowing white robe floating above the scene. He plunges his nail-pierced hand into the waves and pulls me to safety. My *Deep-Water Dreams* revealed the truth of my existence at certain times in my life when I would be living a life far from God.

I always believed in God but was what you could call a *Compartmentalized Christian*. Faith was an aspect of my life that did not shape everything. My life was divided between the secular world and God. I was married twice to men who were not interested in God. When I was not married, I entered numerous romantic relationships. My lifestyle and friends did not always include God. There were times when I abandoned the faith of my youth. I searched for love, acceptance, and identity in all the wrong places. Looking back, I can relate to the Woman at the Well and Denying Peter. Still, Jesus met me where I was and loved me anyway. Such love, grace, mercy, and compassion I could never find in the face of another person.

My recurring Deep-Water Dreams are deeply imprinted in my heart and soul. Throughout my life, Jesus, my Saviour, appeared in so many dreams, which seemed to be prophetic visions of the role fear/affliction/suffering/danger would play in my life. As I have matured in years and faith, I appreciate the spiritual lessons God has taught and continues to make known to me:

- God reveals Himself through suffering/affliction. ***"…they will call him Immanuel" (which means "God with us").* (Matthew 1:23, NIV)**

- God is a God of Purpose. Pain has a purpose. ***"It was good for me to be afflicted so that I might learn your decrees."* (Psalm 119:71, NIV)**

- ***"He is our ever-present help in trouble."* (Psalm 46:1, NIV)**

- ***"Faithful and absolutely trustworthy is He who is calling you [to Himself for your salvation], and He will do it [He will fulfill His call by making you holy, guarding you, watching over you, and protecting you as His own]."* (1 Thessalonians 5:24 AMP)**

- NEVER let go of the hand of Jesus. *"We have this hope as an anchor for the soul, firm and secure."* **(Hebrews 6:19, NIV)**

- *"Praise be to the God and Father of our Lord Jesus Christ, the Father of compassion and the God of all comfort, who comforts us in all our troubles so that we can comfort those in any trouble with the comfort we ourselves receive from God."* **(2 Corinthians 1:3-4, NIV)**

- I can honestly testify that I've witnessed the miraculous life saving hand of our Lord in my life and my family's. *Jesus replied, "What is impossible with man is possible with God."* **(Luke 18:27, NIV)**

- God never sends a storm to sink us; instead, the storms drive us into His waiting arms. Life is more difficult without God.

God continues to do the healing transformative work in my life, turning fear into faith, doubt into trust, cowardness into courage and anxiety into peace. I borrow a phrase *Joyce Meyer* often uses, *I'm not where I want to be, but thank God I'm not where I used to be. God is not done with me yet!*

Marianne Still

Evolution Can't Explain How Caterpillars Become

Butterfly

A few summers ago, I planted several milkweed plants amongst the flowers in my side garden to help with the declining Monarch butterfly population. We watched Monarch butterflies come and land on the leaves and lay their eggs - one per leaf on the underside of the leaf. We waited for the eggs to hatch - but the ants, spiders, and wasps ate them, everyone. We walked past a neighbour's front yard where there were many milkweed plants - but again, not a single caterpillar.

So, when I saw the next Monarch butterfly lay eggs, I took one of the leaves in and put it in a glass container with a cheesecloth topper. Above are the pictures I took of "Elsa's" (as in Born Free) development over the next several weeks. A friend who was a biologist told me how to distinguish a male monarch from a female by the pattern of the wings. I had to rename Elsa to Eli.

I talked to Eli every day through his caterpillar stage and took him outside when it was cool enough so he could feel the fresh air, hear the sounds, and smell the garden. He was a ravenous eater and a prodigious pooper. I had to change the paper towel I put at the bottom of his cage daily.

Eli was so still in his chrysalis stage that I thought he hadn't made it. But I heard a whisper in my head that said, ***"Do I bring to the moment of birth and not give delivery?"*** **(Isaiah 66:9, NIV)**

One morning, when I woke up, there he was on his twig, slowly flapping his wings. My biologist friend told me to make him some sugar water and set him free in a nearby field which had lots of golden-rod plants (which they apparently like to eat the pollen of) and milkweed plants that might attract a mate.

By then, he was clinging to the cheesecloth topper of his bottle, ready to leave. I removed the topper and faced him towards the field. He looked at it for several seconds, then turned around and looked at me. Then he took flight and circled over the golden-rod plants, returned, and perched on a leaf on the shaded tree beside me.

1 Corinthians 15:42-44 says, ***"The body that is sown is perishable, it is raised imperishable; it is sown in dishonour, it is raised in glory; it is sown in weakness, it is raised in power; it is sown a natural body, it is raised a spiritual body"*** **(NIV).**

God speaks to us through his natural world if we will only notice. Evolution can't change a caterpillar into a butterfly. Even if it could, it would take a millennium to do so. Only a heavenly Creator has that power. The miracle of transformation comes to the Christian through the power of the Holy Spirit. For the believer, this becomes a fantastic thing to watch, even more extraordinarily beautiful than the transformation and birth of a Monarch Butterfly.

Roslyn Farmer

Experiencing the Presence of God

My husband of forty-six years passed away eight years ago. We held a 'Celebration of Life' for him here in Canada, and life moved on. However, we did not have complete closure. Although he had lived in Canada for over fifty years, his heart was ever in Scotland. A year after he died, my daughter and I travelled to Scotland to scatter his ashes beside his daughter's grave in a beautiful spot overlooking The Kyles of Bute.

It was a very emotional time for us as both his and my families were able to come to say a final goodbye to a much-loved husband, father, brother, and uncle. We were grieving and missing him and our eldest daughter, who had died in 1991 at age 21, all over again.

My husband loved the steamship "Waverley", which sails up and down the Clyde. We would do this sailing every time we were home, which was why we chose the spot we did to scatter my daughter's ashes. There are now two plaques on a rock, one entitled "Heather's Place" and the second "Heather's Dad".

We had just finished lunch in a nearby hotel and gathered outside for a group photo when we looked out at the water and saw the steamship "Waverley" sailing past my husband and daughter's final resting place. At that moment, I felt a presence, and a feeling of complete peace came over me, and I knew for sure that they were both safe at home with God. I was finally able to let go of my grief eventually. God is ever around us, surrounding us with His love.

This hymn speaks to me of that moment and God's peace.

Be Still, for the Presence of the Lord - Song by David J. Evans

> Be still for the presence of the Lord
> The Holy One is here
> Come bow before him now
> In reverence and fear
> In Him, no sin is found
> We stand on Holy ground
> Be still for the presence of the Lord
> The Holy one is here.

Be still for the glory of the Lord
Is shining all around
He burns with Holy fire
With splendor, He is crowned
How awesome is the sight.
Our radiant King of light
Be still for the glory of the Lord.
It is shining all around.
Be still for the power of the Lord
Is moving in this place
He comes to cleanse and heal
To minister His grace
No work too hard for Him
In faith, receive from Him
Be still for the power of the Lord
Is moving in this place. Amen.

Margaret Russell

Father of Compassion and the God of all Comfort

In 2005, my world fell apart. I lost my beloved mother to a chronic illness that became acute at night. She died. The impact was devastating. She had always been the one to encourage me, to praise my successes, and to lift my spirits as a child and an adult. I felt part of me had died as if my life had lost a substantial part of its meaning. In short, she was my anchor.

Her love had been particularly critical when my father left the family home. I was a teenager and began to drift into trouble. Without her, I might not have made it through my teenage years.

And so, we had an extraordinary bond. And we had many good times together until her death. And she believed in and followed Christ. In my eulogy for her, I called her a "country girl with a heart of gold." She taught me empathy, kindness, and service as core principles.

But now she is gone. And I felt empty. Grief moved in and took up residence.

But God is a God of comfort. One of my favorite passages in Scripture has always been Second Corinthians verses three and four: ***"Praise be to the God and Father of our Lord Jesus Christ, the Father of compassion and the God of all comfort, who comforts us in all our troubles so that we can comfort those in any trouble with the comfort we ourselves have received from God."*** **(NIV)**

As this came to mind, I realized God was speaking to me. I was to build on my service to the Kingdom. But before that began, I had another even more critical God moment. I felt very strongly that He was directing me to seminary. I started to take courses.

The atmosphere of the seminary was healing. The students were friendly, fully engaged, and happy. The professors were eager to talk off-site. The subjects deepened my understanding of my faith. It was, in short, a sacred space.

I graduated with a Master of Theological Studies. The graduation ceremony was inspiring because of speeches by the valedictorian and Tyndale's President. They called us to engage in mission and to give Christ our all.

I wondered when and how God would call me to a mission. It soon became apparent. I saw an ad for Prayer Partners for 100 Huntley Street. I felt called to this role, which involved praying with people who called in from many locations, mainly in North America.

I have been doing this for over a year, and it has been an incredible blessing. I have prayed for people in grief, the unemployed, those with family problems, those with addictions, the lonely, and several hundred unique human problems.

In addition, I have been teaching a Bible study based on a seminary text that takes an in-depth look at how to live well, die well, and live forever.

It is said, "Life must be lived forward but can only be understood backwards." I lived with deep sorrow at my mother's death. Yet, God did not leave me there. I lost the meaning of life with my mother's death yet regained it in a new way. God had new purposes for me. I embraced those purposes.

Our God is a God of reconciliation, restoration, redemption, and renewal. We only need to remember this and prayerfully believe it.

Anonymous

For God so loved the world that He gave His only begotten Son, that whoever believes in Him should not perish but have everlasting life. For God did not send His Son into the world to condemn the world, but that the world through Him might be saved. John 3:16-17 (NKJV)

God and 'Green Day'

We all love a great story. Imagine the most incredible love story, one where love conquers all, where people are seen and valued for who they are and are pursued relentlessly by a great love. Imagine a story where evil, disease, rape, and incest abound, and unjust wars are everywhere—yet truth, justice, mercy, forgiveness, grace, and love are woven throughout. We are experiencing this epic story, one God has been writing since the beginning of time. This is how I envision my life. Sometimes I am a bit player in someone else's story, sometimes the main character, but always significant. If a story is all sunshine and roses - it is boring. An interesting story contains conflict, overcoming, and redemption because that is where the learning, growth, and transformation occur, but we don't always want to live it. This knowledge helps me maintain perspective when difficult or overwhelming situations arise. I can recognise it as a chapter, and my whole life is not now a tragedy. Sometimes, when things go awry, I am even able to think, "This will be a good story someday!"

Since stories engage and draw us in. Most people would much rather hear you tell a story about your life than quote them a Bible verse! I am sure God knew this when he orchestrated the Bible to be written mainly in the narrative. As a teenager, I wondered why Jesus wouldn't just give a straightforward answer. I learned that in Jewish culture, leaders routinely answered questions with a question, story, or parable, and those deep questions rarely had one correct answer. But it still frustrated me. I wanted the bullet points and a clear, incontrovertible blueprint to follow. When Jesus answered questions with a story, they connected with people so they could easily remember them. The parables contained truth and multiple layers of meaning with numerous takeaways for different people listening. If they took the time to ponder them, perhaps they didn't always get a specific answer but a new way of being, thinking and acting from a different posture of the heart and mind. Now, I realize life rarely requires a simple, straightforward answer – life is complex and nuanced.

Our life journey and pace of understanding and learning are unique to each of us. Over my life, I've learned that God is always trying to reach, teach, and connect with us. We are constantly being changed and shaped by the events and interactions of our lives.

I had always read in the Bible how God spoke to people through angels, donkeys, bushes, prophets, and dreams. Yet, I was only listening or paying attention when I was quiet, reading Scripture, listening to sermons, or praying – usually with pen and journal ready.

I hadn't heard of any talking donkeys or burning bushes, noticed angels, or had inspirational dreams. I often thought that God could never speak to me through dreams since I am a nightly vivid dreamer. How would I ever distinguish the profound from the profoundly absurd? So, I didn't have a dream from God or a voice from the sky, but I did have an experience where I believed God uniquely spoke to me.

My husband and I learned about a messy situation involving people close to us. And although we were only indirectly involved, I had never been so hurt by my community of faith. I was shocked and felt such anger and betrayal. I'm not prone to dramatics, catastrophizing, or immediately building up grievances. My initial response to troubling things is to extend grace and not take offence.

Before you attribute moral virtue to me, this is a defence mechanism on my part. I choose to give people the benefit of the doubt since I don't *want* to be angry at people, nor do I wish to consider that they would intentionally mistreat me or hurt me. I protect my heart by assuming there is some misunderstanding or miscommunication somewhere. But in this case, I couldn't find an explanation, positive spin, or adequate excuse for those involved.

Metaphorical hurt turned physical as it seemed like I couldn't breathe properly. I felt that if I tried to take a deep breath, I would choke on my anger. I couldn't sleep. Everything just kept circling in my mind. My husband and I didn't know if this was our fight. We didn't know how to proceed, how much we should get involved, whether to speak up, confront, give counsel, step back, or walk away. We felt sucked into this whirlwind, and we were standing at the centre of a vortex of emotions. I did not doubt God or his goodness – but I was seriously taking issue with the institution and people of His church.

After a restless night, I woke up feeling my heart was broken, my chest hurt, and my thoughts and emotions were swirling. I turned on my speaker and started scrolling through my music library for something to play so I could just sing and try to forget this awful situation for a time. I often played music to match my mood, and that day, I wanted to play something loud, with a strong beat, perhaps an old rock anthem, but I didn't want *anything* 'Christian'. I was thinking maybe some 'Queen' or 'Imagine Dragons', and then I saw 'Green Day'.

It had been quite a while since I listened to 'Green Day'. I appropriately chose the album '21st Century Breakdown' since I felt like I was having one. I scrolled down to my favorite song, '21 Guns,' and cranked up the volume. All I remembered was that I loved the pounding drums in the chorus. I wanted to stomp my feet with the drums and sing at a shouting volume. I wanted to take out my hurt, anger, and frustration in an acceptable way. As the song started, the first line stopped me cold.

"Do you know what's worth fighting for when it's not worth dying for?"

And I thought to myself, "No, actually, at the moment, I don't." I turned and faced the speaker to continue listening.

"Does it take your breath away, and you feel yourself suffocating?
Does the pain weigh out the pride?
Did someone break your heart inside?
You're in ruins."

At this point, the tears started coursing down my face; these were my sentiments exactly! It was just how I felt, articulated in a way I couldn't, with my emotions interfering with cohesive thought. Then, the pounding familiar chorus,

"1, 21 guns, lay down your arms, give up the fight,
1, 21 guns throw up your arms into the sky, you and I."

It continued,

"When you're at the end of the road,
And you've lost all sense of control,
And your thoughts have taken their toll,
When your mind breaks the spirit of your soul
Your faith walks on broken glass,
You're in ruins."

I could hardly believe what had just happened! Through the voice and lyrics of Billie Joe Armstrong, God had just spoken to my soul. I *had* no control. My thoughts *were* taking a toll on my spirit, and I was nearer to the end of myself and my faith than I had ever been. I felt my faith and heart were all broken shards of glass. As the chorus came on again, I realized this *wasn't* my fight, and I needed to keep my hands raised and open to God, and we'd figure out how to proceed. I knew I didn't want my mind to break the spirit of my soul, and I also truthfully knew it was on the path of doing just that. I needed to stop allowing the hurt to fuel my anger. I needed to throw down my offence and lift my arms heavenward. I needed to let God into everything, even my anger, and try to stop my loud, insistent thoughts from drowning out all others, like ones of grace. I *wanted* to be angry. I *had* reasons. I felt *justified*. Others and I had been treated poorly and hurt by the words and actions of people I cared for and respected. They must know how hurtful and wrong they were! My feelings were natural, but I didn't need to feed them and make the rift greater.

I mentally began to lay down my arms, the ammunition I had been gathering in my mind. And as I did, I calmed down. It stopped the turmoil I was feeling in my mind, the twisting in my stomach, and my chest felt free, lighter, no longer constricting my breathing. It reminded me of my children when they were small; they felt such big, uncontrollable feelings and would throw a tantrum. I remember sitting and holding them and letting them cry and be angry until they were spent. I would feel them quiet and relax in my arms. This is what I felt myself doing; I felt like my Father God had held me and wrapped me in his love until the tantrum subsided, and I could relax into his compassion. I felt seen, heard, held, and understood.

I replayed the song and sang it not in defiance but in brokenness, with tears streaming down my face. I did the actions of the chorus, and instead of a closed hand with a rock fist, my posture was one of surrender and supplication. I put my arms down with open hands – letting my ammunition fall to the ground, and then raised my arms to reach out to God, like a child reaching for a parent to pick them up.

Who would ever think God would use an old 'Green Day' song to speak to me? I don't believe for a second that this was random or coincidental, that I just 'happened' to scroll down to that album, that song. My body was listening to prompts from God before my mind could follow them. God wanted to calm my soul and used the only thing that I would listen to at the time.

That is the power of the love of God for us. Only He can whisper truth, love, and understanding into our hearts when we don't even want to listen. He is at work in unique ways to direct our story and help us live through the parts we don't understand. Of course, the situation still existed and needed to be worked through. Much more grace and mercy were demanded of me than I naturally wanted to give. But things in life are complicated – a hug and a kiss don't 'fix' them. Some situations or relationships never resolve to our satisfaction despite our best efforts and intentions. Complex situations, decisions, or misunderstandings will always continue to happen – but more significant than the dimming details of the offence, I will never forget how God cared enough to reach me when I did not want to hear from him. I remember how he used a 'Green Day' song with perfect lyrics to speak truth to me and turn my eyes and emotions Godward so he could comfort, love, and guide me. I will always remember how he affirmed his very presence in the details of my life.

This story is a reminder for me and, hopefully, an encouragement to others that God can and does use anyone and anything to reach us. When we're in pain, suffering, stuck, or following a poor plot line, our awesome God whispers a better story into our consciousness. Our faithful, loving, and persistent God knows us and speaks to us in ways we will hear. God operates in any setting, not only within the church, listening to Christian music, or reading the Bible—because God is everywhere and in everything and wants to speak into our lives. We need to be alert to his voice, as Jesus said multiple times in the gospels; "whoever has ears to hear, let them hear."

Perhaps if we are more open to hearing, we will have those infamous Oprah 'aha' moments, both big and small, that we think only happen to other people - as we acknowledge that all our lives are sacred stories. It is a gift and privilege to journey our messy yet beautiful stories that are mundane and extraordinary as we experience the mysterious alchemy of life with God and faith.

And perhaps *we will* recognize and have more moments of clarity, grace, unexpected peace, deep wonder, or love washing over us, nudges, corrections, and inspirations spoken to our souls through unexpected voices - so we can continue to learn and grow and live out our lives showing His epic love story to the world.

Janey Bordihn

God Even Uses Frozen Pipes!

I share a complicated story involving many people and a few organizations, but it is an encouraging story of God's provision. Please follow along as best you can. It's a good reminder of how each person does their part as the Holy Spirit leads.

Lazarus Solomon was an IVEPer (International Visitor Exchange Program of Mennonite Central Committee) from Nigeria. In 1999, his visa was denied, so he came to Canada in 2000-2001. He worked at our church and in Stouffville and lived at our house for the second half of his stay.

While with us, he received news that his sister, Julia, had been badly burned in a house fire. Because of Muslim-Christian fighting and rioting at this time, the patients at the hospital did not receive proper care for several months.

Lazarus was sad that he couldn't be with his sister but realized that because he was in Canada, it was possible to forward the money the Wideman Church members collected to be used for Julia's care.

When Lazarus returned to Nigeria, he saw his sister's plight for himself. It was a desperate situation. He hoped and prayed more could be done for her. She had little mobility in her neck and arms and stayed at home in the house most of the time. She had several children to care for and could not move effectively to care for them. He asked us, at the Wideman Mennonite Church, to find a North American doctor skilled with burn treatment experience to help her. I made some inquiries and am still waiting to hear back. A doctor in Africa would be the best solution.

Now the most amazing thing happened! On Stouffville Road, Emmanuel International had a missionary training school at their facility. Trainees were housed in a trailer on site. However, the cold February weather froze the water pipes in this trailer, which made it inconvenient to have a family stay there. Wideman's Youth Pastor, Sue Fallon, who worked at Emmanuel International, pleaded with the church one Sunday morning for someone to host the coming

Mellen family of five from England for two weeks. We offered to take them.

The Mellen family had served previously in Nigeria, so we had an immediate connection and opportunity to share about Lazarus' time in Markham. The Mellens planned to visit Toronto with American friends for the weekend. They had met them in Nigeria 10 years ago when both families had been doing voluntary service and had kept in touch. The family was from Cleveland, Ohio; the husband and wife were physicians.

The physicians planned to return to Nigeria in June 2003 to work for the Mennonite Central Committee at a clinic treating AIDS patients. We asked if the Mellens would mention Lazarus and his sister to the doctors from Cleveland in hopes that they might investigate Julia's condition and assess her needs. The Mellens happily agreed to do this, and the doctors expressed interest in meeting Lazarus when they reached Nigeria.

Meanwhile, this same weekend, at Wideman Church's winter retreat, I was standing in the food line recounting this story to someone when Sheryl Wideman, behind me, asked if the doctors from Cleveland were named Beachy. The doctors were Sheryl's cousins, the Beachys, who had served in Nigeria years ago. She contacted them, and their desire to help Julia increased even more.

The story now shifts to Burlington, Ontario. A former Mennonite Central Committee family recently returned from 5 years in the Republic of Congo, and former members of Wideman Church heard the Lazarus story from Sheryl. The wife, Ann Campbell-Janz, currently works with a mission based in Ghana that did surgery on children with cleft palates. She happened to know that a doctor in Ghana specialized in burn cases. It would be far cheaper to send Julia to Ghana than to try to bring her to North America. She suggested contacting that doctor for help.

Back in Nigeria, the Beachys had met Dr. Ardill, who worked at the mission hospital. He was interested in getting together a protocol for HIV care for the hospital and had asked them to dinner to discuss this new care initiative. As a result, the Beachys and Dr. Ardill formed a unique friendship and medical team relationship.

The Beachys met Lazarus and Julia and took photos of her burns to send to the doctor in Ghana. They knew Dr Ardill had a scanner and asked if they could scan the images to send them to Ghana. These photos did not scan well. However, as Dr. Ardill sent them, he was able to review the images. He said he could do surgery on Julia to release the contractures causing Julia's immobility!

Once again, Wideman Church was able to send funds to help pay for the surgical procedure. The Beachys saw Julia smile for the first time following her surgery. Her condition has improved immensely, and she is a happy lady!

What if Lazarus had come to Canada the first year he applied? What if he had gone to another location for his second term? What if the pipes hadn't frozen? What if we had not hosted the English family? What if the English family still needed to meet the physicians from Cleveland and share Lazarus' story? What if the doctors hadn't been returning to Nigeria? What if Sheryl hadn't told Ann, who knew of the burn doctor? What if the physicians had sent the photos without scanning them? What if the Beachys hadn't met Dr. Ardill? What if Dr Ardill hadn't offered to do the surgery himself? What if the Wideman congregation still needed to send the funds?

In Julia's case, everyone had to respond to the Holy Spirit's leading and be responsible for one link in the chain of God's miracle. Usually, we don't see the whole of God's gift from start to finish, but God let us see it this time to encourage us to keep being willing and obedient servants.

Steve and I went to Nigeria to attend Lazarus' wedding in 2004 as representatives of Wideman Church. We met Julia, who was able to greet us and give personal thanks to all the people and the efforts involved in her recovery. Thank you, Lord, for frozen pipes!

A coincidence is God's way of remaining anonymous, says Albert Einstein. *"Most of us go through life a little afraid. I believe a coincidence is often a way God touches our lives to reassuring us of His love and offering us some help or guidance."*

Barbara Ribble

God Found Us the Perfect Home

Our daughter Deborah wanted me to look after her baby girl Michaela starting September first. I was willing to do this, but it was a long drive to her home.

So, we put our two-story, four-bedroom home up for sale. Meanwhile, I drove daily to our daughter's home and prayed that the Lord would find us a bungalow in Markham close to her home.

Our house sold, and we had only six weeks to find a bungalow near little Michaela. We put our furniture in storage and moved into our daughter's home. We slept on a sofa in the basement until we found our new home.

Our realtor called and said that just three minutes away was a bungalow for sale. Did we want to see it? We went immediately. We were sadly disappointed. The house needed a lot of renovations, and the big room in the basement had no walls. But the next day, our realtor called us again to say that the realtor of the house we saw yesterday overheard us say that we wanted a bungalow in this neighbourhood. Well, a place was going up for sale, just doors from the house we had seen the day before. Yes, we would love to see it. And that home was perfect, and we could put an offer in before it went on the market. We met their price and were able to move in just in time for Christmas. The house was three minutes from Deborah's home.

The owner of our soon-to-be home worked in the same company as Alex, my husband, which may have helped us buy the house. We needed God's help, had trusted Him before, and knew He would not disappoint us.

Donna Smith

"For eye has not seen, nor ear heard, nor have entered into the heart of man the things which God has prepared for those who love Him." (1 Corinthians 2:9 NKJV).

God Hears and Helps Us in Life's Big and Little Things

I am incredibly close to my older brother, who, recently, and unfortunately, has been experiencing some severe health problems. He has been unable to speak or swallow due to paralysis in his throat. So, the best thing I thought I could do for him was to send him regular emails sharing whatever I, my two children and friends were doing. I focused on my personal life and felt that it would interest him. His responses back to me were monosyllabic replies of disinterest.

Recently, I woke up in the middle of the night thinking about this and praying for God's help with this dilemma. I asked God how I might better encourage my dear brother. Then, that voice crept into my head, reminding me that my brother was an avid gardener and particularly loved vegetable gardening. I am a flower gardener, but in memory of my late husband this year, I decided to plant vegetables as he always looked after that side of our garden.

As I pondered this, a small voice said, ask your brother for advice on vegetables, so that's what I did. Back came a fascinating and lengthy informative reply. There were no more monosyllable emails. I had stopped concentrating on my own life and interests and connected to what gave him something of interest to lift his thoughts.

Sympathy is saying, "I am sorry for whatever has gone wrong in your life, whereas empathy is feeling and understanding what that person is thinking by letting them know you are carrying them in your heart and hurting along with them."

I wanted to encourage my brother amid his poor health situation by reflecting on him and praying for him. God showed me a way to connect with him in a meaningful way. Once I felt my brother's feelings, I became a more encouraging sister and communicator.

Recently, I got an email telling me that my brother's youngest daughter, Gillian, was diagnosed with cancer and had to have four months of chemo, surgery and then more treatments. I tried to empathize as I contacted her about everything she was going through. Gillian mentioned how my words had encouraged her father and told me that her husband and children were terrifically supportive, as was her church family. She stressed how much her faith was helping her. God works beautifully to assist us in life's big and little things.

Sympathy - an expression of understanding and care for someone else's suffering.

Example - *The president has sent a message of sympathy to the relatives of the dead soldiers.*

Empathy - the ability to share someone else's feelings or experiences by imagining what it would be like to be in that person's situation.

Example – Your friend studies hard for the test but fails. Even though you passed, you can relate as you remember how devastated you felt when you failed.

Wilma Medley

God is With Us and For Us

When one becomes a senior and is a believer, one need never wonder what they will do in their retirement. You may retire but never be out of service, no matter where you reside. God is with us at every stage of life: before and at conception, in our mother's womb, at birth, in youth, in our middle years, and if we reach "old age when strength fails."

King David declared his confidence by saying, in Psalm 71: 6-8, 20 (NIV)

⁶ From birth I have relied on you;
you brought me forth from my mother's womb.
I will ever praise you.
⁷ I have become a sign to many;

63

you are my strong refuge.
[8] My mouth is filled with your praise,
declaring your splendor all day long.
[20] Though you have made me see troubles,
many and bitter,
you will restore my life again;
from the depths of the earth
you will again bring me up.

The fundamental idea for King David is that God is his rock and strong refuge (verses 3, 7). God will rescue and deliver him in God's righteousness. With this vision, we, along with King David, can see that old age is simply a continuation of our service to God and an opportunity to deepen our relationship with Him. In one's senior years, Christians are encouraged to share their wisdom and experience with the next generation. We are to tell of the good news of God's provision of salvation through Jesus Christ for all who will receive it and be His ambassadors.

With years of experience, we seniors are encouraged to tell of God's faithfulness and unfailing love to those younger, especially those who are searching. God is with us always, even to the ends of the earth. His love and faithfulness are ever present, seeking our good. He is ever-loving and faithful in our lives to guide us and lead us in what to share with others and how to live Christ-like examples that point others to Him.

Suzanne Wilkinson

He (God) guided them safely, so they were unafraid;
but the sea engulfed their enemies.
And so he brought them to the border of his holy land,
to the hill country his right hand had taken.
He drove out nations before them
and allotted their lands to them as an inheritance;
He settled the tribes of Israel in their homes,
and David shepherded them with integrity of heart;
with skillful hands he led them.
Psalm 78: 53-55, 72 (NIV)

God is So Good

We had been Christians only six months when, in August, our church asked for volunteers to go door to door in the neighbourhood and hand out Gospel tracts, and if the people wanted to hear the Gospel and respond well, we would offer to serve them in this way. Alex and I volunteered, and in September, we were given several streets to canvas.

Off we went, and the people at the first few doors were polite but uninterested. At the third house, I knocked on the door, and a man came with no shirt on and a paintbrush in his hand. I asked him if he was interested in hearing the Gospel message of Jesus Christ. He just said one word. "Yes!" I was shocked, but I knew God was with me in this. I gave him the message using a small brochure. He wanted to know God and was ready to ask Jesus into his heart. We spent a few minutes answering his questions and mentioned that our church was close by, and we would love to see him there. It turned out that this man worked in the same company as Alex. God was present with us and gave us the words and the courage to say them.

Donna Smith

God is There to Guide Us: Discerning God's Direction

It seemed like a typical day when I was around twelve as I walked down the road after school, carrying my skate bag over my shoulder. A car was following me, and it slowed down. The window opened on the passenger side, and a man was inside. He said to me, "I'm looking for the arena. Do you know where it is?" And I said to him, "Well, you're going the wrong way. It's from where you just came." So anyway, he said, "are you going that way?" I said, "Yes, I am". And then he said, "I can give you a ride, and then you can tell me how to get to the arena."

He had been asking me different questions, and for some reason, I thought he knew me and had seen me skating because he sounded familiar with the skating club to which I belonged.

Instinctively, I sensed that talking to a stranger was wrong. My parents had taught me not to get into a stranger's car. I knew something was wrong, but at the same time, I felt I should help this man, just out of kindness. I sensed fear, yet at the same time, I wanted to help.

As soon as I got into his car, I knew I had done something wrong. I was very, very nervous. As he drove towards the arena, I said, "Well, this is my street coming up. So, you can stop and let me out here." But he didn't stop. He just kept driving slowly. I was figuring out how I would get out of the car. He went to the end of the block, stopped, let me out, and then continued north on the street and stopped at the corner of the first block.

He stopped on the corner and blocked the sidewalk with the open passenger door. Fortunately, I was familiar with the area. There was a wooded area behind the houses on the street that I would have to go down. I ran, for my life, through the woods, came out on my road, and went straight into my home, which was luckily close by.

I can still feel my heart pounding as I recall this incident almost seventy years later. I was so glad to be home. I watched through the curtains of my front windows and saw the man leave the car and walk around looking for me. After a while, he got back in the car and drove away. My knees were shaking, but I was so grateful to be safe.

I didn't tell my parents anything about this incident because they would have been furious with me for getting into a dangerous situation, especially after all the warnings we children had received. Perhaps they knew there was a predator in the area. That's why they told us not to accept a ride with a stranger.

I was ashamed of myself, but it taught me how easily a child can be misled and deceived. As adults, we can be fooled, too. Whenever I sense things are wrong, I must stop, pause, and pray before jumping into the unknown. I can sympathize with anybody who makes a poor judgment they know they should not have made. We learn from our mistakes, but God wants to be our helper. Take the time to consider the consequences before moving forward. Sensing God's direction may prevent bad marriages, financial disasters, and even physical harm. We need to discern God's leading and let Him be our protector.

In retrospect, I know God was my protector that day and saved me from a terrible mistake. Who knows what could have happened to me that day? Life comes at us fast, but we must learn to take time to discern God's direction.

Anonymous

God Moments Through Music

I love poetry, and even more, I love hymns – especially poetry set to appropriate music. God speaks to me through the fantastic truth found in the old hymns of the faith.

I thank God that He has gifted me with an above-average memory, so poems and hymns, learned decades ago, often come to mind when I am experiencing challenging times.

Whenever I have had doubts about my salvation, I am reminded of the third line of verse one of *"Praise my soul the King of Heaven"*, which is *"Ransomed, healed, restored, forgiven"*. Those words have given me the assurance I needed.

There have been financial shortfalls when a specific hymn reminded me of the One from whom all blessings flow.

"We give thee, but thine own, whatever the gift may be.

All that we have is thine alone, a trust, O Lord from Thee."

With those words, God has helped me to reconsider my priorities. In the past couple of weeks, I have had a difficult situation

67

to grapple with, and as I was praying about the matter, an old hymn often sung in a small Bible Study group came to my mind.

He leadeth me! O blessed thought,
O words with heav'nly comfort fraught;
Whatever I do, where I be, ~~e'er~~ ~~e'er~~ *correct*
Still 'tis God's hand that leadeth me.

He leadeth me! He leadeth me! (Refrain)
By His own hand, He leadeth me;
His faithful follower I would be, *delete o* ✓
For by His hand, He leadeth me.
Sometimes' in scenes of deepest gloom,
Sometimes, where Eden's bowers bloom,
By waters still, o'er troubled sea,
Still 'tis His hand that leadeth me.

Lord, I would clasp Thy hand in mine,
Nor ever murmur or repine;
Content, whatever lot I see,
Since ~~it is Thou~~ that leadest me.
'tis God's hand

And especially the last verse…

And when my task on earth is done,
When, by Thy grace, the vict'ry's won,
E'en death's cold wave, I will not flee, *delete comma*
Since ~~Thou in triumph~~ leadest me. (refrain).
God through Jordan

move to after / all the way

Lastly, there have been times of rededication when the hymn.

'Take my life and let it be......' says it more eloquently than I could.

I love singing this hymn, but the last verse has (permanently) moved me deeply, *+ permanently.*

should be in Bold print

"Take my love, my Lord, I pour
at thy feet its treasure store.
Take myself, and I will be, ✗ *BOLD*
Ever, only, all for Thee.

68

(handwritten margin notes: insert after final vrs of "He Leadeth me")

Another hymn that means so very much to me and has guided me is:

All the way my Saviour leads me - what have I to ask beside?
Can I doubt His tender mercy, who through life has been my guide?
Heavenly peace, divinest comfort, here by faith in him to dwell!
For I know, whatever befall me, Jesus doeth all things well

All the way my Saviour leads me - cheers each winding path I tread,
Gives me grace for every trial, feeds me with the living bread.
When my spirit, clothed immortal, wings its flight to realms of day
This is my song through endless ages: Jesus led me all the way.

By combining verses two and three, these beautiful words are a perfect summation of my life. God has faithfully guided me through the past ninety years through happy and challenging times. He has graciously put some unique and gifted people in my pathway who have enriched my life immeasurably, often giving me a new and inspiring outlook on various events.

The above are just a few of the many times God has brought a particular hymn to mind, which has been just what I needed. I believe He inspired the writers of these words and the musicians who enhanced them, just as He inspired the writers of Scripture. Thanks be to God!

Ruth Adams

God Of All Comfort (A Voice In The Dark)

"Don't be afraid, for I am with you. Don't be discouraged, for I am your God. I will strengthen you and help you. I will hold you up with my victorious right hand." **(Isaiah 41:10, NLT)**

"The LORD is close to the broken-hearted, and he saves those whose spirits have been crushed." **(Psalm 34:18, NIV)**

"You keep track of all my sorrows. You have collected all my tears in your bottle. You have recorded each one in your book."
(Psalm 56:8, NLT)

From the age of approximately ten years old, I battled with depression. My first attempt to run from the pain and never wake up was on the night of my First Confirmation, not long after I had witnessed a ruthless, brutal, and violent scene in my family home.

There began a series of attempts to escape a life so riddled with pain, a life that I believed was pointless, a life that was hopeless, a life I felt helpless to control. I felt so alone.

About twenty years later, the Lord's love, mercy and compassion visited me most astonishingly.

I awoke in a dark, lonely hospital room. I remember the feeling of complete despair. Hysterical and sobbing, my pillow was soaked with tears.

My mind contemplated life's heartaches, disappointments, and failures, spinning me into a deeper, darker vortex of despair.

Confused and desperate, I angrily questioned God as to why He would let me live. I accused Him of trying to torture me. Could He not see that my life had no worth? I felt abnormal and broken beyond repair. I argued that my family, friends, and the world would be better off with me dead. I remember my body trembling so much that the bed shook. I was totally distraught and inconsolable.

Suddenly, a voice spoke through the darkness. *My Child don't be afraid, for I AM with You. You are going to be okay. Trust Me.*

It is hard to adequately describe the miraculous atmospheric shift in the room that night. My tears and trembling ceased abruptly. I felt bathed in a warm, supernatural peace and calm. Although I didn't see Him, God's presence was undeniable.

After that experience, the circumstances of my life did not magically get easier. However, the Light of His presence on that dark night sparked a Holy fire desire to know Him more. Out of that experience, thirty-plus years of daily writing in a prayer/dream journal were born. Recording and reflecting on life's experiences spiritually reveals and heals.

I've learned pain has a purpose and grows our God's testimonies. His mercies are far greater than our miseries. No matter what, the enemy of our souls tries to make us believe that we are not worthless.

God doesn't create junk. He has a plan and purpose for our lives.

Marianne Still

God Opens Doors

We had been Christians for about five years when Alex lost his job at Eaton's warehouse. He was in his early forties and worried that, at his age, he would not find another job. We prayed about this and the following week, three job offers came up, and all wanted Alex to work for them. Now we prayed to know which job God wanted for Alex. We felt the answer was for him to accept a position that was an offshoot of Canadian Tire.

Alex worked at this small company only briefly when a notice went up wanting a man with warehouse experience to work at the head office in a retail shop as a manager inside Canadian Tire. Alex thought there were many people at this company and the competition would be very high. I reassured him that no one can take it away if God wants you to have this better job. So, he applied and was accepted. Fortunately, this new position was a significant advancement for Alex, and he was so thankful that God found this job for him. Alex worked there for 20 years. During that time, he heard from many men inside the company who had ten to twenty years of experience how much they wanted this job as it had many excellent benefits.

Alex and I were invited to a weekend conference in Ohio, and at the same time, I needed a new hearing aid. A better hearing aid might be available in the States. We did not have the money to do the trip or buy the needed hearing aid. As I have a profound hearing loss, we prayed especially for the latest hearing aid.

A few days later, a cheque for $2,500 from the company where Alex was now working (the Canadian Tire subsidiary) arrived in the mail. It was money that had been deducted from his pay to buy shares in the company. Because he had not worked there long enough to be able to purchase these shares, the company was refunding the money to him. It was just in time to buy the newest hearing aid and take the weekend trip to Ohio for the conference. God is so good. He heard our prayers and provided for both our desires and needs.

Donna Smith

God Prevented a Car Accident

Here is another way in which I know God is protecting us. Alex and I were on a trip to Ohio, and we were on a busy highway that was four lanes wide. Suddenly, we noticed the exit sign we needed, only 500 feet ahead of us. At the speed we were going and in the wrong lane, making that turn would have been impossible and totally unsafe for us or anyone else. I was in the far-left lane. The traffic was bumper to bumper, travelling at least 100 miles per hour or more.

How could I get over to that exit in time? I was afraid. I would not know how to find my way back if I missed that exit. In desperation, I cried, "Jesus help me," suddenly, a clear path opened, making the turn to the exit possible. The impossible became possible. I quickly crossed the lanes down the exit ramp onto the highway we needed to be on. I was relieved and amazed that Jesus would take an interest in our safety needs and open the way. He did. What a relief! God kept us safe and got us to our destination on time. God is so good, and He deserves our gratitude and praise.

In both these real-life stories, the impossible became possible as we felt God's hand was upon us, opening a way and protecting us as He intervened to save our lives from alcohol addiction and the potential of a terrible traffic accident and perhaps loss of life.

Donna Smith

God Protected Our Little Boy

It was Christmas Eve 1963, and my husband George and I headed out to join in on the church community's annual tradition of carolling at the homes of older folk and shut ins. Our two children – Louise, age five and Ernie, age 3 – were tucked in bed and fast asleep. Their two grandparents were in the apartment (the "doddy house") on the other side of the bedroom wall with the door open. By around 10:00 p.m., they, too, were fast asleep.

Unbeknownst to them, little Ernie woke up and noticed that mommy and daddy (who slept in the same large room as the children) were not there. He crept out of bed to find them. They were not in the living room or kitchen, so he opened the front door of the large farmhouse and ventured outside. The air was freezing cold, and the snow was deep. Determined to find them, he ran down the lane in only his pajamas and bare feet, going around the back of the house and the doddy house, finally stopping in despair below a back window. It happened to be the window of his grandparents' bedroom. His crying providentially awakened his grandmother as she heard his faint cries through the closed window. She immediately jumped out of bed and ran outside to rescue poor Ernie! When George and I arrived home a bit later, Ernie was all tucked up in a warm blanket as he was being comforted by his grandma. He did suffer frostbite on his feet and toes but soon recovered. If Ernie had not stopped below that specific window and if his grandparents had not heard this small boy's faint cry, Ernie's fate would have been life-threatening or worse. We knew without a doubt that a guardian angel had been sent from God above to follow Ernie on the frigid journey around the house and to guide his steps as he stopped in front of his grandparents' window. And we knew that God's nudging woke his grandma to hear little Ernie's cries.

Anna Reesor

"God is our refuge and strength, an ever-present help in trouble." **(Psalm 46:1, NIV)**

"He will cover you with His feathers, and under His wings you will find refuge." **(Psalm 91:4a, NIV)**

God Speaks – "Catch of the Day? Soul!"

It's the age of the spectacular. From the spectacular horrors of modern-day weaponry, drone attacks, massive bombardment, bigotry, hatred, and mob violence to the breathtaking wonders of stage and screen extravagances or the awesome sight, colour, and variations of nature! You, too, have sensed the spectacular.

If you have seen the talent and teamwork of a fine orchestra and heard the sounds of a symphony or the grandeur of a cathedral's well-rehearsed choir singing the Messiah, oh, that music moves the soul to soar. You, too, have been caught up in the spectacle! Suppose you have experienced an IMAX theatre production with its giant video screens involved in science, sounds, and the movement of nature's wonders and humankind's capacity for the extraordinary. In some ways, humanity, like nature, can excel. In those cases, you have experienced the breathtaking spectacular this world has to offer.

A few years ago, I had the dubious opportunity of riding a mule down into the depths of the Grand Canyon. And although the scenery was spectacular, my oneness with the mule which carried me left something to be despaired about. But recently, I had a gift. The gift was to experience the Grand Canyon again, not on the back of a plodding mule on a blistering summer day, but in the comforts of a padded chair in the air-conditioned luxury of an ultra-modern theatre! You not only experience the grandeur of the Grand Canyon but glide silently down and around ravines so marvellously sculpted by time, wind, and rain that you sit in raptured awe and wonder. You are there as you raft down the raging Colorado River, feel the turbulent water haystacks, and plunge into the sound and fury of untamed rapids and boiling waters. Can you feel and experience the power of God's wondrous world? If we take the time to notice, God is alive and speaks to us in many unique and extraordinarily spectacular ways.

And yet...what Isaiah experienced in his vision before the sacred throne of God surpasses by a thousand times the more modern technological spectaculars of our day! In his vision (Isaiah 6:1-8), he sees the Lord God of hosts high and lifted up, enthralled in majesty and holiness! "Holy, Holy, Holy is the Lord of hosts." Can you begin to experience the Majestic? Majesty of wonder and sacredness of Isaiah's vision? Sense the music and praise and joy!

And amid the vision, Isaiah realizes his own significance - his poorness of being. But Isaiah's vision continues - no intermission in this spectacular experience of sensing God. Something like hot coals touches his lips; picture it - a hot coal. And Isaiah knows- he knows it is the touch of God! And from this touch, he knows he is one of God's children! Forgiven and acceptable to God. The Holy Spirit of God has touched his life. And calls for a response.

In our Scriptures, the Holy Spirit of God is often symbolized by fire or wind. Moses, confronted by the Holy Spirit of God in that burning Bush, is calling to rescue an oppressed, ill-treated people from slavery and hopelessness. At Pentecost, the Holy Spirit of God, like tongues of fire and breath of wind, empowers those early Christians to carry God's message of hope and forgiveness, to rescue people from lives of hopelessness and despair.

Amid the spectacle, Isaiah responds. "Here am I, send me." But it is not a straightforward message to carry. No news that calls on people to turn away from injustice and repent of worshipping other gods brings popularity to the messenger. The other side of the message is the promise of help and deliverance by the one whom God would send into the world—a double-edged message: a call for repentance, a promise of redemption and hope.

And now, leave Isaiah's vision before the throne and fast forward your mind for almost nine hundred years! Just push the fast-forward button on the tape or in your mind and move from Isaiah to meet Peter, the disciple, fisherman, and follower of Jesus (Luke 5:1-11).

Peter cleans empty, smelly fishing hats on a cold, clammy Galilean morning as an ordinary fisherman. No crashing chords of the spectacular on a celestial organ! No angelic choirs of wondrous divine music! No holy vision! No spectacular productions here! We find only a discouraged Peter, who has fished all night and caught nothing—no catch of the day, no fish for family or fish market.

Now, if you fish, you can undoubtedly relate to Peter's feelings of discouragement and a sense of utility, "What's the use?" Perhaps you do not fish. Possibly, it is that job that has come to nothing; all those resumes were sent out, and there were no bites. Recessions! Layoffs! Financial reversals! Nothing! It may be that relationship that has eluded you: the separation, the divorce, that hurt the emptiness.

We understand you, Peter, when hope crumbles and life seems pointless! Yes, Peter, we appreciate your response when your Lord tells you to try once more. *"Master, we've worked hard all night and haven't caught anything."* (Luke 5:5, NIV). Look, Lord. I've tried every angle, and still, my life comes up smelling like old fishnets!

You know the rest of the story of Peter and the fish. Peter incredibly draws in more fish than he has ever seen. in a net at any one time! And Peter's response: a thank you at the very least! You would think a net full of fish would rate at least a thank you. Not in Peter's books - not yet, anyway! Peter's response... an echo from the past. "Go away from me, Lord, for I am a sinful man!" Just leave me alone. Doesn't that sound like a clone of Isaiah? Remember his response: there is no hope for me. Every word that passes my lips is sinful. Just leave me be. And what about us? "No use, Lord. I've tried, but I will never make it!"

But you see, the Holy Spirit of God, which touched Isaiah's lips, taught him what to say, and gave him the courage to say it, is now enfleshed in Christ, who stands before Peter with the promise that now Peter will draw people, not fish, into the circle of God's loving care. He is not to pull away in fear but to fall in trust, in reverential fear, to be taught by the Lord Jesus Christ how to rescue the lost, the despairing, the hopeless into life! And into New Hope.

And to us, this day, the Holy Spirit of the risen Christ stands within us, telling others not to pull away, not to fear, and to allow ourselves to be drawn into this same circle of God's loving care.

Allow ourselves to be drawn into the same circle of God's love and care.

The Holy Spirit comes to rescue us from those feelings of insecurity and fear that overwhelmed Isaiah and Peter, those mind-destroying suggestions which say. "I am only a student, only a teenager, only a wife or husband or mother or father, or retired." Our Lord comes to free us from the "I'm only" mindset, sets us on our feet and draws us into the very family of the living God!

Our Lord comes to give a foundation for living so that we, like Peter, may have the courage and faith to launch into deeper waters where we, too, may be surprised by the wonders of our Lord! God speaks to the very innermost parts of our being to tell us we are children of God with a purpose for being!

God got the attention of Isaiah, allowing him to experience the vision of the God of Hosts high and lifted up! Jesus met Peter, not with technological spectaculars, visions, or drama, but in an empty net and the challenge of deeper waters.

The mystery of God, whom we worship, is the mystery of one who comes to us, not only in the beauty of the sanctuary but also in the midst of music and the glorious natural wonders of creation, in the hearing of a still small voice, but also in our sea of despair. The God we worship comes when we, like Peter, are ready to give up and give in to our worries, grief, fears, and guilt! God comes to us to work unerringly in our hearts and souls. God is alive and real, calling us to see ourselves as we are seen, not as some mere cog in the wheel of life, but as wondrous children of God who calls us to live and love with which we were first loved. God calls us to live that love in life's beautiful and empty places and to hold on to that love in the hard and hurtful and disappointing times that come to each one of us.

In Psalm 23, we read: *"You prepared a table before me in the presence of my enemies..."* [1] Yes, our Lord prepares a table-nurtures and feeds us with divine love in the midst of our joys and pain, amid our exuberance and our guilt. God will continue to feed and nurture us with a love that will never let us go! God will continue to give us the courage and strength to push out into deeper places.

Whether we stand amid these spectacular visions of great joy or whatever we are, almost submerged in the crashing seas of despair, whether we are a Peter or an Isaiah or an "I'm only", the Lord God is with us saying, "...*Do not fear, for I have redeemed you: I have called you by name: you are mine.*"[2]

May God grant us the vision for this day. May God meet us at every turn. May God give us peace as we journey with the one who comes to help us and give us great joy. Thanks be to God.

Rev. Freda MacDonald[1]/Rev. Suzanne Wilkinson

Psalm 23:5 (NRSV)[1], Isaiah 43:1 (NRSV)[2] Presbyterian Church of Canada, Counting the Women, 1st edition, 1994, Edited by Dorcas Gordon, with permission from Dr. Anne McDonald for excerpts to be taken from Counting the Women.

God Spoke Out of a Storm

John Newton's mother died when John was seven; He grew up without religious training. As a young man, he entered service in the Royal Navy. There, a life of profanity, immorality, and drunkenness became his life. After a series of fights, outbursts, contempt for authority, and foul mouth misbehaviours, he was expelled from the British Navy, leading him to find the only work available for such a depraved and rebellious sailor- on a slave ship. For even a reprobate like Newton, this demeaning and distasteful work only intensified his immoral character. He inhumanely trafficked thousands of men, women, and children from Africa to the auction blocks of America.

His spiritual conversion began amid a storm-tossed sea in the dark of night when John genuinely feared for his life. As the waves filled his cabin, terror gripped Newton's heart. Facing death, Newton prayed that God would save him and the ship. He knew he and this battered boat had little chance of survival. John realized he did not deserve a hopeful eternity. He prayed for mercy and repented, promising God he would become a new man if he survived. God answered his prayer. The storm abated. Miraculously, no soul, including Newton's life, was lost as the battered ship found a safe harbour. This life-saving experience convinced John that there is a God who hears and answers prayers. Amid the storm, God opened John's eyes and heart and mercifully responded to his cries for help.

Newton realized he was a sinner in need of a Saviour. His conversion played out over several years as he turned from a reckless drunkard and disobedient sailor into someone who later sought theological education.

John was ordained in the Church of England in 1764 and ministered to mainly poor and illiterate people. He was known there for his humility and confessional sermons, in which he identified with sinfulness and the suffering of those who attended his services.

Newton, once a libertine and slave trader, later helped found the Christian Missionary Society. As he reflected on God's mercy and his experience, he wrote the lyrics to the well-known hymn "Amazing Grace". Although the text Amazing Grace dates to 1773, the tune most often associated with these familiar lyrics came later.

John Newton dedicated the rest of his life to sharing the gospel's good news. He led the abolitionist movement in Great Britain, exposed the evils of slavery, and fought to emancipate the enslaved and end the slave trade.

American composer William Walker set it to the musical version best known today in 1835. The modern version of "Amazing Grace" was first published in 1910 and, after gaining acceptance in the United States, spread worldwide. In my experience, I believe "Amazing Grace" is the most familiar and often requested hymn played at funeral services and other similar gatherings.

Suzanne Wilkinson (Excerpts and dates gleaned from John Newton's biography, https://www.museumofthebible.org/exhibits/amazing-grace-online-exhibit

God Stopped Me Mid-Prayer

God's Protection in a Teaching Prayer

My husband had been visiting Iowa on business. Don's habit is to get up early, 5:30 a.m., before the sun is up, and start his return trip home to Toronto. I am also an early riser. I had finished praising God that morning and then prayed for several others. Suddenly, I stopped in the middle of praying. I could not utter another prayer. I had this overwhelming need to pray for my husband so many miles away. I asked God to please be with my husband on his drive home. Having prayed that genuine prayer, I prayed for several other people. God again silenced me. Not a prayerful thought or word came. I could not continue my prayers; something was stopping me each time.

After a few moments, I felt God was speaking to me about my prayer for my husband. I needed to be more specific – not just give my Heavenly Father a simple, unthought-through blessing-type prayer. I sensed that was true of my prayers, as I had been sending up petitions without much thought. I sat momentarily in silence and said, "God, please protect my husband's eyes from becoming blind from the sun's rays as it slowly rises in the east. Put a hedge of protection around him and other vehicles. Thank you, Father, that we can come to you with prayers of all kinds, and you listen and answer." I then went on with other prayers for people I knew in need.

Later, my husband, Don, arrived home safely. Over dinner, we spoke about his trip and the time while he was away. He said, "There were very few cars on the road early in the morning, yet in the distance, I saw three cars ahead of me." He said he felt this strong urge to change lanes and go into the fast lane. Although Don was driving the speed limit with no cars around him, he didn't need to change lanes. Anyway, he did change lanes. My husband noticed that there was a hill coming up. My husband couldn't see far ahead as the sun was rising, and despite sunglasses, he noticed the glare. Just as Don went over the crest of this hill, the three cars he had seen ahead of him smashed at full speed into the first car. The result was

80

a tragic rear-end collision. He would have ploughed into them if Don had stayed in the slow lane.

The other drivers had come over the hill, and the sun was in their eyes. The first car had slowed for the driver to see, and the other two cars ploughed into him. The mangled vehicles indicated that the drivers were likely severely injured. Not to cause a further accident in the fast lane; safety meant it was wise to continue out of the way after calling 911.

Praise God for making me stop and think about my prayer. That morning, I learned a valuable lesson: not to pray rote prayers but to listen to God while I prayed. It taught me to think and to pray more specifically. God comprehended what was happening miles away. He could have stopped this accident from happening to my husband without my prayer if He chose, but God was teaching me a lesson about thinking more specifically about how I was to pray.

As I sit with God to pray, I question whether I put much thought into my prayers, or do I sometimes just read off a laundry list of needs? Being in God's presence and listening to His voice as I pray is an excellent lesson, and I try to practice it now.

This God-teaching moment was one we likely all needed. God stopped me to show me how to pray more purposefully. I praise God for my husband's safe return and God's faithful teaching presence.

Judith Alexander

God Still Works in Mysterious and Miraculous Ways

This story comes from the pages of a fine book, "Love is Blind," by Ruth Vallis. This excerpt is not an exact copy of her book, but the main points have been preserved and are shared here to tell her fantastic story.

Ruth is totally blind. In her early twenties, she studied in England at a school that taught blind students the art and skills of Physiotherapy. Ruth navigated the enormous challenges of being a blind person and discovering London alone. After graduating with a degree, she returned to Toronto to start a successful career, which served her well till her retirement and later time to write her excellent book, from which this story comes. I highly recommend it to anyone who would like to read a riveting tale of a determined and capable woman who courageously overcame many obstacles while coping with her blindness. Along with many setbacks, she faithfully served on many committees as a conference speaker and church worker, and all the while, she was a faithful example of a committed Christian.

In Ruth's autobiography, we read about a curious thing that happened on Sunday. She awoke feeling compelled to call her long-time dear friend in Toronto, whose name was Marilyn. The only way she could do it, on a Sunday in England, was to go some distance into London (where she was studying) to the international pay phone. With reasonable mobility and vision, a fellow student agreed to accompany Ruth to this payphone after they attended church. With fifty pence in hand, she waited in the long line for her turn at the payphone. Yet, though Ruth did not know why, she continued to have this urgent, persistent need to contact her friend, Marilyn, immediately despite being a continent away. Ruth had never experienced such an unexplainable feeling and needed to make such a call.

"Once at the front of the payphone line, I pushed a coin into the slot, and just as I was about to dial, the coin pumped out again. I repeated the process a couple of times with the same result. Thinking the coin might be somehow faulty, I tried another coin. but it happened again." Ruth's accompanying fellow student from the School of Physiotherapy for blind students agreed that there had been quite a queue ahead of them, so perhaps the coin receptacle was full. As they stepped aside, Ruth wrote, "The person behind me inserted a coin and made a call. Discouraged, we walked away, agreeing that the best thing would be for me to call from the school office tomorrow."

On Monday, for some reason, the urgency to call Marilyn had diminished. That feeling of needing to call Toronto was not there as it had been on Sunday. In fact, Ruth had forgotten her plan. However, that urgent feeling was there when Ruth awoke on Tuesday. It was a robust, overwhelming, immediate need to call Marilyn. Ruth arranged to make an international lunchtime call with the school office administrator. She would place this call to her Toronto friend, Marilyn, before she, as a teacher, left for school. When Marilyn answered the phone, Ruth told her about her persistent feelings, her significant need to speak with her on Sunday and now Tuesday, and her frustrating problem with the pay phone.

Marilyn interrupted, "I am okay, Ruth," "Everything went well." Of course, Ruth had no idea what Marilyn was talking about. Then Marilyn explained that doctors had found a large mass in her abdomen. With some urgency for surgery, she went to the hospital on Monday for abdominal surgery. Naturally, many prayed in their Toronto church for a healthy outcome. Still, more surprisingly, the children in Marilyn's classroom requested and received permission to offer a public prayer for their teacher during morning messages over the P.A. Once Marilyn was on the operating table that Monday morning, the surgeon could no longer find the growth, surprisingly and unexpectedly there was no evidence of a tumour. The hospital quickly discharged her without any need for further tests. Marilyn said, "Ruth, I have received a miracle, and you don't have to worry anymore." Ruth had been worried, although she didn't know why, yet she knew she had received a miracle, too. Marilyn was fine! Ruth's anxiety level lessened as she genuinely marvelled at God's healing touch on her dear friend's body so many miles away.

Suzanne Wilkinson - Adapted from Ruth Vallis's book – Love is Blind with Ruth Vallis's permission, available through Amazon.ca in hard copy, paperback, and audio.

God's Eye is on the Sparrow, and I Know He Watches Me

Someone said to me that they had observed that I always seemed to be smiling and asked me why, and since I enjoy and welcome challenging questions, I spent the last several months contemplating that question. As I thought about it, I thought about the quote in 'The Alchemist,' which says, "And when you want something, all the universe conspires to give it to you." So, as I reflect on our faith, we know that that is indeed a divine conspiracy.

And then, I thought of the passage in Scripture, which says, **"*Now to him who is able to do immeasurably more than all we ask or imagine.*" (Eph. 3:20, NIV)** When I prayed twenty years ago, I only asked to find a church where I could worship and bring in the new year. And by God's appointment, I attended and wonderfully so, on an awesome New Year's Eve, God led me to this church. That was, for me, yet another divine conspiracy.

I reflect on the Psalms, which says, **"*Surely goodness and mercy shall follow me all the days of my life, and I shall dwell in the House of the Lord forever.*" (Ps. 23:6, KJV).** And so, "I smile because I'm happy, I smile because I'm free, His eye is on the sparrow, and I know He watches me." Thanks so much to each of you who knowingly or unknowingly have participated in this divine conspiracy, which I am blessed to call my life. Thank you and bless you.

Milton Fletcher - Milton Fletcher submits these words offered at Yorkminster Park Baptist Church in Toronto on Oct 29, 2023, when speaking of God's leading in his life.

"God-Speak" Moments

Some time ago, our Pastor spoke about listening to God's voice. We know that God's voice is not necessarily audible, but He speaks in various ways; if only we could be quiet and listen to the multiple ways He speaks. This kind woman, the author of this book, asked me to share a "*God-Speak*" moment in my life.

My life and times have been in God's hands, even when difficult. I lived reasonably comfortably for many years, but then difficulties came. After years of marriage, I was alone. I remember Hagar, who bore a son, Ishmael, to Abraham. When, in the desert, alone, God saw her and spoke to her: "You are the God who sees me," she said, ***"I have now seen the One who sees me."*** **(Gen 16:13b, NIV).** She saw God. I see God anew in my difficulties.

I struggled with my newfound independence. I have a job, but more importantly, a church family. They prayed for me, and in them, I see God. I sense God in the way they have supported and encouraged me. Their prayers joined with mine and were invaluable. God knew my situation. When I prayed to Him, there was no surprise in my requests. He knew what I needed. He invites us to come to Him with prayer, supplication, and thanksgiving (Philippians 4:6).

My life since then has been different, but I know who holds my tomorrow. He holds my future and will be with me all along the way. My circumstances have challenged me, but I have been able to view my situation as part of life and know that God controls everything. James 1 says to "count it all joy when we face adversity," when conditions are not joyful, our joy comes from Him, who is our strength, hope, and comfort.

In times of difficulty, we grow, becoming much more than we were before. God uses our challenges to refocus us and mature us in the faith. God always sees us and what we need most for our good. When we take the time to be in His presence and wait on Him, we see the wonders of God and the richness of a faith that we had not seen before.

Though one never wishes hardships to come, we can see God in a new, more expansive way. We can see Him through the experiential eyes of faith. Life becomes more peaceful even through grief, sorrow and being alone. I now see God in my circumstances and through the faithful in my church family.

God has promised to keep those whose minds are stayed on Him in perfect peace. We should not be afraid of loneliness, pain and suffering since when we share in the suffering of Christ, we are also going to share in His Glory.

Carole Clyne

Gratefulness

It is helpful to look back on our lives occasionally, reflect on past events, remember our journey, and thank God for the 'blessings' we have received and enjoyed. I am reminded of the many people who have supported me in all areas of my life. Few activities are accomplished without other people's encouragement and help. It's good for us to remember those blessings and offer thanks to them and, most importantly, to God, who put them in our lives at the right time.

Speaking personally, I would not have become a minister without sensing God's call on my life. As far back as my teen years, I believe God spoke to my heart and planted the seed for me to enter the ministry. Yes, I ran into almost insurmountable resistance because I was a female and because of tradition and policies. Yet, God led me onward, and doors finally and graciously opened.

There were some people who believed in me and encouraged me despite it being a second career. Chaplaincy was the ministry area for which I seemed best suited since my former career was as a Registered Nurse. It was not easy, but I thank those who believed in me and could sense God's urging me to move forward in this privileged direction. The last twenty-plus years have been personally satisfying, rewarding, and hopefully fruitful. Most importantly, I pray that God and His kingdom have been blessed by God's gracious call on my heart.

It also helps to evaluate our lives, our mistakes, and our failures and avoid similar pitfalls in the future. Above all, looking back enables us to see the hand of God guiding us. We often need to acknowledge the Spirit's leading while we are amid a challenge. Only when we have completed a task can we discern how our Lord has supported us throughout the process, providing us with the power and strength to finish well.

We respond to God's generous blessings by practically demonstrating our gratitude through the way we live our lives and the sharing of our good fortune. The apostle Paul also encouraged the Philippians and us to fill our minds with *"whatever is true, whatever is noble, whatever is right, whatever is pure, whatever is lovely, whatever is admirable—if anything is excellent or praiseworthy—think about such things."* **(Philippians 4:8, NIV).**

Let us remember that we are blessed to be a blessing to others.

Suzanne Wilkinson

Guidance and True Peace

This story is meant to be a collection of moments experiencing God's guidance, comfort, and providence.

My mom is the eldest sister of nine siblings. She had a very close relationship with her mother, a devout Christian who grew up attending church and praying regularly. However, it wasn't until she immigrated to Canada that she truly understood what it meant to have a relationship with God. Looking back, God had guided her through a long journey.

She left the Philippines to go to Europe to find a better job to provide for her family. My mother first worked in Madrid and then found her way to Paris. It was a struggle to be alone, but she knew God had a plan, and through a unique circumstance, she was given a chance to immigrate to Canada.

God blessed her and our family as she sponsored her parents, siblings, and my dad, whom she met through a friend who put them into contact as pen pals. They were fortunate to be expecting their first child, but sadly, this little one passed away at birth. A few months later, my mom also lost her mother. This was a harrowing period in my mom's life, and she leaned on God and her Canadian church family.

A few years later, God blessed my mom and dad with another child; they have been excellent parents. They raised our family to grow in our knowledge and relationship with God and to rely on Him in every circumstance.

We lived with my grandfather until he was hospitalized, and the family gathered to pray for him. My mom had a strained relationship with her father and prayed constantly for his salvation. After he was in the hospital, he was not at peace and was experiencing hallucinations. My mom decided to have a one-on-one conversation with him about his relationship with God. This frank conversation ended with them praying together when he asked for forgiveness and salvation and declared his belief in Jesus Christ.

It was through this experience that my mother witnessed a miracle. After my mother and grandfather prayed together, he felt at peace that he had not known. His hallucinations stopped. He was at ease and at peace in a way he had not known. A few weeks later, he passed away, and we were comforted to believe that he was home with the Lord and that we would see him again one day.

Looking back at these moments, especially in my mother's life, we remember that we have peace in every situation, whether joy or sadness, knowing God is always with us. "*And the peace of God, which transcends all understanding, will guard your hearts and your minds in Christ Jesus.*" (Philippians 4:7, NIV).

Dr. Melissa Isada

For God hath not given us the spirit of fear; but of power, and of love, and of a sound mind." (2 Timothy 1:72 (NIV)

"Above all, love each other deeply, because love covers over a multitude of sins. (1 Peter 4: 8, NIV)

Have You Ever Wondered?

Have you ever wondered what soil the seeds you planted fell? I know it is not up to us to grow the seeds, but we must cultivate them. God does the growing, but we are to nurture others, discipline them and encourage them to grow.

Two other ladies in my neighbourhood were expecting at the same time as my first child was born. These neighbours and I became good friends. We did many things together, like shopping, having coffee, going for long walks in the park, and sharing stories. We thought these neighbourhood friendships would last and we would see our children grow up together. Then my family moved, not very far, just fifteen minutes away. That move changed my life. I met some ladies who invited me to a Bible Study. I went and loved it. Due to that study and the influence of these ladies, I gave my life to Jesus Christ and endeavoured to make Him my Lord.

I had kept up with my friends from the old neighbourhood, but now our children were all in school. We only saw each other for lunch or an occasional theatre date. As a Christian, I started to speak about Jesus to these ladies and found that we were on a different wavelength. They wanted to avoid hearing about Jesus. Their eyes glazed over, and they swiftly changed the subject. I learned not to speak of Him in our conversation and only bowed my head quietly when I said grace if we were out for lunch. Soon, I was uninvited to the lunches, and we rarely saw each other. I prayed for those former neighbours and still think of them often.

Three times over two years, as I was out and about, I was led by the Lord to drop into one of these ladies' places unannounced (Rose, I will call her). Each time she answered the door, she would burst into tears and say, "How did you know I needed someone to talk to? She then poured out the troubles she was going through. I listened as I knew she needed to vent to someone. As I was leaving, I told her I felt a nudge from Jesus to come and see her. She disregarded what I said. Rose never called me after these visits to say that she was glad to see me or to thank me for listening or dropping by. I sensed no more nudges and never saw her again.

Have you ever wondered where the seeds land or what happens afterwards? My love for these former neighbours and my curiosity makes me wonder. We do not need to know. We may find out in eternity if the seeds of faith have grown. I hope to see them one day. God only knows, but we are to do our part, which is to obey. God has done His part by sending His son, whose death pays our sin debt and reconciles us to our holy Heavenly Father. If people would only realize and accept Him and trust in Him, what an eternal difference that would make for them.

Several years later, out of the blue, the other lady (Phyllis, I will call her) called to ask if I would have lunch with her. I was delighted and said, "Yes, I would love to come." I met her at a restaurant, and after catching up on what our families were doing, she said, "Judith, I want you to know why Rose and I stopped calling you. We didn't like how you kept speaking about Jesus Christ as your personal Saviour and how He changed your life." I was so amazed that she said that, as I had quickly realized back then, they did not want to hear about Jesus. I refrained from speaking about Him. I realized they had to see the change in me firsthand. They needed to initiate the conversation about Jesus, which they never did. She then used Jesus' name many times and mentioned what I had said about Him. I felt a warm love coming over me and could not help but smile. She had recalled the seeds I had sown. The more she said Jesus' name, the more I smiled. Then Phyllis stopped and said, Judith, you look so beautiful and peaceful. We sat there for a moment in silence. I felt this was Jesus' moment to speak to her heart. We finished our meal and went on our way.

Months later, I heard she had died. Someone told me that, when she was delirious, she had mentioned my name. Did she remember our conversation about Jesus? Did she realize her time was short and accept Him before it was too late? Have you ever wondered what the soil was like for the seed you planted? Perhaps we will know when we meet our Lord face to face.

As I go through life, I must listen to what God asks me to do. How many times have I failed to respond to that nudging of God? Perhaps it is with the name of the person God wanted me to call or send a note of encouragement. There have been other times, but after these two experiences, I try not to miss a nudge from God. I want to do my part in the miracle when Jesus changes a heart. Yet, I do wonder about the seeds I have the privilege to plant. With God's nudging, I intend to sow as many seeds for as many people as possible on this side of heaven.

Judith Alexander

He Rescues

As a wife and parent of four who are now young adults, there were times over the years when I failed at doing the God-wife-parent thing. I would do the Heather thing instead. The Heather thing would include losing my patience, feeling sorry for myself, or maybe even seeking quick fix-it tips on improving oneself before going to God about the matter. I'm not proud to share this, yet it's part of how God continually guides, rescues, and provides in His mercy and grace. One cannot save oneself regarding the state of your heart and soul and all your iniquities. We need almighty God, creator of heaven and earth and everything in it. God, who made us and knows us and all our thoughts, knows precisely what we need and provides answers to our deep soul desires.

There were times I would cry out to the Lord in deep distress. In those times, I questioned where God was, yet the Lord was right there in the dark valleys, protecting, strengthening, and healing me. In Psalm 130:1-2a, the psalmist cries to God to be rescued; ***"Out of the depths, I cry to you, Lord. Lord, hear my voice!"*** **(NIV).** In the book of Jonah, we find Jonah up to his neck in deep water and close to drowning due to his lack of faith and disobedience to God. It was the mercy of God that put Jonah into the depths and then into the belly of the fish, and Jonah humbly cried out to God for help, and by God's mercy, Jonah was saved. From inside the fish, Jonah prayed to the LORD his God. He said: ***"In my distress, I called to the LORD, and he answered me. From deep in the realm of the dead I called for help, and you listened to my cry."*** **(Jonah 2:2, NIV).**

We may find ourselves in a 'belly of a fish' condition when we look at our sins and question, "How can I get right with God?" The enemy wants to convince us that our sins are unforgivable. When we are in the deep depths, we can cry out to God, and He will hear our pleas, liberate us from our bondage to sin and lift our burdens.

May we look to the cross where Jesus hung and reflect and remember the tremendous price our sins caused our sinless Lord.

The shedding of Jesus' blood for our forgiveness cost him dearly. God's LOVE for us is so great that His one and only Son stepped down from glorious heaven, and when it was time, He obediently stepped up to the cross to die for you and me. God pardons sin by His grace and mercy based on Christ's work on the cross alone. God incarnate, in the flesh, in the person of Jesus Christ, revealed Himself by coming to earth to show us the way to be reconciled and at peace with Almighty God.

Thank You, God, for rescuing me.

Heather

Heavenly Interceptions

One year after driving nonstop from Florida to Canada before Christmas, my husband and I fell asleep at night during that drive. A police officer managed to stop us while we were still driving. He urged us to open the windows. He was kind, did not give us a ticket, and wished us a safe trip home. We could have been in or caused a severe accident. God was protecting us that night.

Another time, in December, we prepared for a move and had a packed car. Unfortunately, it broke down on the highway later that night. A large transport truck stopped and towed us to the next service centre. That was a gift from God.

Daily, I had a 30-mile drive to work. I was working the night shift when I had a flat tire. Fortunately, it was near a driveway in an isolated area. I hesitantly walked the long way up a hill to the house. The family received me graciously, and the gentleman there kindly changed my tire.

Again, on that same highway following a day shift, I had a tire blowout, and my car turned in circles. It was on a dangerous road. Fortunately, I did not go off the cliffs on either side of the road. Traffic came from both directions; no other cars were hit or involved. I was shaking so severely that one of the oncoming drivers changed my tire at that time.

Many years ago, when living many miles away from a major city and when we had started a family, we began to look for a home. We had very little money to spend. There was a very cheap furnished house for sale. All the floors were uneven; it was a real mess and a true fixer-upper. I wouldn't, or anyone else would not want to live there, even if it were cheap enough to fit into our limited budget. We talked to the bank manager about a loan, but he told us about a well-built office building for sale. He advised and lent us the money for that office building, which became our home. We were much more comfortable in the office building than in the shack that needed significant fixing.

When our child was two years old, my husband told me that he didn't love me anymore, and he left. Of course, I was devastated and overwhelmed. I continued to work, but I also needed to make better choices. Many people we knew were happy to take advantage of me being on my own and in a needy place. My husband returned periodically to visit but only occasionally stayed. He left us in the country while he went to the city. I struggled for quite a while, not knowing what to do. I frequently failed as I was on an emotional roller coaster. As a single mother, I worked, supported, and cared for our son. God looked after us.

I tried reading, trying to discover the magical cure for my situation. I remember one book, "I'm OK, You're OK," but I was not convinced. A significant book I read was "Beyond Ourselves" by Catherine Marshall. One night, I had an authentic vision of Christ. It wasn't a dream but a vision. I saw two others walking behind Him, and this vision of Christ became a significant turning point in my life. From then on, I began to make better choices. God was real after that to me.

Shortly after that, I met the wife of a Pentecostal minister who invited me to a Bible study. I went and soon had a new family of friends who gave me real emotional support. I did a lot of individual studies, underlining ideas that I had never noticed before. There were many get-togethers, sharing conversations, studying, enjoying food, and singing together. These were uplifting times when I needed to be encouraged.

93

My new friends invited me to a Women's Retreat out of town. Organizing babysitting for work was one thing, but a weekend away was another. However, I was able to obtain childcare. The company on the trip was great. While away, the message was loud and clear, "Submit to your husband." I told these friends, "I don't have a husband to submit to."

We returned home, and life continued. There was work, chores, and a small child to care for. Our home, in the office building, needed a new roof. The church men volunteered to replace all the shingles if I would buy the supplies. I did and made chilli to feed this incredible army of workers. They were God-sent at a time of need. God provided.

My husband and I had been on our own for over two years, and though I missed him, I was more content. The occasional visits and phone calls continued, yet we still needed to determine whether there would be any resolution. My husband had once said that if I wanted to come to him, I could come. He did not say that he wanted me to come. I did not go without him wanting me to go.

Our friend was hospitalized after a severe accident, so I called my husband to let him know about this accident. That night, after three years of separation, he said he wanted us to rejoin him. I agreed, quit my job the next day and packed a box, and my son and I prepared to drive quite a distance to meet him. I was then submitting to my husband and happy to be a family again.

My husband wanted to do further studies. We rented a friend's apartment while my spouse went off to do other studies at university. We had our second child, and I continued working and looking after the care of our children and finding daycare when I was at work. When he finished and got his degree, we again needed to find another place to live. There were two apartments in the same building. One was unavailable, yet the one available was $100.00 a month more for the same unit size. Of course, we can manage much better, saving that $100.00. The night before we were to sign a contract, the cheaper one became available. That I felt was a God send, He provided yet again.

We were still receiving mortgage payments from the office building. The buyers wrote asking for a further reduction in their buyout. It seemed God wanted us to have a home now, this time in the city. The Bible study group prayed for a house, and God gave us our home. We were in that home within a month. Amazingly, God engineered that move as He provided.

Time passed, and our children grew up and had children. I planned to spend my day off making cardboard cars with my two grandsons. I picked up two large, narrow plant boxes and painted them blue. I bought plastic plates for the steering wheels, tires, numbers for licence plates, etc. The two young boys made their car, so with two cars, we used up all the supplies I had purchased. I looked at a VCR to find a movie they could watch as if they were at a drive-in. My grandsons spent many hours watching that video in the two cardboard boxes made into cars. They loved driving those cars, which was great entertainment for them. God provided the time, resources, and know-how to give them a good time.

At the same time, our daughter, who had grown up, needed a car. We leased one for her. She had it for a year, but we returned it to the car dealership when the lease was about to expire. That day, there was a contest at the dealership. My husband played in the competition and lost. I was tired from work and many duties and wanted to go home. I declined to play, but my husband insisted I participate in the contest. Reluctantly, yet with the salesman's encouragement, I played and won a blue car. Fortunately, there were no more bus rides to get to work. God knew my need and gave me a blue car.

God is there to answer my prayers for things like finding good parking spots and keeping me safe on the roads. He has put special people in my life and the beauty of nature surrounding us; these things make life worth living and seem part of God's input to make the challenges faced possible and comfortable.

God has gently guided me on my Christian journey and has been a constant, faithful friend I can rely on. I still make mistakes, for which I am genuinely sorry, but my friends, Bible study group, work, home, children, and grandchildren are there because of Him. God faithfully walks with me as my most genuine friend.

Over the years, I have had the opportunity for meaningful employment in an area where I thrived. I have enjoyed my work, made many friends, and helped others. Along the way, and with the challenges, there have been promotions, which have given me significant benefits and a pension in my retirement.

I cared for my husband before he died, and I am now retired in our home, which will be a source of income for both my eventual care if needed and a gift to my family when I pass on. I have been able to travel, often with friends. I live alone but am in the city where my children and grandchildren live. I have my friends, my Bible Study group of gals I have known for at least twenty years, who love me, my church, and my Heavenly Father, who has been faithful to me throughout my life in good times and bad.

God has faithfully provided, not just in this world, but has promised through Christ to give me a place in the next. I am indeed grateful and can never thank Him enough.

Anonymous/Suzanne Wilkinson

His Wonders to Perform

It was a hot and humid day in the middle of June. The Uxbridge Township Council was holding its final meeting before the summer. The agenda was short, and discussions were brief. Near the conclusion, one counsellor raised a concern about a family whose children were absent from school for a long time. "It seemed strange to me that they're not attending," he said, "and haven't been at school for more than a month." The township's bylaw enforcement officer, seated at the council table, admitted the report was correct. He agreed to visit the home.

Although then, a greenhorn in the newspaper reporting business, I listened in on the conversation with considerable interest and found myself thinking, "I, too, will visit and see why this family's children are absent from school." I was quickly able to obtain the family's name and address.

The next day, I made that visit, and what I discovered then and even now remains indelibly etched in my memory. Throughout my lengthy seven-decade career as a newspaper reporter, I haven't seen such a disaster as I saw that morning.

A middle-aged mother of three answered my early morning knock at that address. She was dressed but looked overwhelmed. I introduced myself and the reason for my visit. She cordially invited me in. The scene that met my unbelieving eyes was more than imaginable.

The heat inside was unbearable, and the swarms of flies were plentiful and everywhere. This place was dark and dirty, and a bad odour took my breath away. I grew up in a clean but simple farm home; this was foreign and unbelievable.

In one corner of the kitchen was an elderly lady, perhaps the grandmother, sitting in a rocking chair. She appeared to be unwell and maybe disabled in some way and possibly confused. She did not speak. I quickly learned that on the floor behind the stove were three girls aged nine, seven, and five. They appeared frightened as they huddled together. None spoke, and when they tried, it was not speech that was understandable, only a faint mumble. They made every attempt to hide themselves. They looked unwashed and un- fed.

I was young and inexperienced, having just started my newspaper career. It appeared that there was nothing I could do, only stand, and quietly stare. When I could speak, I learned that the family's father had recently been convicted of arson. He had burned a neighbour's barn down to the ground and had subsequently been sent, for a time, to jail. Still speechless and without a pad, pencil, or camera, I felt helpless and retreated.

I did not return to the office but to a neighbour's nearby farm to use a phone since I had arrived on foot. From there, I summoned assistance from the suburban editor of the then Toronto Telegram, a

97

daily newspaper with which I was attempting to become a country correspondent. After hanging up, I remembered whispering to myself. "Please, God. Please help these poor people. I can't do what needs to be done alone. This is too big for me." I felt so inadequate.

The following day, a Telegram staff reporter stood outside the office door, camera in hand. He was middle-aged and walked with a confidence that I needed to acquire.

"Please accompany me," he kindly requested, "This area is unfamiliar to me."

While on our way, I explained, as best I could, what he was about to see. He merely shook his head in disbelief. "Oh God help, help us." he prayed respectfully. Soon, he was to face the reality I had seen. By his prayer, somehow, I felt I had met a kindred soul.

We were both welcomed warmly, as I had been the day before. This senior reporter requested that I remain silent during our visit, having seen that I was pretty "green" at all that was happening. I was happy to oblige. Having met the mother and nodded to the grandmother, he went over to the girls who were again trying to hide. He knelt on both knees and crawled slowly towards the girls, smiling gently with a look of compassion and slowly approached them. They began to respond and move forward from their huddle behind the stove.

Once he gained their confidence, showing that he was their friend and not an intruder, the atmosphere changed; acceptance replaced fear, and smiles replaced frowns. He was gentle and reassuring to each one in that home. He asked permission to take a couple of pictures and to tell their story. The mother gave that permission, trusting this kind reporter and being persuaded that we meant no harm.

We left the house on good terms and even saw a smile or two as we waved bye. Once outside, this reporter told me, "Thanks be to God, but we need His help. I believe people will be interested and respond to this need."

The following day, The Telegram carried what we knew to report of this family. Funds, food baskets, and clothing rolled in. The family thanked all the kind people who generously provided for many of their needs.

I followed this family from afar and watched how the simple kindness and generous response to this need made an overwhelming difference in these women's lives. Several years later, the paper published a follow-up story describing how the mother had found a job, and all three sisters had returned to elementary and later to secondary school. Years passed, and they have now graduated from universities (on scholarships) and acquired self-satisfying positions. The girls gained confidence in their God-given intellect and abilities as the community offered them love and acceptance. These simple kindnesses and the support of many genuinely caring people changed these women's lives.

I learned a great lesson that has stood me in great stead throughout my career as a newspaper reporter. The way the Telegram reporter demonstrated love through his actions brought out the best in many. Early in my career, I saw Christ in action in a desperate situation that could have proven disastrous for this family. The response to the love shown by the community was remarkable for all to see.

"Heavenly Father, You heard our prayer and answered magnificently. Thank you, Lord, for demonstrating Your love at a time of great need." Yes. God works in mysterious ways, His wonders to perform. Take it from me: He does!

Jim Thomas/Suzanne Wilkinson

How God Found the Perfect Husband for Me – A True Ten!

In 1990, my first husband died from a brain tumour at age fifty-three. We had met in the fall of 1962 and married in July 1963, after a 9-month courtship. We did not know each other well. For me, it was "Love at First Sight." For my husband, it was "Opposites

99

Attract." I reminded my husband of his favorite movie actress, June Allison, from the 1960s. My husband was six feet and one inch tall, and I was five feet and one inch in thick socks.

Before long, we had three lovely children and trouble in our marriage. A daughter first, then two sons who are now a great blessing in their adult years. When the youngest was a year and a half, my husband and I separated for more than seven years as there was too much stress in the home.

Because our teenage, rebellious daughter was heading for trouble, my husband decided to return home, having experienced life without the family, and wished to join us. We had a complete family again for eight years until cancer took his life after a challenging time when I cared for him while managing the home and family. These were exhausting days. Our children were ages twenty-three, nineteen, and seventeen, and I was forty-nine when he died.

Several years passed, and I was busy working; the children were away at university, and I belonged to several cultural groups. I was lonely but felt relieved of some of my former responsibilities. I joined a grief support group for six weeks and attended church regularly. My faith helped sustain me; this support was essential to my recovery.

One summer day, I met some acquaintances in a restaurant, and they asked how I was getting along. They also asked if I was "dating?" I said, "Not right now, but eventually, I might be interested."

After my husband passed away, I made a list of qualities I would like to find in a man based on what was lacking in my first marriage. There were ten essential points. The last one (for fun) was, "Can he cook?"

One time, when my friends were talking after the meeting, my friend Barbara told her husband, "There is a staff member at work whose wife died, and he does not know how he will get through the summer." He and his wife were teachers and did everything together, including teaching at the same high school. My friend said,

"What about that lady (referring to me)? Maybe they could talk to each other and go to a movie or have dinner somewhere. I think it would be good for each of them."

My friend asked if I would give this gentleman, whom she admired, my phone number. I agreed, and soon afterwards, I received a few phone calls from "Arthur." For our first meeting, we went to a restaurant, and then, since it was summer, he invited me to a picnic and offered to bring the food. How could I not accept?

We had our first picnic and, shortly afterwards, at least three more picnics on perfect summer days before I eventually supplied the food. We went to symphony concerts, ice-skated, took ballroom dancing lessons and enjoyed each other's company. It was beautiful to be out having fun.

Arthur is ten years older than I am, with white hair and a slim build, and in fact, he was a perfect fit for all the items of qualities I had on my list. He was a perfect 10. I heard a voice repeating the name Arthur, Arthur, Arthur whenever I was driving, composing a letter, or doing almost any activity. In retrospect, it was the voice of the Holy Spirit guiding me, yet in those months of indecision, it almost became annoying.

Because of my experience in my first marriage, I was unsure if I was ready for another one. I also thought that Arthur might be too "mature because he was a decade older." Even my former mother-in-law approved of him, and all my friends thought he was great, and so did my children. I felt I needed more time. We decided to take a break from each other, which lasted about three weeks before I realized I missed Arthur. I was still hearing that voice saying his name. During that time of separation, I discovered I did love him.

Luckily, we decided he was the one for me and made plans to get married. We have been married for thirty years, and my heart still skips when I see him. I continue to thank God for sending such a caring, loyal, and helpful husband to me.

Life has given us a surprise. Instead of the older spouse developing health problems, the younger spouse (me) has experienced three significant illnesses. Two years after marriage, I underwent triple bypass heart surgery. Arthur cared for me and has continued to carry a heavy load as I have had cancer and a stroke. Fortunately, Arthur is a very caring Christian and enjoys looking after people (most of the time). His ability to cook and help has been a blessing for most of our marriage, especially during my illnesses. He is all I could have ever hoped for and more.

God had blessed Arthur with a perfect wife in his first marriage, and now he has sent me, Arthur, to make my second marriage the best possible match. In my heart, I know that the voice I repeatedly heard was the guidance I needed. Thanks be to God.

Anonymous

This is the verdict: Light has come into the world, but people loved darkness instead of light because their deeds were evil.
John 3:1 (NIV)

I Profoundly, Thank You Lord

In 1968, I was diagnosed with systemic lupus erythematosus (SLE), which is the most common type of Lupus. SLE is an autoimmune disease in which the immune system attacks its own tissues, causing widespread inflammation and tissue damage in the affected organs. It can affect the joints, skin, brain, lungs, kidneys, and blood vessels. At that time, the treatments in medicine were poor for combating this challenging and progressive disease. My prognosis was poor. I learned I would be in a wheelchair within a year and would die in four or five years.

I am now in my eighty-fifth year and have experienced good health for many years. I am well-controlled on some heart medications for atrial fibrillation, which my siblings also experience. I am more active and involved than many of a similar age. What changed, and how did this terrible disease disappear? Here is my story of how God answered my simple prayer.

My diagnosis of Lupus had been confirmed by two revered rheumatologists practising at noted hospitals in Toronto, Ontario, Canada. I was very ill. I was twenty-eight. Mobility was a significant issue, and I was extremely exhausted. On top of this, I developed this illness following the delivery of our first son. I had so much to live for as we had just purchased our first home. I was delighted with our new baby and wished to care for him as a mother should. As the weeks passed, my illness only became more severe. One night, I found myself on my knees praying a very heartfelt and desperate prayer yet making a simple request.

Lord, if you are hearing me, please answer my prayer. I wish to care for our son devotedly and actively through his infancy, be well enough to make cookies to take to, and participate as a helper for the children during his early years at elementary school. I may not have expressed my prayer precisely that way, but it was my prayer. I did not ask for total health and long life, other children, the ability to have a career, or a wonderful long marriage; no, it was a straightforward, simple prayer that was a profound need of mine then.

God heard and answered amazingly. Over six to eight months, my Lupus slowly disappeared. My specialists were amazed at my test results, which improved with each visit. Quite unexpectedly and inexplicably, this disease was disappearing. In the ordinary course of Lupus, remissions occur, but not like mine, nor for the length of time since the onset. The Cortisone drugs were withdrawn, and my activities gradually increased. I was then allowed to drive the car again. The day came when the doctor said he thought my blood work was normal enough that if we cared to change it, we could try to have another child, which we were hoping to have. Fortunately, we had our second son amazingly, almost to the day, nine months later.

We have been incredibly blessed by our two boys, now grown men. They are both fine Christians, and we consider them true gifts from God. I have recently become a great-grandmother of a delightful baby girl and have just returned from a short visit to see her, in British Columbia, where my grandson and his wife live.

I am active and my life is fulfilling, as it has been since that time of severe illness. I am actively involved and still working part-time at an age far beyond when most people have retired. I can't help but think of what life might have been if the Lord had not healed me.

This spontaneous and lengthy remission is inexplicable except as a healing miracle from the loving hand of my Heavenly Father. I can not express my deep gratitude to God for His constant presence, guidance, love, forgiveness, and healing. He has astoundingly blessed me and our family by answering a simple, heartfelt prayer offered over fifty-five years ago. From my heart, I sincerely thank You, Lord!

Suzanne Wilkinson

If We Are Listening, God is Calling

Do you remember watching the movie, "Fiddler on the Roof," and listening to Zero Mostel sing, "Tradition!" as he resisted new ideas and expressed the need to maintain what had always been? Traditions are our links to the past and a path forward into our futures, but as we all know, there often comes a time when some traditions need to die; they are no longer valid, helpful, fun, or relevant. It's time to let go.

On the other hand, there are times when our traditions get stolen from us. Think of the impact of COVID-19 on so many individuals, families, and cultural, social, and religious traditions. And sometimes, if we are forward-thinking, we might start a tradition to carry it forward for years. We enjoy reunions with friends from school days or look forward to celebrating an anniversary with dinner at our favorite restaurant. Yes, traditions are great once they're not.

In Exodus 12:1-14, God insists on starting a new tradition to be carried forward forever. Read about the first Passover with God's people in a life-or-death crisis.

God insisted that they respond with a new ritual that would forever burn into their sense of self-identity. There are times when traditions have great value, but the prophet Ezekiel insists that change must happen if the people remain faithful to God (read Ezekiel 33:7-11).

We, too, live in a threatening and dangerous time. God calls us to wake up and care for His earthly creation and inhabitants. The deadly nature of the impacts of climate change remains in the daily news. Yes, disasters have occurred since the beginning of time. Yet, in recent years, God has spoken to us about the unparalleled damage to the melting polar ice cap, forest fires, floods, hurricanes, earthquakes, and parched grounds of drought affecting each continent. Climate change is a factual reality, disputed by its deniers.

We must change our habits concerning pollution, fossil fuel energy, and waste. Our traditions and our way of life, in some cases, need to change if we and the planet are to thrive. The alternative is global biosphere collapse. It is late in the game, but action now would slow down the destructive forces plaguing our planet and threatening the lives of humans, animals, and all we enjoy in nature.

Let me give one small example – I have been watching, but I have only seen one monarch butterfly this summer; years ago, they were prevalent as they flitted among the flowers. Why are they so massively dying off?

If we are listening, God calls out to us through these Simic shifts in our planet. Let us hear the voice of God through the old and now young prophets who will help guide us into a healthier future. Let us enter "a season of creation" with commitment. Let us worship and celebrate and earnestly pray that it is not too late to save all that is dear in God's creation.

Jesus said, "My sheep hear my voice, and I know them, and they follow me: And I give unto them eternal life, and they shall never perish, neither shall any man pluck them out of my hand." **(John 10:27-28, KJV)**

Suzanne Wilkinson

105

In His Care

Cheerful voices were slowly fading away. One by one, the happy faces of girls and boys were gone. Silence.

I looked around and realized I was left swinging alone in the playground.

"Where is she? She was supposed to pick me up but is not here." I waited… and waited…. and waited.

Abandoned. Rejected. Nobody. That's how I felt at that moment.

It was hard growing up without a father walking me to school. Or a mother who would brush and tie my hair with a bow. I used to envy my friends who had moms and dads drop them off at school and kiss them goodbye. I used to hold back my tears when I walked up a stage to receive an award. No one attended my recognition day to pin the ribbon on my dress.

When asked by our teacher to describe my father, I had no words to describe him. I never met him. I have no photo of him. I knew nothing. When asked to write an essay about my mother's love, my paper was spotless and clean. She was present but absent. She would appear and then disappear. It was as if I was looking at an illusion. She was a mother to my five lovely stepsisters but not to me. I could only look at her but could not have her.

"Why did my father abandon me? How could my own mother reject me? Who am I?" These piercing questions haunted me for many, many long years.

I received my response on one gloomy and scary day. I discovered that a breath of life was slowly blossoming in my womb. I replayed the day my mother discovered that she was pregnant and without a husband. The struggle that she had to endure. There were huge waves of judgment from her family. The strong winds of disgrace swallowed her entire being. She was stripped, left with no worth, unwanted, all by herself. It's happening again. But the image I see is mine.

"What am I going to do? Who can I run to? Who would help me?" I was scared. Desperate. Lost.

Then, I heard God's soothing and comforting voice. It came from a Psalm. ***"Though my father and mother forsake me, the Lord will receive me."*** **(Psalm 27:10, NIV)**

Yes! I might not have an earthly father who would come running to find me. Or a mother whose arms are wide open to embrace me. However, I have a Heavenly Father who loves me unconditionally. He cares deeply for me. I can run to His loving arms. I can pour my heart out to Him.

> ***"Cast all your anxiety on him because he cares for you."***
> **(1 Peter 5:7, NIV)**

And so, I finally let out all the choking words I had kept for many years: *"This is so unfair. I just wanted to have a family of my own. Why do I have to follow the fate of my mother? You better give me a man who would love me and my dear daughter."*

I grew up without loving parents. My childhood friends were pigs and chickens. Envy and striving were my best friends. Failure kept following me. But could I plead? I dream of a family of my own. What I most longed for was to have to love me. To get married, find security, and for my daughter to live a life full of love. Was it possible?

"For with God nothing will be impossible." **(Luke 1:37, NKJV)**

Two years passed, and my Heavenly Father sent me a precious gift: my husband. He prepared the most beautiful and memorable wedding celebration. Tears of joy fell on my cheeks as My Father God walked me down the aisle. Yes! I am married. I have a loving husband. I have a family. My sweet bundle of joy, Sophia, will live a life full of love. Not only that, but God gave me a new life with Him.

Are you an outcast in your family? Are you alone fighting for your marriage? Do you think you are a failure as a mom? None of your children care about your existence. All your friends are gone. The pain of losing a loved one is unbearable for you.

Run to God! Come to Him and give Him all your worries and anxieties.

Jesus Christ himself cried out to God. He screamed out loud. *"My God, my God, why have you forsaken me?"* (Matthew 27:46, NIV). He experienced the magnitude of abandonment and rejection as he hung on the cross. His friends fled, and one of them betrayed him.

But Jesus knew his suffering was nothing compared to what God had set before him. His death wiped away all our sins. He resurrected and sat at the right hand of the Father!

Even if everyone rejects and abandons you, remember you have a loving Father who deeply cares for you. He longs to sustain and deliver you! Therefore, you can live a life with Him.

My friend, your world might be bleak and dreary now. You feel like you are drowning in deep sorrow—no remedy to be found to numb the pain. The darkness blows the little glimmer of hope out of your hands. No rescue is coming.

Remember......... YOU ARE LOVED. YOU are CARED for. YOU are GOD's child.

Just as my Heavenly Father patiently waited for me and graciously answered my plea, *"You have granted me life and steadfast love, and your care has preserved my spirit."* **(Job 10:12, NRSV).**

Anonymous

Incredibly True - An Immediate Answer to Prayer

Throughout the 1980s and '90s, being part of the Women Alive movement was a blessing. Each May, notable Christian speakers like Jill Briscoe, Kay Arthur, Joni Eareckson Tada, Corrie Ten Boom and others were invited to speak at a conference at the University of Waterloo. Their messages were always inspirational, powerful, and transformative to those who had the opportunity to attend. I was one of those privileged people who served on the committee for several years.

One year, I was on the leadership team at one of these conferences and had a more intimate opportunity to see the behind-the-scenes happenings. I heard an incredible true story of God answering an impossible prayer. Corrie Ten Boom was the keynote speaker that year.

Cornelia "Corrie" ten Boom was a Dutch watchmaker who, along with her family, harboured hundreds of Jews amid the Nazi Holocaust to protect them from arrest during World War II. It's believed their efforts saved nearly 800 lives. Eventually, betrayed by a fellow Dutch citizen, the entire family was imprisoned. However, Corrie survived and told her story in an autobiographical 1971 memoir, *The Hiding Place.* Having grown up in a devoutly religious family, Corrie ten Boom also started a worldwide ministry and travelled extensively as a public speaker. She died on her 91st birthday.

I learned of this story firsthand from someone who was there and saw this prayer answered. It is a true story of how God compassionately answers even a little prayer for an elderly giant of the faith. Corrie Ten Boom was staying in one of the residences of the university, where she had a

room for her stay at the conference. A representative from the Women Alive executive was to bring her from the student residence to the large auditorium, where she was to speak to the assembled crowd, mainly women, at that gathering of about three thousand.

As they started down the long hall leading to the assembly, Corrie paused and said she was tired and would like a glass of milk and a cookie to give her some energy for the evening. However, dinner time had passed, and all the kitchens and cafeterias were closed. There needed to be a place for Corrie to get even a small snack. Moreover, going outside the university to obtain food would take time, and Corrie was due to speak shortly.

The person from the executive accompanying Corrie heard her quietly say a heartfelt prayer for a little snack. She thought her

109

request was an impossible one. She wondered how God would bring a little refreshment for Corrie before they arrived at the auditorium. As they walked along the long hall heading for the assembly, a student living in the residence waiting for the start of summer courses came towards them carrying a food tray. As this student approached them, she paused and offered the food on this untouched tray to the elderly Corrie. On the student's tray was an unopened carton of 2% milk with a straw and a wrapped cookie.

God heard the prayer of one of His precious adopted children and answered it just at the right time. Corrie paused, and together, they stood in the hallway, enjoying the amazingly offered milk and cookies. This passing student knew nothing of the prayer, but Corrie knew, and that was enough for her to appreciate that God heard and answered both her physical needs and her simple prayer offered with faith.

One of Corrie's well-known quotes was, "Never be afraid to trust an unknown future to a known God."

Suzanne Wilkinson

For the eyes of the Lord are on the righteous, and his ears are open to their prayers; but the face of the Lord is against those who do evil." And who is he who will harm you if you become followers of what is good? 1 Peter 3:12-13 (NKJV)

It is Not Okay with Me!

Janine Maxwell has given me permission to share this fantastic story, taken from one of the chapters in her book, *It's Not Okay with Me.* Her book is compelling, and compelling is far too mild a word to describe the impact of this document. It describes God's call on a heart that came alive in a woman who dared to listen. "Somebody's Calling My Name" is an old spiritual that forecasts her experience. It is a real faith-based adventure that is rooted in love.

Heart for Africa is the soul of the ministry Janine and her husband, Ian, launched in AIDS's ridden Africa, where 15 million orphans were left parentless and without the means of sustaining life. Janine's story is brutally honest, and we'll take you straight to her heart, the issues of Africa's greatest need. *It's Not Okay with Me* provides truth and fresh insight into Africa and is filled with hope. Even the most seasoned African traveller will have their eyes opened to the truth. The truth is that there is hope in a place that seems hopeless. We must come alongside, say it's not okay with me, and then act. Janine Maxwell lives and works with her husband in the "Hope for Africa" ministry in Swaziland, Africa.

This story is not an exact quote, but it conveys her story of one of her remarkable encounters with God. I highly recommend you read her book *It's Not Okay with Me* to learn of other extraordinary encounters this once highly successful Canadian business owner had that brought her to the depth of Africa. I will tell this fantastic story in the first person, almost exactly as she told it.

Sitting at the back of the conference room filled with 5,000 people, I heard God tell me to write a book. You might think I am completely nuts. Yes, God told me to write a book, and I said, "No way!". Can you imagine me saying that to God after all God has allowed me to go through? And after saying yes to closing my business and yes to everything else, I said "no". I said "No Way" to God when he asked me to write it. God repeated Himself to me right there in the conference. He said in plain English, "It is time for you to write the book." I was thinking to myself, "You have got to be crazy if You think I am going to open my chest cavity and reveal my red and beating heart to the world by sharing my life with them. I can't handle that. Plus, I did many stupid things that I'm not proud of. I am not going to risk exposing myself to the world. "No way."

Suddenly, a vision flashed through my brain, pictured me sitting on Oprah's couch with a book in her hand. Oprah asks me, "Say, don't you think it was foolish to close your business?" Or worse. Something about the book is that the article says Janine is unstable and needs more authority to write about Africa. She's just a businessperson, and oddly, obviously not a very good one, or she

111

would still be doing it. Or worse yet. No one will read it. Okay, so the Oprah thing may be far-fetched, but it did flash through my head; honestly, it did. So, I said to God, as if He hadn't thought of this, "Okay, God, who would want to read my story? Everybody has an amazing story. Who on earth would want to read mine?" I can't believe I was conversing with God, with 5000 people around me, yet no one else knew. He said, "Don't worry about who will read it; just write it as an act of obedience."

"No! No! No!" I am not going to do it. I can't. It will hurt too much. Haven't You put me through enough? Wasn't my business, life, family, and heart enough for You, God? Please don't make me do it. I can't. I won't. And I didn't tell a living soul, not even Ian, because I knew he wouldn't be on my back about doing it.

I went down to the exhibition booths, and Stephen was there. I had heard him give his conference message the day before and had read his book. He was from Malawi, Africa. I took a team to Malawi later that year, so I wanted to introduce myself. His warm smile and big handshake made me feel like I had known him my whole life. I told him about myself, Heart for Africa, and our upcoming trip to Malawi.

I didn't know how God did this, but our short ten-minute conversation made Stephen tell me that I needed to share my testimony. This story of having it all and giving it up to serve people experiencing extreme poverty in Africa was critical, and people in North America and Africa needed to hear it. He said that African people consider the American dream their goal, and I had given up the vision to obey God's call. Great. Now, God had total strangers in my case. No, I wasn't going to do it. Many months later, when I was in Malawi, I met with Stephen to thank him for being the catalyst for my writing to begin. He told me then that when we had met in Hawaii, the Lord had shown him a book beside my head. But he wasn't sure if he was to tell me that or not. I would have fainted if he had. In time, I did write the book, "It is Not Okay with Me".

Suzanne Wilkinson - Adapted from Janine Maxwell's book, "It is Not Okay with Me." with written permission.
https://www.goodreads.com/book/show/2661918-it-s-not-okay-with-me.

Let Us Cry Out for God Given Empathy.

I have travelled to Israel three times with groups of pilgrims going there to learn and absorb something of humanity's history and the origins of faith. These are found uniquely in this little but pivotal country of Israel, which God so praised and set apart from the beginning.

I ask myself; can society no longer feel the pain of others? There are many places in our world where the appalling, needless loss of life is an unspeakable atrocious. Has evil which necessitates a war caused humans to reason together no longer?

God created humans with a higher intellect than animals. We were created in God's own image. We thank you, Lord, for the incredible capacity to feel and to reason. These are God-given distinctive, yet, for many, where have they gone?

Humankind can create robotics, fly to the moon, and develop Artificial Intelligence, yet we can't get along with each other. God has given us the ability to love, care, and empathize, but where have these qualities gone for many? Sin, pride, hatred, and selfishness get in the way. Let us cry out for God-given image distinctions. Let love and empathy towards our neighbours be restored before we destroy ourselves and the planet that sustains us.

Today, some people have great difficulty empathizing with the many innocent Israelis or Palestinians caught in the conflict of war. Bombs continue to destroy homes and the landscape of Ukraine. Marches have turned ugly. Some see only the pain of the side they're on. They fail to see that child who is bleeding out on a dirty, unattended stretcher in a dust-filled tunnel. Do we not care for the medical people who are dehydrated and have served beyond exhaustion? Have we as humans lost our ability to care for our fellow humans caught in this unresolvable war with evil, whistling missiles and cocked guns? Can humans no longer reason together? So many of us cannot look into the eyes of "the other side" and acknowledge those captured in an age-old conflict that seems so unresolvable. Where has wisdom gone? What happens to our ability to empathize?

Too much hate exists in our world, and there appears to be insufficient understanding and love – the kind of love that lifts another human higher, whoever they are. Has passion and understanding been lost to hatred and revenge?

Empathy is simply listening well and withholding judgment. It is an emotional connection that communicates understanding to the other. It lets that person know they are not alone and are understood. It is a faithful God-given gift one gives to another. We sense their predicament and feel their pain and that they are not alone.

Are we not taught in the Scriptures to "love our neighbour as ourselves" (Mark 12:31)? Doesn't the Old Testament and the Talmud both teach "love of neighbour" as a tenant of and crucial to faith? Is not the connection to and understanding of another's pain the force and power of our common humanity? Let us not lose this mysterious power, this connection to a fellow human, whoever they are. Why do we think ourselves so much better than others? Have we walked in their shoes? Can we not sense their value and their pain?

Is empathizing with those in need no longer part of being human? When we see an injured child, an oppressed homeless person lost in a maze of addiction, or a senior who is now without resources, do we ignore them, turn, and walk away? Do we want to be uncaring? Where is our pain for those our neighbours near and far, no matter their skin colour or creed? Do we in our society ever ask ourselves, "Who is our neighbour?" Don't we recall the story of the Good Samaritan? (see Luke 10:25-37). Let us challenge ourselves to be a Good Samaritan.

The acuteness of war brings this unfeeling, unresponsive quality to the surface as we are bombarded so starkly with conflicts in the daily news. I fear humanity is losing the ability to care, to see that innocent child suffering is not a "Palestinian" child or a "Jewish" child. To see and care that the prostitute on the downtown corner could be your daughter addicted to drugs. They are each a child suffering.

We need to rediscover our humanity. I want to tell those unfeeling, uncaring people, "If you see somebody in pain, try to feel that pain." Empathy is understanding another person's feelings and imaginatively entering those feelings. Yet even without a genuine heart of understanding, just simple decency and some compassion extended to another in a situation of need will do. Humans are losing that capacity. Empathy may not be enough to change the circumstances, but it at least gives one a sense of humanity and lets the other know someone cares.

Pray to God that we might see the vivid faces of children and their parents murdered while they slept or sense the fear of youth at a music festival at a time of war. Care for those who today sit kidnapped as a hostage, or the innocent Palestinians who have lost everything that they once called normal. Pray for our fellow human beings and the innocents on both sides. The knowledge and the situation of each should cause us pain and drive us to prayer.

Thank you, God, for the power of empathy. May our neighbours and all humans, wherever they are, feel empathy and compassion for those who find themselves caught in the grip of unfortunate circumstances, whether self-inflicted or forced upon them. You call us to be heavenly citizens, so help us be so.

Let us be the ones to whom God makes known the riches of the glory of the mystery, which is Christ in us, the hope of glory, and may that include justice, mercy, understanding, and kindness.

Help us not to become unthinking, unfeeling, robotic creatures. May empathy be sewn into the DNA of all of us in our humanity. Please connect us humans in a way that the others know we care, love, and understand them. Oh, Sovereign God, hear our prayer, and may 'love of neighbour' reign supreme upon this earth. Oh, Lord, hear our prayer. Amen

Suzanne Wilkinson

Life and Death

The thought of death for many elicits fear, anxiety, unsettledness, denial and more.

The experience of death brings varied emotions of sorrow, grief, regret, and depression and deeply affects the majority.

Christians have the assurance that "death has been swallowed up in victory…Thanks be to God! He gives us victory through our Lord Jesus Christ." (I Corinthians 15:54b, 57, NIV).

From my early years in my Christian walk, I was impacted by a particular verse tucked away in one of the Apostle Paul's letters. It reads: *"For to me, to live is Christ and to die is gain."* (Philippians 1:21, NIV). This became my "life verse" and has been remembered so many times when reflecting on the death of people in my life.

My grandparents were godly Christians whose lives drew me to seek them out for counsel, a listening ear, some encouragement, or simply a quiet, comforting retreat. The last days of Grandpa's life were in the hospital, where I visited shortly before his death. Without knowing if he was consciously hearing me, I shared how God had done some incredible things that summer in the Christian camp where I served. He began to sing some of his favorite hymns and repeat Scripture he had put to memory. I left that hospital room thinking: "When I die, I want to go like that ... singing hymns and repeating Scripture ... with the Lord foremost in my heart and mind." The legacy of faith and testimony of those who have "gone before" helps to strengthen my resolve to live for Christ.

Less than a year later, my brother died in a tragic drowning accident. He was 18 years of age – at the other end of the spectrum from aged grandparents.

Questions flood the mind in that kind of death experience. And, for me, it recognized that my youngest brother would not be around any longer – to enter into university, to continue with the young people and music programs at church, to become a counsellor at camp using his gifts for the Lord, and so much more. His last

116

photograph of him is in a teen boys' Sunday School class, with his open Bible in hand. The <u>last days</u> of his life were at a youth retreat with some one hundred young people who were strangers – because he was tagging along with a friend (a long distance from home).

Following his death, our family received a packet of letters, notes and cards from the youth and adults at that retreat. They expressed the impact of his life on them – in such a short time. Teens were saved, others were challenged to "take hold of life again", some experienced "healing" of hurts and wounds, and many said (in one way or another) that their new close friend was "alive in the very presence of Him who died that we might <u>live</u> forever."

The truth that dying is gain for the Christian has brought comfort and solace that can be shared with others and joy knowing "what a day that will be when Jesus I shall see."

I have lived long enough to see both parents promoted to their heavenly home. Their lives were well lived for the Lord and family members who are part of the family of God and walking with the Lord.

Witness and testimony that had a ripple effect in church, community, work and circles beyond. When I was preparing the Memorial Services for each of them, selecting the music that would reflect what message they would want to leave behind was not difficult.

Mom had written her three favorite hymns in front of her Bible. First, "Praise my soul, the King of heaven, to His feet thy tribute bring; Ransomed, healed, restored, forgiven, evermore His praises sing." Then there was "Guide me, O Thou great Jehovah, Pilgrim through this barren land; I am weak, but Thou art mighty, Hold me with Thy powerful hand."

And thirdly was "Jesus, wondrous Saviour! Christ, of kings, The King! Heaven itself without Thee dark as night would be. Lamb of God! Thy glory is the light above. Lamb of God! Thy glory is the life of love." I concluded my "tribute" by saying: "Mom is now bathing in that light. She is enjoying the life of love in its fullest measure, even now … with Jesus, her wondrous Saviour, Lamb of God."

Dad had one song that had to be included in his service – "Until Then". It reads: "My heart can sing when I pause to remember a heartache here is but a stepping stone. Along a trail that's always winding upward – This troubled world is not my final home. But until then my heart will go on singing, until then with joy I'll carry on – Until the day my eyes behold the city until the day God calls me home." Until then – *"whatever you do, work at it with all your heart, as working for the Lord, not for human masters, since you know that you will receive an inheritance from the Lord as a reward. It is the Lord Christ you are serving."* (Colossians 3:23-24, NIV). Dad's oldest grandson gave tribute by saying: "This is how Grandpa lived his life and how he has set an example. There is comfort in knowing that Grandpa is now receiving his inheritance for a life spent in service to God, an inheritance provided by God's grace."

So, in BIG part, my life is full of music – singing and playing and being part of worship, praising God – my Lord and Saviour … because of mom and dad. I must live THIS life to the full, as my parents did – and because Jesus said: *"I have come that they may have life and have it to the full."* (John 10:10b, NIV). And live life in anticipation of what is beyond earthly death – eternal life. That's gain!

In life and death, God has proven Himself to be faithful to me. In life – He provides "strength for today"; in death – there's "bright hope for tomorrow." I am grateful for "blessings all mine, with ten thousand beside! "Great Is Thy Faithfulness.

In the Book of Lamentations, we read: ***"Because of the Lord's great love we are not consumed, for his compassions never fail. They are new every morning; great is your faithfulness. I say to myself, 'The Lord is my portion; therefore, I will wait for him.'"*** **(Lamentation 3:22-24, NIV).** With promises like this one has no reason to fear death.

Anonymous

Light . . . It Changes Everything!

"You're here to be light, bringing out the God colours in the
world. God is not a secret to be kept . . .
If I make you light-bearers,
you don't think I will hide you under a bucket, do you?
I'm putting you on a light stand. Now . . . shine!"
Matthew 5:14-15 (The Message)

Light . . . it changes everything. Just watch a five-year-old child who's terrified of the dark. They will be fearlessly frolicking in a room alone until . . . you turn out the light! Regardless of how often you turn on the light, show them there's nothing there; when you remove the light, the irrational fear returns. There is an innate fear of what may be hiding in the darkness, an instinctive suspicion of what cannot be seen.

In setting foot on earth, Jesus brought light to a world shrouded in darkness, fear, suspicion, and aimless wandering. In his own words, he explained, *"I have come into the world as a light so that no one who believes in me should stay in darkness."* (John 12:46, NIV)

Darkness is simply the absence of light. Jesus has 'turned on the light' and dispelled the darkness. Darkness cannot remain in the presence of light. Even the tiniest flicker of light is enough to dispel darkness.

We are charged with the privilege and responsibility of continuing his mission, of being light to those around us, those living in fear and wandering aimlessly through life looking for . . . something.

So why are we timid? Why so bashful about this great message of hope in a perishing world? We are bearers of light, 'bringing out the God-colours in the world', a world desperately looking for colour, light, purpose, and peace. The Apostle John writes the obvious when he says,

119

"Whoever walks in the dark does not know where they are going." **(John 12:35b, NIV)**

We, who have been shown the way, are called to lead others out of the darkness into the way of light. May God give us the passion and courage to be a light to those wandering in the darkness. And when in doubt, when feeling timid and sceptical, remember that this light has the power to transform, to entirely renovate, an entire city – a prosperous, hedonistic, intellectually arrogant, occult-steeped metropolis (see Acts 19).

Lord Jesus, forgive me for failing to see that those around me who have yet to discover You are wandering in the dark. Some are afraid, while others live aimlessly, grasping for anything that will dispel their darkness and give them direction. Forgive me for often passing judgment on those who have messed up and lost their way. Even today, it helps me live as a light-bearer, unashamedly, boldly, and willing to offer hope to those who don't realize they are in the dark. I ask that You please bring someone into my life who needs to hear Your message of the hope that You have entrusted to me and give me the courage, faith, and boldness to share it. Amen

Suzanne Wilkinson

Like the Sparrow, I Know He Watches Over Me

Throughout this story, I prayed for God's guidance, and He answered my prayer in ways I could not have imagined.

Some years ago, when I became aware that my husband was having some health issues, I put our names on a list at Parkview Village Community in Stouffville, Ontario. (One of our sons lives in that city.) This community was founded about forty-five years ago by some very forward-thinking Mennonites who realized the senior population would need future housing. Many residents here, including me, believe the planning team was inspired.

Parkview Village Community is comprised of four types of housing:

- Apartments – Independent Living
- Life-lease condo suites
- Cluster homes - A settlement of small bungalows
- Parkview Home – Long-Term Care

A decade ago, there was at least a ten-year waiting period for placement in one of the housing options. I placed our names on this waiting list, wondering if or when we might need such accommodation.

About a dozen years ago, when my husband and I realized our health would decline as we age, we felt the need to be proactive about our future. We sold our home and moved into a lovely, spacious apartment in Toronto. Eventually, it became apparent that my husband was showing signs of severe health issues, which became very marked during the Covid 19 restrictions. To the best of my ability, I cared for him as I looked after him at home. However, in 2021 and 2022, I found that I could not continue to provide for his increasing mobility issues and care needs.

Through the help of a social worker, I was urged to place my husband's name on the critical care list for him to obtain a long-term care facility. We would need to wait until a placement opening, which would take at least six months. I listed three places that would be suitable and assured him that he would not be moved over the summer so he could have full enjoyment of the gardens where we had lived. Eventually, a place would be found for him, but where would I go? Which of the three places would open up for my husband before we could move forward? I looked at several condos and considered buying an excellent one, but I sensed a need to wait.

Shortly after the five-month mark, we received a call as a room was becoming available at Parkview Home Long Term Care in Stouffville. A son and daughter-in-law of mine live near this home, and it is only a thirty-minute drive for our other son to visit. On October 3rd, 2023, Dave signed the consent forms, and he moved into a very nice private room at Parkview Village Home, where we have been pleased with the service he has received.

That same day, I contacted the placement agent at Parkview Village Community and received the news that no accommodation was available in any of the four areas. No sooner had I arrived back home in north Toronto when I received a call from the agent saying, "An independent living two-bedroom apartment had become available. Would I be interested?" I immediately returned to Stouffville. After some minor reservations were resolved and confirmed by my daughter-in-law's agreement, I signed the papers and agreed to move within six weeks. It was a monumental effort to downsize, but it was only possible because we had previously decluttered in stages after selling our home.

On December 14th, 2023, I moved into that two-bedroom apartment in what I have discovered is a beautiful community. I have made many friends over the last year and enjoy living here. I am a short two-minute walk to the Long-Term Care Home where my husband lives, and I make that trip often due to his gradual decline.

In our latter years, we both appreciate our living space and the opportunity to live close to one another. Of course, we would rather be young forever, but God has provided and has answered our prayers. Without His guidance, things might have been so much more challenging. Thanks be to God, the great provider who knows and responds to our needs and cares.

Rev. Suzanne Wilkinson

Listening

In the summertime when I was a girl, we would visit my grandparent's farm near Lambeth (now a suburb of London, Ontario) each summer. I spent many warm, beautiful afternoons riding my bike, playing with friends, and exploring. I had more freedom and independence than young teens have today, though the risks were just as significant. We felt safe as we'd hike into the woods, rode a pony named Tony, try out the neighbour's home-made teeter-totter (which wasn't safe; my broken arm proved that), visit the one-room schoolhouse and the ballpark, which had a public pool. Still, I was not allowed to swim in it due to the risk of coming down with polio.

I would venture into my grandfather's barn to watch the hired hand milk the cows. I especially liked to watch Bessy. She was my favorite holster as she was a friendly cow.

But whenever I heard the clanging bell by the back door of the farmhouse—that clear sound slicing through the summer breezes—I immediately dropped whatever I was doing and headed home. The sound was unmistakable, and I knew to come home. Years later, my ears still perk up and listen if I hear a clanging bell.

In the gospels, Jesus told His disciples that He is the Good Shepherd, and His followers are the sheep. "*The sheep listen to his voice*," He said. "*He calls his own sheep by name and leads them out*." (John 10:3b, NIV).

We live in a time, like Jesus', when the Jewish leaders and teachers of the law sought to confuse Christ's disciples by asserting their authority and undermining Jesus' authority. Jesus still declares that His loving voice can still be heard clearly, more distinctly than all the others. **"His sheep follow him because they know his voice" (v. 4b, NIV).** Jesus still calls out to us in many ways because He loves us and desires to protect, provide and guide us.

May we listen to Jesus' voice and avoid foolishly dismissing it, for the fundamental truth remains: The Shepherd still speaks clearly in our day, and His sheep hear His voice. Perhaps through a verse of Scripture, the words of a believing friend, or the nudge of the Spirit—Jesus speaks, and we would be wise to listen for it. Like in everything else, listening is a skill worth developing.

Suzanne Wilkinson

And walk in love, as Christ also has loved us and given Himself for us, an offering and a sacrifice to God for a sweet-smelling aroma," (Ephesians 5:2, NKJV)

Looking Backward

It wasn't until I was sixteen that I realized I needed glasses. The chalkboards at school had become very fuzzy. Despite my father's doubts about my claims of not seeing clearly, I pushed forward with my doctor, was tested, and was eventually declared "short-sighted." Glasses for seeing anything much beyond the end of my nose were required.

Similarly, I think I have been "short-sighted" much of my life about who I was and who I was being called to become. Born and raised in the church, I carried on through my teen years, early twenties and into married life and parenthood, but if there were signs all along the way, I either missed or misinterpreted or didn't see them at all.

As a young adult, I pursued my career as a federal civil servant for 30 years. Yet, during those years, there were signs. I hungrily read anything and everything theological. I became a Sunday School teacher, then an Elder.

I participated in national events for my denomination and tithed in my local congregation. I bought a beautiful communion set – plate and goblet but wondered what to do with them. I took early retirement from my civil service job to have more time to do church work, be on both local and national committees, and even be an employee in the national office. Then one night at bedtime, I found myself reading "Reformed Theology" by R.C. Sproul, and I wondered what on earth was wrong with me that this was my choice of "fluffy" bedtime reading material. I realized that I was "hungry" and needed more substantial spiritual food to feel satisfied.

Knox College is part of the University of Toronto, the seminary for The Presbyterian Church in Canada. I signed up for one course in a two-year program that would satisfy that hunger. However, I was told that I would be required to get the written permission of my minister to enrol. I met with him, and *he immediately* asked why I wasn't signing up for the three-year Master of Divinity program. I laughed. I laughed *at* him, not *with* him, telling him I had already completed my so-called "career" and was not looking to launch into a new one. He backed off, but I could see he disagreed with me.

That September, I entered Knox College, and that very first morning, I walked into the foyer and stopped, staring around. Down the hall were classrooms; upstairs was the library. In another direction was the chapel. Standing there, absorbing it all, I had the overwhelming sense of finally being in the right place at the right time in my life. God wanted me *here*. That first day, I changed programs and began the path toward ordained ministry.

In retrospect, I can see more clearly now what I did not see in the past. Yes, God calls us, but sometimes we're too busy, disengaged, or doubtful even to hear the call, let alone ponder and respond.

Now that I have completed the first decade of ordained ministry, I marvel at God's wisdom and timing. I have loved every minute of serving as a pastor, and I look forward, hopefully with a better-attuned antenna than before, to discerning what God would have me do now. There is no expiry date on responding to God's call to service. It is up to each of us to ponder what God has in store for us and how we can be our best selves as Jesus' disciples.

I look forward to this forward-leaning adventure! Thanks be to God for all of it!

Rev. Joan Masterton

My God Will Meet All Your Needs

according to his glorious riches in Christ Jesus. (Phil 4:19, NIV)

As camp director of a Christian boys' camp, I had many varied responsibilities, demanding the use of God-given gifts and acquired abilities, along with "learning the ropes" with new experiences that brought challenge to the role.

The camp planned a building project for the coming spring, and a fantastic new washhouse facility for the older boys' camp was set

125

in motion. An estimator made plans, and a budget was worked out. Construction was soon underway and hopefully would be on target for the first week of camp.

Fundraising was the BIG issue. Under the direction of the camp board, I was responsible for raising the money to cover all the expenses. And the motivation for doing so was my job. I felt the pressure mounting as each week passed. This task was out of my league.

Philippians 4:19 (a Scripture memorized when I was much younger) came to mind repeatedly. God WOULD provide. He has promised to meet our needs. Much prayer accompanied the whole thinking process: how can we raise this much money quickly?

I approached a Christian businessman and asked for counsel on fundraising. He offered excellent and helpful advice and a sizable donation with a cheque as I left his office. What encouragement to help spur me on – when the big picture looked daunting.

It was a wonderful summer of camp ministry, with boys and young men coming and going – enjoying the whole camp experience. We saw God's hand working in our lives as decisions were made for Christ – our real reason for running camp … "Winning and Training Boys for Christ."

But Labour Day came, and the camp had not received the funds required for the washhouse project. Fervent prayers were made during the fall season as camp was closed, evaluations and reports were made, and our financial books were put in order for year-end.

God – we trust you to meet THIS need.

I'll not forget the day I arrived at the camp office – my job was on the line, what more could we do? The camp secretary was waiting, almost impatiently, for my entrance. She had tallied the contributions toward the building project, and with "last minute" cheques that had come in, the camp's fundraising goal was achieved. Praise God!!!

That was our first response as we "danced around the office." It seemed like we were giving God "three cheers".

I was humbled and overwhelmingly grateful for God's provision. It cemented that verse (Philippians 4:19) in my heart and mind and increased my faith – realizing that God is at work in our lives beyond what we could ever ask or think.

Anonymous

My Roots Boots

After one final walk through the house, I was satisfied there was nothing left for me to do until the movers came early the next morning. It had been a busy and emotional time packing up the family home in the city to start a new phase in my life. Looking at my watch, I noticed I had an hour to kill before heading off to some friends for dinner. I decided to use that time to drive to the local transfer station to drop off the three bags of garbage in my front hall. I couldn't leave them behind for the new owners and didn't want to take them to my new place. So, I loaded the bags of discarded stuff into my trunk and headed off to dispose of them.

In my forty years in Toronto, I had never been to a transfer station and was shocked to see the mountain of garbage in the massive drop-off building. It heightened my awareness of how we have become a consumer-driven society. I took the bags from my trunk and heaved them onto the huge garbage pile. In the process, my Roots boots and two of my daughter's stuffed animals fell out and lay there forlorn on the heap. Overwhelmed by emotion, I walked over to retrieve the stuffed animals. I did not have the heart to leave them behind, but a voice deep inside convinced me to leave my boots where they were, and that image is strongly imprinted in my mind to this day. The boots are a metaphor for the life I left behind, defined by status symbols such as designer clothes and footwear, education, and profession.

Dreams have been an essential part of the healing process that has taken place in my life, and for years, looking for lost shoes or difficulty finding the right ones was a recurring theme in my subconscious at night. As I was preparing for this significant life transition, God brought a book that helped me understand the dreams and path He had chosen for me. *Soul Prints*, written by Marc Gafni, an American philosopher living in Jerusalem, remains a favorite in my collection of books on spirituality. The following passage helped me understand the significance of leaving behind my Roots boots at the garbage dump:

When Moses hears the voice from the Burning Bush, the first words of the call are, "Take off your shoes, for the earth on which you walk is holy ground." This charge is not some audio command that blares, "Shoes prohibited!" Instead, these instructions imply the essence of Moses' call. "The ground on which your feet are walking – the path of your life, your story – is sacred ground." Shoe in biblical Hebrew is a na'al., literally translated as "closed' or "locked." We are too often closed off from – locked out of-ourselves. Shoes are at once a sign of culture and a symbol of our alienation from our own footprints. The footprint like the fingerprint and the palm print is a physical expression of the soul print......... The print left by your Nike is the same print left by every Nike, but the print left by your bare foot is unique to you.

I bought my Roots boots the first winter of my six years in university studying for a career change in midlife, and I wore them faithfully each winter to my classes in downtown Toronto. The boots represented a phase in my life that I was leaving behind. It was the beginning of a journey with God, exploring my unique calling, with a shift from professionalism and the world's concept of success to an ordinary everyday life focusing on family and relationships. I filed away my business cards and resume, and I have learned as much from my personal struggles and those whom God brought into my life as the years at university. I learned through experience how God uses His school of hard knocks, also known as wilderness or desert time, to teach and refine us. And I have come to understand my calling as soul-mate, which is so clearly defined in the first chapter of 2 Corinthians: **"He comes alongside us when we go through hard times, and before you know it, he brings us alongside someone else who is going through hard times so that we can be** *there for that person just as God was there for us."* **(2 Cor 1:4, MSG)**

I no longer dream about searching for my shoes; they are no longer essential to me. I have found my unique footprint through discovering who God created me to be. I have learned "who I am and whose I am," and peace has replaced the inner turmoil that manifested through my dreams. The little stuffed animals rescued from the dump are safely stored away in my basement, waiting for a visit from my grandchildren in this new phase of my life.

Magda Wills

No Mega Bruce Almighty Moments

As transformative experiences go, I can't say I have had one. At least there are no mega Bruce Almighty moments for those familiar with the Jim Carey/Morgan Freeman movie.

My God Story is probably stories, a natural build-up of multiple incidents that all reaffirmed my faith, taking us to where we are today. I've considered myself a Christian from my earliest memory. From being baptized and Sunday-schooled to becoming an official church member, to being married in the church and having our children baptized there, I have seen a deepening of my faith and Christian experience.

I have zero plans ever to get a tattoo. But should that change, that ink would have to read "Keep the Faith." Those three words have been the key for me, constantly reminding myself that God has a plan. That's been especially important but sometimes difficult to accomplish during life's low moments. Bruce Almighty didn't have that faith. He had to learn the hard way. I got lucky. I am blessed.

Jim Mason

Nothing Special, Yet Special

It was another day; the rain had already started before I stepped outside. The rain continued as we packed the SUV and drove the three hours home. *Nothing special.* The temperature was a welcomed 22 C (72 F) rather than the high 30s C (86+ F) with humidity just a few days ago. The raindrops tapped my arms and head as I loaded the SUV. My sundried skin welcomed the moisture of those large, cool raindrops. My son is sitting in the passenger seat, sharing the joy of music options on the radio. Our kitten, Misaki (me-sock-ee), is safely in her cat carrier in the backseat. *Nothing special.*

We continued to the gas station. I paid at the pump, and my son pumped the fuel. *Nothing special.* Back in the car and after a stop for a drink and snack, we were driving down the highway. More drivers are on the road today than just a month ago. Large raindrops began to come down. I reduced my speed and increased the wipers' speed to keep a clear view of the road ahead. *Nothing special.*

Misaki, meowing in the back seat, prompted my son to bring her to his seat for loving attention. After a bit of time, Misaki was gently and reassuringly placed in her cat carrier and returned to the back seat. *Nothing special.*

After a quick stop at my sister's home to pick up our dog, Max, we were on the 20-minute drive home. *Nothing special.* As we drove down the dirt driveway to our home, our large dog, Max, was spread across my son's lap in the passenger seat. Max closed his eyes in bliss as my son lovingly patted him. *Nothing special.*

A downpour was released from heaven as we pulled into the driveway. We each opened the SUV doors and lovingly brought our pets to the front door. *Nothing special.* After opening the front door, best friends Max and Misaki reunited after two days apart; they are exceptional pets together. Tonight, I placed food in Max's dish. Misaki took the first bite. Max graciously shared his dinner with his best friend and companion, Misaki. *Nothing Special.*

As I type this note in the darkness of my room, I hear Max and Misaki playing with each other downstairs. Max's toenails tap the floor as he runs about, and the jingling bell on Misaki's collar is a joyful accompaniment. *Nothing special.*

Nothing special, yet today was *very special*. I sensed you, God, in all those special and not-so-special moments. I don't want to ever take You for granted, Lord. *Thank you* for unfolding another beautiful summer day, the rain, the music, the companionship, and the opportunity to be together. *Thank you* for the chance to leave Max with my sister and her son. *Thank you* for the opportunity to afford the travel. *Thank you* for the safe travels. *Thank you* for visiting my other sister, her new puppy, son, and family. *Thank you* for reuniting our pets and our return home as a whole family. *Thank you* for this home. *Thank you* for soaking in the love of this day with me. I encountered You all day and that is special. Lord, accept my love and thanks from someone you have made special as Your child.

Mary George

Oh, to See Through the Eyes of a Child

" '[Mary] will give birth to a son, and you are to give him the name Jesus because he will save his people from their sins.' All this took place to fulfil what the Lord had said through the prophet: 'The virgin will conceive and give birth to a son, and they will call him Immanuel' (which means, "God with us")."
Matthew 1:21-23 (NIV)

Christmas 2021 was a thrilling experience for our two-year-old granddaughter, Rae. It was the first Christmas she could walk and talk, and she was delighted to discover miniature "Santa friends", including reindeer, a sleigh, and elves. They were just the right size for her little hands.

Rae spent even more time playing with the figures of a Nativity scene. She observed, "The angels are beautiful!" We sang "Angels

131

we have heard on High" to help explain why the angels appeared in the sky to sing about Jesus and tell the shepherds (and all of us) where to find Him. She was puzzled at the three men who were holding different things. "What's that, what's that, what's that, what's that," she asked, pointing at the boxes they held. We tried to explain that the wise men brought gifts to Jesus on his birthday, just as people gave her presents on her birthday.

"Do we only give Jesus and people gifts on their birthdays and at Christmas?"

Long before dawn on December 17, I received a surprise call from Rae's parents, Dave, and Dana, to come quickly and watch Rae. They had to go to Sunnybrook Hospital as soon as possible. A few hours later, Rae's first sibling, baby brother Peter, was born. A new son, brother, and grandchild is a beautiful Christmas present. Our hearts overflowed with joy and celebration. While the parents and baby stayed in the hospital for a few days, Rae slept at our house, and we shared many Christmas stories and songs.

As soon as Rae met her baby brother Peter for the first time, she looked at Jesus in the nativity scene with fresh eyes. Her attention was now focused on Jesus and his relationship with his parents, the wise men, shepherds, and angels. Every day, she pretended her little Mary figure was holding, kissing, feeding, and caring for baby Jesus. She said, "Joseph loves Jesus too". "Yes! And Jesus loves us too."

We sang, "Jesus loves me this I know." Rae would hold baby Jesus in the manger in her left hand and, one at a time, bring Mary, Joseph, the shepherds, and the wise men up close in her right hand until she had them "kiss" baby Jesus.

Before New Year's, Rae and her parents got very sick. All tested positive for Covid 19. Four days later, I developed a very sore throat and burning sinuses. I, too, tested positive. Baby Peter had to be rushed to Sick Children's Hospital. His parents stayed there with him for five days because he was not getting adequate oxygen. Rae moved into our house again and stayed for two weeks while we both had Covid 19. I felt weak, dizzy and had a lot of pain, so caring for my sweet little two-year-old granddaughter was unusually challenging. We couldn't play outside in the snow and felt too weak for active indoor games. She couldn't see her little brother, baby Peter, who was cared for by mommy and daddy and the kind, helpful nurses and doctors at the Toronto Sick Children's Hospital.

Every day, Rae gently held baby Jesus, Mary & Joseph, the angels, and all the characters of the Christmas story. We played Christmas Carols on the piano. Often, we lazily cuddled on the couch and listened to calming Christmas carols of hope, peace, and joy. We prayed every day that Peter could come home from the hospital and that we would all heal.

Thankfully, our prayers were answered. Peter's breathing and oxygen levels improved, and he could leave the hospital. A few days later, we hugged Rae goodbye, and she, too, returned home. Healing and homecoming brought peace and joy.

I could clean up after Christmas when I caught up on sleep and recovered from the Covid symptoms. My husband put the Christmas tree out on the street. We packed the candles, decorations, stockings, garland, and lights away and put them in the garage. Our house looked bare and empty.

The next time little Rae arrived at Grandma's house, she noticed everything "Christmas" was gone. It was a sad day for Rae. She looked for her favorite.

 characters, Santa and Jesus. She wandered from room to room, searching for her "best friends."

"Where is Santa?" asked the crestfallen, two-year-old little girl.

"We put Santa, the reindeer, and the elves away in the garage until next Christmas," I answered. With eyes wide with dismay and an anxious voice, she asked, "Where is Jesus?"

"In a blue bin in the garage," I responded.

The corners of her mouth drooped. I clarified, "We put Jesus away until next Christmas." She begged, "But I want Jesus NOW!"

It was a somber day for little Rae. She did not forget or give up hope. Day after day, she asked for Jesus and her "Christmas friends."

A couple of weeks later, when Rae revisited Grandma's house, she desperately requested, "I want to find Jesus!"

So, we put on our winter coats, hats, mittens, and boots and walked out to the ice-cold garage. We opened the lids of about ten bins, all marked "Christmas." We found Christmas tree decorations, lights, wrapping paper, cards, and music. We were cold, but Rae did not want to stop looking for Jesus. Finally, when we opened the second last bin, a smile beamed across Rae's face; her eyes sparkled, and she exclaimed, "We found Jesus! Bring him back into our house!" We did.

The wise men, shepherds, Mary and Joseph, and the sheep now reside in a drawer in our front hall. Often, Rae pulls the drawer open and plays with Jesus, his family, and his friends.

I learned a lesson that day. The tree, lights, and decorations are beautiful but can stay in the garage for eleven months of the year. But Jesus is most important and must not be hidden and lost in the garage.

Now, we can see Jesus every day. The day we found Jesus and the Nativity figures in the garage, Rae climbed onto the piano bench and had a few more special requests. "Grandma play." "Joy to the World", "Away in Manger", "Silent Night, ..." Rae's eyes sparkled, and she smiled. Lost and found, Jesus was back in our house and our hearts forever.

We now sing Christmas songs year-round and are reminded of God's loving gifts of a baby, peace, and joy.

Pause and take a minute to list the things vital for you and your family at Christmas.

What gives us love, hope, peace, and joy?

From January to December, do we leave Jesus out of sight, outside our hearts and our homes? Is Jesus "Immanuel, God with us" every day of our lives? Anonymous

Our Heavenly Father Protects His Children

Alex, my husband, and I had accepted Christ, being new Christians, we were trying to walk with the Lord and be as faithful to Him as possible. I made a surprising discovery three months later. Before knowing about God and His Son, Jesus, Alex, and I were regular drinkers of whiskey for me and beer for Alex. This discovery was terrific, yet a delightful shock. I asked Alex, "Do you know what?" He said, "No, what?" We have not had a drink of whiskey or beer since that day, February 4th, 1979, when we accepted Jesus as our Saviour and became adopted children of God.

Alex said, "You are right." In the past, we believed it would be impossible to give up our drinking. We loved the way it made us feel when we were consuming alcohol. This euphoric feeling was so strong for each of us. We had tried many times before but were unable to abstain from drinking. We could not give up our alcohol consumption. Amazingly, after our conversion, we discovered that our appetite for alcohol was gone.

We could only put it down to God, taking away our appetite for alcohol and the financial cost involved. We did not miss drinking whiskey or beer during those three months. On our own, we could never have had the willpower to stop drinking. Neither of us has had a drop of alcohol since February 4th, 1979, the day we chose to accept Christ and walk in His ways. God is so powerful, and He knows what is best. We credit God for this drastic change and blessing in our lives. Our Heavenly Father protects His children.

Anonymous

"Now all glory to God, who is able, through his mighty power at work within us, to accomplish infinitely more. than we might ask or imagine." (Ephesians 3:20 NIV)

Out of the Blue

In God's time. In God's time. I've heard this a lot over the years. Your prayers will get answered – in God's time. And they may only sometimes get answered the way you want, but there will usually be a resolution. The power resides in the God to whom we pray.

Prayer is calming; it eases our doubts and anxieties. And when God decides to answer you, you will have the answers and peace you are seeking. And sometimes you may feel a miracle has occurred.

I remember one of these instances. I had decided to quit work in 1991 when I had two very young children. I wanted to be a full-time mom for a while. My husband's income was okay; we knew we could get by. In 1993, we welcomed our third child. As the years passed, it became apparent that we were running out of money. No - I didn't pray for a lottery win or money to fall from the sky. But for months, I did pray for some resolution to the problem. It was during November 1997, with Christmas coming, that we knew it would be a tough year.

Out of the blue, I got a phone call from one of my former bosses whom I had not worked for in over ten years. "Could I do a bit of consulting work?" she asked. It was just for a couple of weeks, but the pay was very good, and it would help us with the extra expenses we needed for Christmas. I jumped at the opportunity, knowing this was the answer to my prayers. The work was rewarding, and I realized that I had missed it.

About a week after that temporary assignment, my former boss called again. Would I be interested in working two days a week, on a permanent basis? she asked. My answer was a definite yes. I know this doesn't constitute a miracle by any definition, but rightly so, this was an answer to my prayers. But, for me, it was, especially since I had not worked for that company or talked to that person in over ten years. My prayers had been answered - not just at the right time - but in God's time.

Charlene Mason

Paxwood

Why did I stop walking? All was quiet beneath the leafy branches in Paxwood, just the gentle rustling of aspen and birch. I had work to do, yet I stood still, clutching the bundle of gathered dry sticks. I listened, not knowing what I would hear, heart open, mind alert.

The other girls in my wood patrol, also collecting firewood, yet we had spread out; good dead wood was scarce because other Girl Guide groups had camped before us. I was alone, yet not alone. I received the message given to me and was puzzled over it as I swung the weighted end of my rope over a dead branch. I pulled both ends of the rope, and the branch snapped and fell to the ground. I was not injured. Then I understood the message: the Holy Spirit is real and present. I sensed His presence. I wondered and treasured this revelation.

Previously, I had heard of the "Holy Ghost", but I did not believe in ghosts. I was practical and not prone to believing in spirits. I was not superstitious. This sure certainty that the Holy Spirit IS of God, thoroughly good and thoroughly reliable, was a sure foundation and something definite that gave direction, stability and understanding.

We cooked our evening meal over the open fire, sang our Girl Guide songs and "Taps", and then curled up in our bedding in our tents. After breakfast the following day, we dressed in full uniform, lanyards and berets and walked a couple of miles to a small village Anglican Church for Church Parade. The colour bearers led us down the centre aisle, placed the flags to one side behind the altar, and we took our seats for the service. It was Pentecost Sunday. The words of this hymn flew off the page and embraced me. Deep in my heart, I found myself praying as I sang:

1 Come down, O Love divine,
seek thou this soul of mine,
and visit it with thine own ardor glowing.
O Comforter, draw near,

within my heart appear,
and kindle it, thy holy flame bestowing.
2 O let it freely burn,
till earthly passions turn
to dust and ashes in its heat-consuming;
and let thy glorious light
shine ever on my sight,
and clothe me round, the while my path illuming.
3 And so the yearning strong,
with which the soul will long,
shall far out pass the power of human telling;
for none can guess its grace,
till Love creates a place
wherein the Holy Spirit makes a dwelling.
United Methodist Hymnal, 1989 Author: Bianco da Siena

The words were alive; I was alive. I knew that the Spirit was alive in me and in that place. Now, I know it is impossible to be away from the Holy Spirit; there is no place where He is not. Feeling His presence is irrelevant; He is! I was astounded that I should be reminded in such a vivid way of the message I had received the day before under the aspen tree.

A woman gave the homily, probably a lay reader. She spoke about death. Death is not to be feared. As she spoke, I had the same sensation I sometimes experienced in math class when an elusive concept suddenly made sense. She said death was not something to be feared; being in the presence of God our Creator is good.

The knowledge I received in Paxwood is a constant in my life. When I have abandoned God and given up on Him, the Holy Spirit has waited and patiently given understanding, and, in due time, I have received. I found peace.

As a result of my experience at Paxwood, my attitude towards life was being shaped, and my mind altered. I knew I was in the care and authority of a Higher Being than a human being. My parents had the care and authority over me then, but there would come a time when that would cease.

Then what? I knew I should pursue this relationship with this Higher Being, the Holy Spirit, who had entered my conscience of His own free will. I knew ultimate wisdom came from that source. I would listen!

Another result of my experience was an answer to the question of death. The answer came in the sermon at the little Anglican church in the village. Death would not be an end to nothingness. It was going through a gateway to a new life. As I matured, I saw the pointlessness experienced by many in this existence called life. We work, we breathe,

we clean, we eat. We work to eat, we clean to stay healthy and work, we work to eat. What for? To die!

The Holy Spirit gave a different perspective. The point of life is the life hereafter. Some things I strive for remain here after I die: my house, bank account, body, or ashes. After I die, other things stay with my soul: love, forgiveness, cleansing from wickedness by Jesus' blood, kindness, and self-control. These things and many other souls will go beyond the grave, and this life will have been worth living.

My encounter in Paxwood was a minor incident, and I wonder if it even was an incident. Nothing tangible was there for me to photograph or carry back to the campsite. I had nothing to tell the other girls. Would they understand if I did? They would probably give me a strange look or laugh. It was a minor incident that I had forgotten and not thought about for many years.

Yet the substance of that encounter with a Being who is both beyond and on this planet has made a profound difference to my thinking, being, actions and relationship with others. Stressful times drive me to my knees and make me look up, up, up. Hope replaces despair. The promises of "In my Father's house are many mansions..." (John 14:2, NIV) and "The Lord is my Shepherd..." (Psalm 23:1, NIV) changed my outlook on life.

Indeed, life is a mountain to climb, a swamp to wade through, and a desert to endure. However, at the same time, there is a pathway, a trail, sometimes hidden, and sometimes I avoid it, but I keep coming back to it, and I follow this way that is like a dream but full of reality to its Source, God the Father Almighty.

Andrea Kidd

Pure and Refined

"But who can endure the day of His coming? And who can stand when He appears? For He is like a refiner's fire, and like launderers' soap. He will sit as a refiner and a purifier of silver; He will purify the sons of Levi, and purge them as gold and silver, that they may offer to the LORD an offering in righteousness. **(Malachi 23: 2-3, NIV).**

A group of women once studied the book of Malachi in the Old Testament. While reading chapter three, they came across verse three: "He will sit as a refiner and purifier of silver." This verse puzzled the women, and they wondered what it meant about God's character and nature. One of the women offered to learn about refining silver and report back to the group at their following Bible study.

That week, this woman called up a silversmith and made an appointment to watch him at work. She didn't mention anything about the reason for her interest beyond her curiosity about the process of refining silver. As she watched the silversmith, he held a piece of silver over the fire and let it heat up. He explained that in refining silver, one needed to keep the silver in the middle of the fire where the flames were hottest to burn away all the impurities.

The woman thought about God holding us in such a hot spot – then she thought again about the verse, that he sits as a refiner and purifier of silver. She asked the silversmith if it was true that he had to sit in front of the fire the whole time till the silver was pure and refined.

The man answered "Yes" and explained that he had to sit there holding the silver and keep his eyes on it the entire time it was in the fire. It would be damaged if the silver was left even a moment too long in the flames.

The woman was silent for a moment. Then she asked the silversmith, "How do you know when the silver is completely refined?"

He smiled at her and answered, "Oh, that's easy. When I see my image in it."

If you are feeling the heat of this world's fire today, remember that God the Father and His Son Jesus Christ are refining you. "You are predestined to be conformed to the image of Christ."

This unknown author's story has been adapted by Suzanne Wilkinson

Savior's Complex: Dream and Vision Upon Awakening

"The Lord is My Shepherd" (Psalm 23:1, NIV)
"I am the Good Shepherd." (John 10:14, NIV)

Codependent relationships are something that I have struggled with all of my life. I was raised in a dysfunctional home. Personal boundaries were loose and unhealthy. As the eldest girl in a family of 10, my sweet, overwhelmed mother needed my help to keep the house and home. By the age of eight, I was a well-trained caregiver in a turbulent violent home. I developed a heightened sense of responsibility for the needs and well-being of those around me. This had both positive and negative effects on my relationships.

- I had a natural tendency to feel empathy/compassion for others; and a desire to help those in need.

- I developed a *Savior Complex*. I formed unhealthy addictive attachments. I became an enabler/rescuer.

A recent article I read explains the Saviour Complex: (*The Saviour Syndrome, C-2 Care*)

Among us there are saviours. These are people who are eager help, empathetic, and who want to assist everyone in any situation. They are people who will give everything for others, even if it means forgetting themselves. We call this the saviour syndrome.

The causes of saviour syndrome are often found in childhood. They may be children who have experienced various traumas, and abandonment. They may also be children who have been "parentified". That is, they had to take on the role of parents to their brothers and sisters at a very early age.

In a recent dream and waking vision, I believe God communicated a spiritual lesson to help heal me from the *Saviour's Syndrome.*

I was at a Christian event in a large stadium. I was excited. I brought several of my unbelieving family and friends and hoped that they would meet and give their hearts to the Lord that night. Just as the group I was with were about to settle into their seats, they suddenly decided that they wanted to go and get some hotdogs, popcorn, and beer. Fearing they may miss an encounter with Jesus, I offered to go in their place--as a Christ follower, I told myself it was the right self-sacrificing thing to do.

With food and drink orders in hand, I headed out. To my dismay, I found huge lineups at the concession stands and many of the items on my list were sold out. I became frustrated. Everything seemed to be so complicated. I became angry and judgmental of my unbelieving family and friends. I thought that they had their priorities mixed up. I could not understand why.

hotdogs, popcorn, and beer were more important than meeting Jesus. My arms were full and overflowing; items kept dropping and I struggled to pick them back up. I was totally overwhelmed. When I finally returned to my family and friends, I was exhausted. It seemed that no one understood or appreciated my efforts. As emotions began to flood over me, I cried and screamed. I started to hit myself. Nobody seemed to notice or care.

I woke screaming, drenched in perspiration and my face wet with hot tears. As I opened my eyes, there was a male figure standing quietly beside my bed. With arms folded, He intently watched over me.I will never forget His eyes; they seemed to pierce through the darkness, communicating some message that I did not quite understand ---later, I would. He wore layered garments with a heavy cloak over top. A draped covering was tied to his head. There was a regal presence about Him. Startled, I leapt out of bed, my heart thumping wildly in my chest.

That same morning, I sat down to journal my experience. The dream content itself was familiar to me. I often exhaust and overwhelm myself in a misguided attempt to rescue and reduce pain and negative outcomes in the lives of people that I love and care about; in addition, I seek to direct their spiritual destinies. This was never a role that God intended for me.

At the end of my dream, it's obvious that my frantic racing was all about me---about not being appreciated. I lost sight of WHO it has always been about! ---JESUS, The Good Shepherd---not me!

"No one can come to me unless the Father who sent me draws them, and I will raise them up at the last day." **(John 6:44, NIV)**

The Bible tells us to: *"Work out our own salvation with fear and trembling."* **(Philippians 2:12, NIV)**

The above verse is key and instructive: I am answerable to God for my own life and not the lives of others. I believe that the supernatural vision I saw standing by my bed that night was the Good Shepherd, Jesus. Just as other people in the Bible were initially startled or frightened by heavenly messengers, so was I. Yet, when the fear subsided, my spirit understood the meaning of it all. Jesus, Himself, stood watch and guarded over me that night. Jesus' eyes were heavy with concern. His arms were patiently crossed, signifying that He was waiting for me to trust Him. He was communicating these questions: '*Why do you wear yourself out doing what only the Father can do? They are my sheep—not yours. It is not you that saves them but ME. When will you ever trust me?*'

Jesus spoke truth into Satan's lies. Symbolically, Jesus was gently reprimanding me as He reprimanded another:

"Martha, Martha, you are worried, bothered and anxious about so many things; but only one thing is necessary" (**Luke 10:41**)

My over-attentiveness for the people around me, took away from the precious time I could sit quietly at the feet of Jesus. It's been my experience that there is no better place on earth. It is there that I find peace, joy, comfort, and the Lord's indescribable all-consuming love. My frantic attempts to rescue, serve or save the people in my life have often overwhelmed and exhausted me to the point of illness. It is *self-destructive* and *other-destructive* to do for others what they could do for themselves. I pray for God's continued guidance, wisdom, and discernment. My dream/vision is a powerful reminder that, yes, I am to love and care for the people God brings into my life, but in a balanced way. I need to keep my pride in check and allow God to be God, the True and All-Sufficient Source and Supply of all our needs. When I pray for and entrust the people that I love into God's hands, it is best that I leave them there---doing so demonstrates confidence in the Heavenly Father who is able to accomplish far more than I can ever imagine or ask for. God hears my prayers and is faithful to answer.

Marianne Still

Speechless

For 25 years, my husband John played pick-up hockey on outdoor rinks in the country and at schools in Toronto's Yonge/ Eglinton area. Many Canadian guys and girls love the sport in the crisp, cold, fresh air of winter. The ice sometimes sparkles under the moon and stars. Even under the lights of an outdoor arena, there is a magical feeling when someone glides on skate blades over the frozen water. The atmosphere is almost out of this world if large white snowflakes fall from the dark sky. As the skaters stretch their legs and carve the edges of their sharp blades into the ice, they create a unique scraping sound. The stronger the skaters, the louder the rhythmic sound of the rich, deep percussion of the "ice music" created by skates carving hundreds of unchoreographed paths around the rink. When skaters move both skates parallel and instantly grind to a stop, the ice moans under pressure and throws up a wave of "snowy ice spray". Eventually, the snow from the sky and the snow from the skates scraping the ice get deeper. Skaters use shovels on frozen lakes, rivers, and ponds to clear the outdoor rink. A Zamboni circles the rink in cities and towns until the ice is once again as smooth as glass.

The players are not there to bodycheck or attack each other. The point is to score goals with skilled forward and backward skating and passing. Players show up to have fun.

John was in his mid-thirties and skating circles around guys in their teens and twenties at the outdoor rink of Hodgeson School near Davisville and Yonge in Toronto. It was pure sportsmanship. Minimal hockey equipment was worn because games were about something other than hard body checking.

They were only a few minutes into the neighbourhood "everyone's welcome to play" game when a teenager raised the puck with a vicious slap shot. It flew straight at the front of John's head.

John was not the goalie and had no protective equipment. The pain of the hockey puck crushing the bones in his neck was excruciating. John was speechless. He was speechless for days because the hard black puck had destroyed his voice box.

John could not talk. He had to communicate by writing on a clipboard. I called a friend who is an Ear, Nose, and Throat doctor in Ohio, and he referred John to an ENT surgeon at Sunnybrook Hospital in Toronto.

About a week after the accident, the doctor took a long scope and looked deep into John's throat. His face looked grim, and he asked me to look. The doctor explained: "If you imagine the voice box as a violin, the violin is broken to pieces, and therefore, the strings cannot be played and make music."

My heart sank. How could John live without a speaking voice? Would I never hear his rich baritone voice sing a full range of music again?

"Help!" Our hearts cried out to God. "What can be done?"

The surgeon gave us some hope by saying, "We should schedule surgery as soon as possible."

"Please, God, please let an operating room and staff be available." Thankfully, a few days later, the surgeon did a tracheotomy and inserted a titanium plate to hold the broken bones together. Following the surgery, I sat beside John's bed in Sunnybrook Hospital and prayed. "Dear heavenly Father, our Creator and all-powerful Healer, we ask for complete recovery of John's voice". Did I dare to ask for 100 percent recovery? Yes.

As I sat with John in the hours following the surgery, I noticed minute by minute, hour by hour, more blood was oozing out of the site of the sewn-up tracheotomy.

Over and over all day, I begged the nurses to get a doctor." The surgeon is in the Operating Room and cannot be interrupted", they answered. The oozing blood became a trickle-down John's neck and chest. The trickle grew. A towel became blood-soaked. Then we needed a second towel. Long before I had to get a third towel, I said, "John, you are losing too much blood; something is wrong. We need a doctor!"

"I have been begging the nurses to call the doctor for five hours." Desperate, we prayed for another miracle. "Please, God, bring the doctor!"

I went to the nurses' station and announced, "I am going downstairs to the Operating Room and standing by the door until the surgeon comes out." "I am going to tell him myself that my husband is bleeding to death!!!"

The time for gentle requests was over. The nurses could see the problem and a desperate, hysterical wife lobbying very strongly for the survival of her husband.

"Ok, we will call a doctor."

Thankfully, the same ENT surgeon arrived in John's hospital room. Instantly, he knew he was looking at a critical problem.

146

"Bring me a surgical kit and suction here at the bedside immediately!"

The surgeon removed a blood clot the size of a baseball from deep inside John's throat. Then, he sewed up the tracheotomy correctly, so the bleeding stopped. We both breathed a sigh of relief and a prayer of thanks.

A nurse came in and quietly told us, "Many people with that kind of injury die on the spot before they even get to a hospital. Furthermore, you could have died from the blood clot. You are a fortunate man."

We don't believe in luck but believe God heard our prayers. We do believe God can heal.

God restored John's speaking and singing voice to the rich tone and full range he had before the hockey puck smashed his voice box. We dared to ask for 100% recovery, and God granted our request in His power and providence.

"Shout for joy to the LORD, all the earth. Worship the LORD with gladness.

Come before him with joyful songs. Know that the LORD is God.

It is he who made us, and we are his. We are his people, the sheep of his pasture.

Enter his gates with thanksgiving! And his courts with praise.

Give thanks to him and praise his name. For the LORD is good, and his love endures forever,

His faithfulness continues through all generations." **Psalm 100, (NIV)**

Esther Philips

Starting With Jesus

It was the end of the sixties, the time of flower power, free love, sex, drugs, and rock 'n roll. I slid into my teen years on the music of the Beatles, Janis Joplin, Jimi Hendrix, the Byrds, Carole King and the Guess Who. I was still trying to guess who I was, looking for myself in all the wrong places and coming up empty.

I had a church background, and I did believe in God. My moral compass existed, but it was spinning wildly. I would try to help friends who were even more messed up than I was, but I needed help myself. Some Christians told us about having a personal relationship with Jesus, something I had never heard in church. I didn't understand. I listened more closely and asked questions about why Jesus died and whether he really rose from the dead. I had started reading the Bible and praying. Then, one day, I prayed and asked Jesus to forgive me and take charge of my life. Everything changed, and I joyfully joined the ranks of the Jesus people.

So, it was to the strain of 'Come to the Waters' and 'It Only Takes a Spark' that I was swept into the Jesus movement. I traded the music of Janis Joplin and the others for Andrae Crouch, the Maranatha! Singers, Chuck Girard, Evie, and Keith Green. I repeatedly listened to 'Jesus Christ Superstar' and 'Godspell' and memorized all the lyrics.

At that time, three guys – "Jesus' people" – came to Halifax from Detroit to share the Good News of Jesus and the experience of the burgeoning Jesus movement. Their names were Matt, Bernie, and Joe 'Bananas'. 'Banana', he told us, because his nose looked like a banana. They rented a tiny apartment on Henry Street near Dalhousie University and started telling people, "Jesus loves you!" Their door was always open, and they welcomed university students and high school kids like me to come and talk about Jesus and learn more about the Bible. They spent time on the streets passing out gospel tracts and inviting people to their meetings. I was among those who joined in this 'street ministry' with an army surplus knapsack filled with Bibles and tracts and a 'One Way Jesus' badge sewn on its flap.

Despite their long hair and my mother's misgivings, their place became a regular hangout for me and my friends. Matt played the guitar and taught us songs about Jesus. On Wednesday evenings, Joe would lead a Bible study. Up to 30 or more teenagers could be gathered in their tiny place, filling every seat, every bit of floor space in the living/sleeping area, the hallway, and the bitsy kitchen. We'd pray together and read the Bible, and Joe would talk about Jesus and what it means to follow him. We could ask anything, but the Bible was always where we would turn for answers. We mostly understood that Jesus loves us just as we are and calls us to follow him wholeheartedly. This was a different, more radical kind of faith than the Sunday religion some of us knew. The anti-establishment perspective of the hippie movement carried over to the Jesus movement. We questioned whether mainline 'church folk' really knew Jesus, not recognizing the irony of judging those whom we felt were thinking of us.

The music we sang was an intrinsic part of shaping our faith. "For Those Tears, I Died" (Marsha Stevens) was, to me, the voice of Jesus personally speaking to my heart. And so many other songs called us to discipleship, to self-denial and servanthood, that reminded us of who Jesus is and what he did to show his love for us. If he died for me, how could I not give my whole heart and life to him?

The combination of Scripture, music, mission (tell your friends about Jesus), unconditional love and an undeniable stirring of the Spirit of God was transformational. Not just for me but for my group of friends, many of whom came to faith at that time.

I recently watched the "Jesus Revolution" movie and was touched by the role of the pastor, who risked his job to welcome and nurture the 'Jesus' people.' It reminded me of the adults who were willing to stand – not so much among us – as near us, almost like guardians or shepherds keeping watch.

I remember Lou, an older man who came to Joe Bananas regularly, always with a big Bible and a prayerful heart. At one point, a couple arrived among us – self-proclaimed prophets – and many of us were swayed and influenced by their seeming spirituality. Uncertainty arose, and Lou expressed concern, and then, he disappeared for a while. Eventually, it became clear that the couple were not indeed who they claimed to be and were misleading these vulnerable new believers. Joe, Matt, and Bernie asked them to leave. They had not listened to Lou's earlier warnings and felt badly that their discernment had been faulty. In those days, many cults and false prophets were appealing to the heady spirituality that was so far-reaching. Lou returned to the group once they were gone and assured us that he never stopped praying for us. Then, we saw him as the anchor he was.

Another adult mentor was an Anglican clergyman in a downtown church. A couple of my friends volunteered at the 'Boys and Girls Club' there, and sometimes we attended the church services. Rev. Dennis Andrews was a humble British priest who loved Jesus and always welcomed us. His sermons provided some sound foundational teaching for our growing faith. He was also associated with InterVarsity Christian Fellowship, whose high school expression, Inter-School Christian Fellowship (ISCF), some of us were involved in. InterVarsity was a student-led movement, and we planned and ran our meetings with the support and consultation of a teacher advisor. These adult 'guardians' watched over us and stepped in with gentle corrections or advice if we got off track. But for the most part, they sat back, encouraged, and prayed for us, and I am sure they gave thanks in wonder at what the Holy Spirit was doing.

And so it was that, as a teen, I stepped intentionally and joyfully into a life of faith. Despite times of struggle, doubt, pitfalls, and setbacks, I always surrounded myself with a community of people who accepted me and prayed for me. They assured me by their words and actions that Jesus loved me and that we are family in Christ. They were willing to journey with me as we learned to follow Jesus.

That was fifty years ago. Most of those friends are still fellow pilgrims, and we are still family, along with many others I have met along the Jesus way. I am forever grateful for the Jesus movement of the 70s that set me on the path of peace with the One who said, "*I am the way, the truth, and the life*" (John 14:6, NIV). God has been faithful all these years, and I love and trust him more today than I did then. And by the way, Jesus loves you! He always has, and always will.

Rev. Barbara Fuller

Step by Step

"*Your people will be my people...*" Ruth 1:16[1]

This is a true story written by a friend, Christine Kenel-Peters. She was the wife of James Peters (who was a member of the First Nations community, recently deceased), Christine's story first appeared in Hot Apple Cider and Cinnamon[2], published by That's Life! Communications, Markham, Ontario, 2015 and is adapted with Christine Kenel-Peters permission.

It was as if God planted a seed in Christine's heart, for even as a child, she loved the First Nations people. This story is about the 'step-by-step' obedience to God's leading and the love she offered to needy people in an unexpected place in northern Ontario, where the Attawapiskat people live. This rendering of her story is not an exact quote of what she wrote in Hot Apple Cider and Cinnamon.

It is truthfully based on Christine's story, using excerpts to tell it in the space available. You will be amazed by it.

One evening near the end of October 2011, I returned home from work as usual and began preparing dinner. I turned on the television, paying little attention to the news. However, the corner of my eye suddenly caught images of a First Nations reserve. Curiously, I put down what I was doing and approached the TV.

The reserve's name was plastered on the screen: Attawapiskat. I had never heard of it before. They said it was a remote community in northern Ontario.

Teresa Spence, Chief of the Swampy Cree, who lived on the reserve, had just declared a state of emergency. As alarming images flashed in the background, the news spokesman described the crisis in the community. Due to many factors, including recent river flooding, many houses have gradually become uninhabitable. And the situation was worsening. Numerous families lived in trailers, sheds, and even tents with inadequate bathrooms, no running water, or electricity. With winter and bitterly cold temperatures approaching this subarctic region - disaster loomed.

I was distraught as the newscast ended, and I returned to preparing dinner. I shivered as I pictured young children in the drafty shacks I had just seen, with the wind whistling and temperatures dipping to -30 degrees Celsius[3]. The phrase in Mark 12:31, "*Love your neighbour as yourself,* "[4] kept running through my mind. This wasn't some faraway country - It was my home province of Ontario! How could I show my love for my neighbours in this bleak situation?

Suddenly, money wasn't an option - we had very little, and the newscast had yet to mention any aid agency. I remember the Ojibwa children I'd played with as a nine-year-old and the sadness of their living conditions. Memories of the many other First Nation people who had welcomed me warmly over the years came flooding back. They felt like my own family - my people.

I fell asleep that night, knowing I had to find a way to help. Early the following day, at my desk at my church office, I quickly did some research. Where was this reserve again? I looked on the Internet and found Attawapiskat on the map - way up in northern Ontario, near the shores of James Bay. It was hundreds of kilometres from the nearest city, in unfamiliar territory to my family and me. Then I sat back. What's next?

Suddenly, I felt in touch, a nudge to call a good friend—Terri Lamarche, who lived in downtown Toronto. Although I hadn't spoken to her for some time, I remember her from The First Nation church her family had attended many years ago. Terri was an "Elder," a term of great respect used for wise, older First Nations people. I often turned to Terri and other elders for advice during my almost twenty years of marriage to James. Terri was kind, compassionate and helpful, always willing to talk through and help with any issue I put before her.

Terri answered the phone with her customary enthusiastic greeting. It was hard to believe that she was nearly seventy and had severe health issues. She was always full of life, glamorous, and- in her matching leopard print outfits and fashionably dyed hair- just hearing her voice lifted my spirit.

We spoke for a while about our families, and then I dove in. "Terri," I said with some trepidation, "Did you watch the news last night? They were talking about a crisis in a northerner reserve - I'm not sure how you pronounced the name. Do you know anything about this place?" "Of course!" she exclaimed. "It's Attawapiskat. My mother was from Attawapiskat. Don't you know?"

My mouth fell open: Terri - connected with the very same reserve? I knew Terri was Cree and came from northern Ontario, but I needed to familiarize myself with the dozens of reserves in that remote area. What a coincidence!

"As it happens," she continued, "I wasn't born in Attawapiskat. My mother had tuberculosis. She was sent to a sanatorium 600 kilometres south, and that's where I arrived. Then, I was with my grannie in Moosonee until my mom was better. But I still have cousins in Attawapiskat. "Terri laughed. "It's pronounced Atta Wa pis kat! "It means "People of the Parting of the Rocks."

Our discussion quickly turned to what the people of Attawapiskat might need most. "I think it's a great idea to help them. Count me in," Terri said eagerly. She told me that she had already contacted Rev Ross Maracle[5], a well-known figure among Canada's First Nations, to discuss the need for Attawapiskat. With Mohawk friends, Ross planned to ship warm blankets, clothing, and Christmas gifts for the children.

"So," Terri said, "I think we'd better concentrate on collecting food - you know, the nonperishable kind." "Sounds like a good plan. Terri," I agreed, with a twist of appreciation. I had never organized a food drive before. "I can look into getting some food boxes together."

Terri and I ended our conversation with prayer, asking God for help with the many tasks ahead of us.

After putting the phone down, I glanced up. The pastor for seniors had walked into the church office on his way to the pastoral meeting, and he caught the tail end of my conversation. "So what? What is all this about?" He inquired with a kind smile." It sounds pretty severe." I told him about the crisis at the reserve. He was quiet for a minute. Finally, he said, "Leave it with me. Maybe we can do something to help." My heartbeats faster as he disappeared into the meeting room; when he came out sometime later, he had a broad smile.

After the meeting, I heard, "Great news, Christine. The Church is right behind you in this initiative. We can announce it from the pulpit, and you can distribute flyers, whatever you think will work best to collect that food. "How does that sound?"

Within 24 hours of watching a newscast and being nudged into action, I could hardly contain my enthusiasm. Not only had I received affirmation from Terri, with her inside knowledge of Attawapiskat, but my Church had given its full backing for a food drive!

I had taken a small step of faith, and now I felt like a new door had opened wide, with friends rallying around in support. "Thank you, Lord, "I prayed as I contemplated the next step.

Later, they enthusiastically chimed in as I related the events to my husband, James, and our teenage children at home. "What a great idea! "We can help pack the boxes," said Jonah.

"Yeah - we've never done this before, but we do know that God can take care of things, don't we?" commented Naomi.

We're all surprised at how little we knew about this remote community of Attawapiskat.

"Sounds like this needs a lot of prayer," concluded James. He was keenly aware of the needs of The First Nations but equally concerned that his limited vision would make it harder for him to help. "I'll certainly do what I can."

A short time later, Terri and I tackled the next challenge as we studied the map together. "It seemed like a long way, I told Terri. I'm not sure my little car will make it there and back. Should we be hiring a van?" Terry laughed. "Christine, you can't drive there. In winter, the only road to Attawapiskat is an ice road- for big trunks and the like. I'm not even sure it's been built yet."

I was shocked. "What? No regular road. But why not?" I glanced at the map and frowned. "I just don't understand -- this is still Ontario." "That's right," Terri replied in a severe voice. "But that's the reality up there in the North- no roads." She paused for a moment. "Oh, but now I remember! I have a contact at Air Creebec. They might be able to help us."

"You mean Air Quebec?" I asked, mystified that I hadn't heard about that airline before. 'No, no,' Terri laughed as she corrected me. 'Air Creebec! It's owned and operated by The First Nation; I know somebody who works there. They have planes going regularly between Attawapiskat and Timmins. Yes, that might work. If we can't get food to Timmins, Air Creebec might be willing to fly it to Attawapiskat, especially if it is to help in a crisis."

Timmons! I glanced at the map again. Timmons was about 700 kilometres North of Toronto. It seemed more manageable than going all the way to Attawapiskat. I was already planning the route in my mind.

To our delight, Air Creebec immediately approved the shipment of 50 food boxes. We now had a specific target to achieve. However, it was already November, and it soon became apparent that more time was needed to organize a large-scale food collection for

155

Christmas. I felt frustrated and disappointed. How are the people of Attawapiskat going to survive the winter?

Terri and I were relieved to hear that many religious and secular organizations had stepped up to help as the holidays approached. Ross Maracle launched an Attawapiskat Compassion Outreach. Several churches sent us supplies; even the Red Cross coordinated an appeal and intervened.

Nevertheless, we realized that the troubled Attawapiskat community's needs would continue.

Terri and I resolved to resume our efforts in the New Year while James continued to pray. "How I wish I could fly to Attawapiskat with these food boxes once we've collected them." Terri reflected during our following phone call conversation. "I feel it is important to tell these people that this food comes with our love and the love of Jesus."

Terri sighed. "Since the airfare is out of our reach, at the very least, I'd want to drive with you to Timmins Airport to thank the staff at Air Creebec in person and explain to them why we are doing this."

"Now that I think of it," Terri continued, "her voice suddenly sounded concerned, "what about the other end of this trip? We shouldn't leave the food boxes at the airport in Attawapiskat. Imagine the chaos!"

"You're right." I shuddered at the thought. "This was something we hadn't considered." We could contact specific people at Attawapiskat to let them know the food was coming. To my delight, I searched the Internet for churches in Attawapiskat and found two. No one answered when I called the Catholic Church, but Stephen Stoney replied at the Pentecostal Church. I introduced myself. "We're collecting food for your community, I explained, and we are looking for someone to take care of the boxes once they arrive to ensure the food reaches people who need it." "Praise God," he exclaimed. "We've been praying for God to supply the needs of our community, and food is definitely one of those needs. My wife Kathy and I would love to help."

Stephen explained that he and his wife were from The First Nation Reserve of Fort Severn, the most northern community in Ontario. They had come to teach at the elementary school on the Attawapiskat reserve and pastor the Attawapiskat Pentecostal church.

The plan was unfolding step by step. We felt that God had once again provided just the right connections.

Imagine my surprise when I arrived at Church the next day to find the desk in my office surrounded by food bags, boxes, and parcels of every description. It is filled to the brim with food items, diapers, and other items on the list. Our initial goal was to fill 50 office-type filing boxes. However, we quickly surpassed that target, and things continued to arrive. Our team of volunteers zealously pitched in. In a short time, we had over 100 boxes packed full of nonperishable groceries of every description.

My car was going to be too small to carry them all. We marvelled at God's provision as a church couple offered to lend us their midsize van for the drive to Timmins. Then, the custodian remembered the Church owned a small trailer, usually used by the youth group. We gladly accepted both offers.

Terri nervously called Air Creebec several times to ask if they would allow 'just a few more boxes.' Finally, they said, "125 and no more!' I counted all the boxes piled up in the back of the church office. There were exactly 125.

We were ready on Thursday, March 29, 2012, about ten days before Easter, with 125 boxes of supplies packed tightly inside the van and trailer. With much trepidation, I would tackle the nine-hour, 700-kilometre drive from Toronto to the airport in Timmins. (When the time came, Terri was not well enough to go). I said to James, "You'd better come with me. There's no way I'm making this journey alone." To my astonishment, James just smiled and pointed to his overnight bag, which was already packed and ready to go: "Let's go."

We set off in awe of God's provision at every single step of the way. The rest of the drive to North Bay went well. As we stopped for a short break in Huntsville, happy memories flooded back. James and I had spent our honeymoon there.

James and I arrived in Timmins, and as we approached the hangar for Air Creebec, I noticed that James was very still. He was listening intently. His eyes could barely see the barren landscape around him. But he could hear the planes roaring overhead. My heartbeat was faster, dispelling all feelings of tiredness after two long days of driving. Giddy with emotion, my mind retraced every step of our journey. The end is almost here.

Two young men from the airline helped us unload our van and trailer. We watched in appreciation as they placed all 125 boxes on three palettes and skillfully shrink-wrapped the entire shipment.

"How much weight do you have here?" one of the young men asked as if it were a regular business shipment. Of course, we had no idea. The men laughed as they weighed the shrink-wrapped load. How much would it usually cost to ship this weight to Attawapiskat? We looked at him in wide-eyed ignorance. Both men chuckled. "Thousands of dollars! Our mouths fell open.

As we completed the paperwork and procedures, we were struck again by the generous attitude of the airport officials. "Thanks for your help," we called out. Humbly, James and I left the airport amazed at how God had made this journey possible.

A short time later, back home in Toronto, we heard that the boxes had arrived in time for Easter.

Since then, our Church has hosted six similar donation drives with generous contributions from our congregation and, on occasion, other churches in the community. Every single time, this shipment has reached its destination before the targeted date. Moreover, after that first journey, a church member offered his truck company's services for each 700-kilometre trek from Toronto to Timmins at no cost.

All this hinged on a small step of faith back in October 2011. When I heard the news story, I acted on God's request to "love my neighbour as myself." This step of faith knit my immediate family together more closely, unleashed incredible generosity from many church families, and opened new doors of friendship and understanding.

Being part of this project has been a fantastic experience and a resounding confirmation of the lifelong love and respect God placed in my heart for The First Nation people. These people have indeed become my own.

As I pursue this journey of love, I pray that my heart will continue to listen and that I will continue to have the courage to obey God as he nudges me toward the next adventure.

Christine Kenel-Peters/Suzanne Wilkinson

1. Ruth 1:16, New Living Translation (NLT)
2. Lindquist, N.J, Hot Apple Cider with Cinnamon - Paperback: Stories of Friendship and Love, published by HACC (Hot Apple Cider with Cinnamon), THAT'S LIFE COMMUNICATIONS; 1st edition (Nov 2015)
3. -30 degrees Celsius is about 22 degrees below Fahrenheit.
4. Mark 12:31 (NIV)
5. Reverent Ross Miracle hosted the Spirit Alive television broadcast for 20 years (1988 to 2008) and founded several other First Nation initiatives. He died in a tragic car accident in 2012 at age 66, having done much to help Attawapiskat. Miracle was half Mohawk and half Scottish and lived for a long time in Deseronto, next to the Tyendinaga, Mohawk Territory, on the door shores of Lake Ontario between Belleville and Kingston, ON.
6. Note: The term Indian is not used to refer to the indigenous people of Canada. It is now considered outdated and potentially offensive. Since the 1970s and 80s, it has been generally replaced in Canada and Canadian usage by First Nation (person). If used at all in this context, the term "Indian" should refer to someone with "Indian status," which is a specific, rightly defined legal term.

Supernatural Encounters Amid the Ordinary

"On the eighth day, when it was time to circumcise the child, he was named Jesus, the name the angel had given him before He was conceived." (Luke 2: 21, NIV).

Even after the extraordinary events Mary and Joseph experienced, from the immaculate conception to their baby's birth, they were still just Mary and Joseph from Nazareth on the journey of first-time parenthood.

After their baby was born, the shepherds told of their wild experience of angels proclaiming the Saviour was born. Life continued. Even though their baby was the son of God, they had to learn how to be first-time parents within their culture at that time. This required them to bring their newborn son to be circumcised and named on the 8th day. This was the custom of that day. It's what Jewish parents did. And yet, amid this ordinary act, we are reminded that this baby was no ordinary child.

There are many customs for naming Jewish babies, but Mary and Joseph did not follow these because an angel had given them a name before he was conceived. This is just one of many seemingly ordinary experiences for Mary and Joseph that collide with the supernatural. I suppose this should have been expected when you're raising the son of God.

We see Mary and Joseph living an everyday Jewish life as they prepare for the purification rites. Jesus was almost six weeks old when they headed to Jerusalem to present Him to the Lord and offer the required sacrifice. In our day, in some churches, parents still observe this as they dedicate their child to the Lord before the congregation.

As they made their way to Jerusalem, the Holy Spirit prepared another for a supernatural encounter. We don't know when, but we do know a man called Simeon had been told that he would not die before seeing the Lord's Messiah. On this very day, I suspect as Mary and Joseph made their way to Jerusalem, the Holy Spirit moved Simeon to go to the temple court, and when they arrived, Simeon somehow knew to take Jesus into his arms and praised God for he had now seen the son of God. Reading this Scripture, we see how God had orchestrated this encounter and had been planning this moment since before Jesus was born.

Not only had Simeon been told by the Holy Spirit that he would not die before seeing the Lord's Messiah, but he was also moved by the Holy Spirit to go to the temple on this particular day. This is a beautiful depiction of how God is always at work orchestrating divine encounters, which can take many years to come to fruition.

Here, the story continues with Mary and Joseph at the temple, not because the Holy Spirit called them there but because they were following the law. They were doing what they knew was required of them, and God met them there, in their obedience, in an extraordinary way.

The Scriptures begin with Simeon's blessing, and then prophet Anna came when Simeon finished speaking to confirm that Jesus was someone extraordinary indeed. I love what verse 33 says Mary and Joseph did: they "Marveled at what was said about Jesus." They'd met with angels, experienced an immaculate conception firsthand, and had multiple confirmations about their incredible child. Yet, they can still marvel at what God is doing in their midst.

This passage ends with Mary, Joseph, and Jesus obediently completing their purification rights and returning to their hometown in Nazareth. These parents, raising the son of God, live their lives in this beautiful tension between the ordinary and extraordinary.

Supernatural encounters, divine interventions and miracles punctuate their everyday lives. The most incredible part is that we live with this same tension. God is still at work in our ordinary lives if we will notice.

Rachel Bernard/Suzanne Wilkinson

Take Heart

I have never had the flashing of lights, the conversation moment, or the 'big band' of conversion so many people speak about.

I was born into a family where Mom and Dad were "born again." They had each committed to Jesus' years before I was born. I do not know that testimony. Mom played Christian music in a violin quartet to service members during the War.

Their quartet was sent to London, Ontario, to play before service personnel. Dad was preparing for the War and was stationed there. When Dad saw Mom play, he decided she was the one for him to marry. It was love at first sight for Dad. They had a love story that was so beautiful and blessed. I always knew that their meeting was their answer to prayer.

I was raised by two wonderful Christian parents and by the Church. My parents lived their faith. I lived with them. Jesus was my friend. "What a friend we have in Jesus," and God was my Heavenly Father. I had no trouble believing this reality because my parents walked, talked, prayed, and lived it. We went to Church every Sunday, morning, and evening, and I was eventually in the Orchestra. That meant I was at Church from 9 am - 9 pm every Sunday at my second home. My close friends came from Christian homes. We could talk naturally about our faith but did not need to. We were challenged or not challenged by our Sunday School class, but we had friendships at Church, so we looked forward to Church as we felt we were a family. I did not think I needed to go ahead at an altar call because I believed I belonged to Jesus already.

I firmly believe that a "little child's" faith is essential when talking to God, even when we are grown up. As a little child, He was my Dad in heaven. What humble trust and lovely prayers his little girl offered to him. In my late teens, a Christian at another church told me that being saved means one declares oneself to Jesus by word and public baptism. I then chose to be baptised. Following this, my whole Sunday School Class went through the waters of baptism, each professing their faith.

We all invited our friends to witness our public declaration of faith. Afterwards, I felt a heavy responsibility and a big challenge that day to be a worthy representative for Him. I felt very strange about baptism. I was thrilled to be baptised. I followed Jesus' example but believed I was a Christian before entering the baptism water.

Jesus was the Lord and Saviour before He met John the Baptist in the river Jordan. He was the original Christian, so He loved God, and God loved him before baptism.

Here is my question. Does a father ask a child to say, "Dad, today I accept you as my father?" No. Dad accepted the child when the remarkable discovery of pregnancy occurred. I did not say, "Dad, I accepted you as my father when I was born." Why would God let me go if I did not do or say the exact words that some Christian groups suggested that I pray?

More complications arose in my mind. Would anyone ever need to tell their brother or sister that they believed in them years after they were their brother and sister?

If Jesus calls us brothers and sisters, we are accepted. I began disagreeing with some preachers and evangelists, and still do. To make matters worse, Christians told me I was not a Christian if I had never had a conversion moment.

I struggle with that. Sometimes, I wonder why some have such considerable changes in their lives. They can tell me a day, an hour, a minute. I feel conflicted when I hear these stories; many leave their faith because of words like this.

I felt very blessed when reminded that Timothy did not receive the faith through some form of dramatic conversion like that of Paul but through his family, grandmother, and mother. Timothy had received his faith through his family like I did. I believe God has many ways to reach His sons and daughters, not just a moment in time or a special place. The apostle Paul wrote to Timothy to give him confidence, encourage this young man and set him on to do good deeds for the Kingdom. Paul's experience was uniquely dramatic; not everyone experiences that. Some have a gradual turning on their journey to mature in their path that leads them to true faith.

The apostle Paul is saying to all of us, keep yourself from beginning to lose confidence in Christ. ***"So, do not be ashamed of the testimony about our Lord or of me his prisoner. Rather, join with me in suffering for the gospel, by the power of God."*** **(2 Tim. 1:8, NIV).** From Paul, it seems he was saying, "We all need to take heart." I believe our heart attitude is essential to God, even more than the date of our conversion.

In our Christian walk, we meet many who have colossal born-again moments. I am so thankful that my coming to Christ must have happened in heaven when I was born into my family. For that, I am genuinely grateful and praise my Heavenly Dad.

"Faith is born and reborn: not from a duty, not from something that is to be done or paid, but from a gaze of love to be welcomed. In this way, Christian life becomes beautiful, if it is not based on our abilities and our plans, but rather based on God's gaze. Is your faith, is my faith tired? Do you want to reinvigorate it? Look for God's gaze: sit in adoration, allow yourself to be forgiven in confession, stand before the Crucified One. In short, let yourself be loved by Him. This is the starting point of faith: letting oneself be loved by Him, by Him who is Father." Pope Francis

"Fight the good fight of the faith [in the conflict with evil]; take hold of the eternal life to which you were called, and [for which] you made the good confession [of faith] in the presence of many witnesses." *(1 Timothy 6:12, Amplified Bible)*

Anonymous

"For if we believe that Jesus died and rose again, even so God will bring with Him those who sleep in Jesus."
(1 Thessalonians 4:13-14 NKJV).

Testimonies of a Young Christian Mother in Kuala Lumpur, Malaysia

Matthew

At ten months old, Matthew was still experiencing night terrors. I had been told that my sister-in-law's oldest son, Robert, also suffered from the same condition. I quietly wondered if the spiritual atmosphere of my mother-in-law's home and her regular visits to a medium contributed to these night terrors. I invited my prophetic friend, Jeannette, to my home to discern if there were any spirits causing these night terrors. Although Jeannette found no untoward spirits residing in our house, she prayed powerfully over my son, and for the first time since birth, Matthew slept peacefully throughout the night.

In fact, Matthew slept peacefully for a whole month—I know because I journaled this. At the end of the month, I was so in awe of God's goodness that I could not help but turn to my husband and say, "Isn't it wonderful that God healed Matthew from these night terrors?" My husband then hushed me in case I jinxed our night-terror-free month. So, when Matthew had a night terror *that same night*, I was furious.

After comforting my son until he fell back asleep, I stormed into my husband's empty study, shook my fist at Satan and bellowed, "How dare you touch my son after God has healed him. Get your hands off him and leave him alone." My little son never suffered from night terrors again. I shared this story with Matthew when he was older, and he confirmed that he had not had a nightmare since. When God heals, God heals.

Bethany

One day, around three years old, Bethany had an "off day" where she seemed to have discomfort in her stomach. I fed her simple foods in the hope her stomach would settle down but even then, she did not have any appetite. By nightfall, she was still uncomfortable and so I turned to God and prayed for His wisdom as to what was happening with my daughter. Taking note of her symptoms, I turned to my trusty medical book and found a condition

165

called, *intussusception* that seemed to mirror what Bethany was experiencing: sudden bouts of unexplainable pain, diarrhoea, and lack of energy. The following day, I took her to the pediatrician and after explaining why we were seeing him, suggested she had intussusception. The doctor was shocked I had accurately diagnosed Bethany's disorder where one part of her intestine was sliding inside an adjacent part. This telescoping action blocked food and fluid from passing through so no wonder she felt such discomfort yet was unable to articulate this. This condition meant blood supply to this part of the intestine was affected which if left untreated, could lead to infection, death of bowel tissue or perforation in the bowel (Mayo Clinic) and so Bethany was rushed off to the ultrasound where intussusception was indeed confirmed. By God's grace, the doctors were able to straighten out her intestine that very day. I remain grateful to God to this day for imbuing wisdom in a young mother so that the cause of my daughter's pain could be identified and swiftly treated.

Dominic

When Dominic was a year and a half old, we discovered he had a hernia that needed surgical intervention before it became strangulated and burst. A date for the operation could not be set until Dominic recovered from a persistent runny nose. After a week, mucus was still running from his nose. I prayed for wisdom to find the cause as I opened my medical book. To my amazement, I turned to the page on food allergies. Since I was not sure which food Dominic could be allergic to, I fed him one pure ingredient at a time. Within a day, his nose stopped running. The following day, I rang the doctor to schedule an operation for Friday. When I found out my husband was in back-to-back meetings that day, I rescheduled the surgery to Monday.

However, on Sunday evening, Dominic experienced incredible pain, causing him to vomit until he was retching from an empty stomach. My husband and I rushed him to the emergency room where the doctor on call confirmed he had a strangulated hernia. Dominic needed to be operated on immediately, but all the operating theatres were in use and the next available one was a six-hour wait.

We were told no painkiller was strong enough to dull the pain and hence no medication would be administered.

Since we had to stay overnight at the hospital, we were given a hospital room to wait in until an operating theatre became available. My husband returned home to pack an overnight bag. Given our countless visits to the hospital, he knew to pack my Bible. As soon as I could, I rang one of my praying mother's friends, who in turn activated our prayer chain. No longer alone, I mentally prepared myself for a long night. I prayed in tongues for six straight hours. God was so gracious to me, for Dominic miraculously fell asleep in my arms and continued to sleep until the nurse came in to prepare him for the operation. Again, by the grace of God, the strangulated hernia did not burst, and the operation was successful. In fact, such was its success that the first praying mother to visit at the break of day was rendered speechless as Dominic was crawling around the room despite the recent surgery and stitches he had received mere hours ago. Stunned, she relayed how one of her sons had an appendix removed and it was days before he could even move, let alone crawl.

Testimony One

One of my favorite Tuesday Ladies' testimonies came from a visiting missionary. Her friend's husband had arrived at a remote village in one part of China. Naturally, the villagers were untrusting of this Caucasian man wanting to teach them about Jesus. Unknown to his wife, the village elders had decided to poison her husband, and, unknown to the husband, God had awakened his wife back home to pray for him at the exact moment he was being poisoned. The husband woke up the next day alive and well. The villagers, in shock, realized the power of God and converted to Christianity. Such testimonies convinced me of God's spiritual protection over His own.

Testimony Two

Another woman, whom we'll call Hope, was married to a man who was vocally and viciously against Christianity, forbidding her to share her faith with their four sons and frequently humiliating her before them. Despite this, Hope was unthwarted and brought up her sons in the ways of Jesus. One day when buying groceries at the open-air market, her then 5-year-old son disappeared into the crowd. Not knowing whether to turn right or left, she cried out to Jesus for wisdom and following the Holy Spirit's lead, turned left and ran until she came across the man who was carrying her son in his arms. She confronted him with all the furore of a protective mother and rescued her son from his clutches. Such stories of children being abducted were commonplace in Malaysia and not many of them end well.

Testimony Three

Through the Tuesday Ladies' weekly offering at Calvary Church, we supported a missionary couple from our church to Africa. The people of the local village were so hungry that preaching Jesus to them on an empty stomach held no relevance in their lives. The missionary pastor shared how he cried out to Abba to meet the people's physical needs first if he was to meet their spiritual needs. To his and our amazement, Jesus gave him the gift of healing, so all manner of ailments were miraculously healed – even that of severed limbs.

Dr. Maria Kon

Thank You, God

I was born in Glasgow, Scotland, in 1933, to wonderful parents. My mother was raised in the Catholic church; she dropped out of that denomination and sent her three children to the Church of Scotland Sunday School.

My father was a genius and was raised in the Church of Scotland, and he dropped out; both were believers. The following are records of my encounters with GOD's saving grace. Around nine years of age, the war was raging, and the bombing badly damaged the building we lived in, so my father moved us to Barrhead, a small town where my mother was raised. That move was a happy one, as we lived among my mother's relatives. Around nine years of age, I was playing a stupid game, leaping from roof to roof of some outbuildings, when I slipped and fell about nine feet onto my head. I woke up in hospital, my head swathed in bandages except for my eyes, nose, and mouth. I had a concussion for three–four days but no broken bones or cuts.

Another time, I was cycling around a left-hand curve with a six-foot wall on my left. A truck comes around the curve towards me. The driver sees some children in his lane, so he swerves to avoid them and hits me. I go flying and land six feet in front of the stopped truck. I was severely shaken but saw no blood or bones broken. My prized first two-wheeled bicycle was a twisted wreck.

Around eleven years old, my cousin Frankie, older than me, wants to show me an owl's nest. We were both interested in nature study. The nest was located on a 45 ft. high granite cliff created by a now-closed quarry. The base of this cliff was covered in rocks left when the quarry closed. Frankie led the way, and I followed every hand and foothold about 35 feet up the side of the cliff. I reached out and gripped a handhold with my left hand, and as I put my weight on this handhold, it came away. I started falling, believing I was going to die. I told GOD, "GOD, it has been short, but I've enjoyed it" (meaning my life). I landed face down, spread-eagled. I had no pain. I thought I must be dead. Is this what death feels like? I opened my eyes, rocks all around me, and tried moving, but still no pain; slowly, I got up to my feet, realized I had no broken bones, and saw no blood. Frankie, high up on the cliff, almost fell off when he saw me getting up. When we realized all was well, guess what he said, "Come back up". I immediately thought, "Do not put your Lord to the test."

In 1965, I emigrated to Toronto, Canada. In 1970, I married a wonderful lady from Nova Scotia and inherited an equally wonderful family of in-laws, particularly my mother-in-law. In 1971, we were living in an eleventh-floor apartment above the Don Valley. One night, as I lay in bed with my wife, I became aware of two presences outside the building inviting me to accompany them. I agreed. Suddenly, as we were flying through black space, I became

169

aware that my wife realized something was odd and knelt beside me, shaking me. I tried to tell her I was okay but couldn't as I had suddenly arrived in heaven. Words cannot describe the peace and glowing soft light in heaven. A man was in a small cloud-like office manipulating parts on a cloud-like desk. My escorts informed me there was nothing to worry about and that this was what it was like there. Suddenly, I sat up in bed, asking - where am I? I went over the details of what I had experienced, and my wife told me what she had experienced, saying that I tried to talk, but she couldn't make out what I was saying. I don't feel this was a bad dream or a vision but a real experience I can't explain.

In 1975, we now own a bungalow and have a son who is a joy to both of us. I am the general manager of a well-established printing company. The owners, a father and son, and the employees were very pleased with how I ran the business. However, I have a problem. I realize I am fighting an addiction to alcohol. I was what is known as a functioning alcoholic. One night, as I was walking past the bar in the basement of our home, having consumed two beers, I stopped: I heard a voice saying, "You've done it again, Jim." I fell to the floor, curled up with my face down to the floor, every fiber of my being crying out to GOD for help. As I lay there, I slowly felt a great peace come over me, and slowly, I realized my addiction had been taken from me. I stood up, and I felt like a new man. Glory Be To GOD.

Jim Paterson

The Least of These

"In as much ye have done it unto one of the least of these my brethren, you have done it unto me." (Matthew 25:40, KJV)

As the ferry pulled away from the Isle of Mull for the ten-minute trip to Iona, I felt relieved that the long journey to my destination was nearly over. I had flown into Glasgow around noon the day before and, after a three-hour wait, had boarded a train which got me into the town of Oban around six p.m. After an overnight stay at a B & B, I boarded a ferry for a forty-five-minute trip to the Isle of Mull, where a bus was waiting for a unique journey on a single-lane road to the other side of the island. It was a short distance, but we encountered frequent delays while the bus driver cleared the road from sheep or longhorn cattle, which blocked our way. We also had to pull over at times onto specially designated areas on the side of the road to allow oncoming traffic to pass by. Fortunately, I had been prepared for this lengthy trip by a friend who had visited Iona a few years earlier. She had told me it would take a lot of patience to get to the island for my spiritual retreat. Getting to my destination was the first step in preparation for a retreat on an island that felt far removed from home.

As the ferry approached our destination, I was overcome by a sense that I had been here before. At a time when I was exceptionally weary from the busy pace of life, I dreamed of being in a rowboat with a young man on a peaceful lake. In the distance, we could see the city with crowds on the street engaged in frenetic activities while fireworks exploded into the air. In the dream, I turned to the man in the boat and said, "I can't do this any longer." I felt overwhelmed by the burden of a life with its constant focus on performance. The man replied, "You don't have to," and then silently rowed to a dock on a peaceful island, where I stepped out of the boat. When I woke up from the dream, I realized the man in the boat was Jesus. As the ferry approached Iona, I was moved to tears by the recognition that this was the dock's site in the dream.

The Catholic House of Prayer, where I stayed for a week, was just a five-minute walk from the dock. As I pulled my heavy suitcase on wheels, the narrow cinder path leading to the house on top of a hill was a challenge. I strolled, taking in the beauty of the scenery surrounding me, leaving behind a crowd of tourists from the ferry heading in the opposite direction on the paved road to the Abbey.

When I signed up for a week's stay at the Catholic House of Prayer, I expected an experience similar to retreats at Loyola House in Guelph, where guests were encouraged to share on a deep spiritual level with others under the guidance of a spiritual director.

171

Sister Jean, who ran the guest house in Iona, was a warm and caring house mother who made us feel at home, but spiritual direction was not her role. When I arrived at the guest house, there were three other female guests: an American Episcopalian priest, a Church of England priest from London and a young woman from a small town in Scotland. The two priests did not socialize with the other guests except for the meals together. Their conversation focused mainly on their careers as religious leaders in the church. The young Scottish woman and I spent time together, sharing our personal journey. She had been through a painful divorce when her young son was three, a child conceived after ten years of infertility. Her husband left her for a younger woman who worked at the bank, where he was the manager. This woman's serenity struck me despite some harrowing times in her life, and I appreciated her vulnerability by sharing her personal story with me. I was sad to see her leave two days after my arrival.

A woman in her early sixties came for one night. She had been recently divorced, and her bitterness towards her former husband and her lot in life poisoned the air at the dinner table that evening. It was highly uncomfortable to be around her, and we were relieved to see her leave on the ferry the next day. The two female priests were replaced by a retired Catholic priest and his sister, who was a nun. The atmosphere changed as the male priest became the centre of attention. Once again, I was struck by how the religious leaders were largely defined by their professional roles.

The following morning, I got a chance to get acquainted with another new guest while waiting in the lounge for breakfast. She was born and raised in a tough neighbourhood on the south coast of England. She had been married, but her husband left her to raise their three young children alone while he moved overseas with another woman. The single mother made a bold decision to move to a Catholic community in Scotland for the sake of her children, fearing they stood a good chance of falling in with the wrong crowd if they remained in the city in which she had grown up. It had been a wise decision as she watched her children thrive in a caring communal setting, especially her son, who enjoyed the outdoor life with men in the community who provided a positive male role model. The people in the community had offered to look after her children while she was on retreat in Iona.

When she asked what people did on the island during the day, I shared how I spent the days in a quiet spot by the water to journal and sketch. Her face lit up when I mentioned journaling, and she explained how her "sister," her spiritual mentor, had encouraged her to journal while she was in Iona. When she admitted that she had no idea how to journal, her sister replied there would be someone to teach her. I was humbled when, with a childlike faith, she stated that "sister was right." She believed I was God's messenger.

After breakfast, we headed off in different directions for the day, and when we met again in the lounge before dinner, she was anxiously waiting for me to share what she had written in her journal. I was struck by the depth of her spiritual insight and felt ashamed of how I had initially judged her by her humble appearance. She became a true soul mate for the next few days as we shared personal stories of challenges in difficult circumstances. We kept in touch for a few months afterwards, and she was a compassionate support for me when my own marriage crumbled.

My final dinner in Iona was memorable as we welcomed yet another new guest who shared her personal story at the dinner table. Her husband had walked out on their marriage three months after the arrival of their son, who was born with cerebral palsy. He could not handle being the father of a "deformed" child. The woman shared with great pride how her son had just graduated with a degree in psychology from the University and was now enrolled in a master's Degree program with the encouragement and support of the University. This young woman was full of gratitude for all the blessings in her life and had learned sign language to "give back" to other disabled people. She described how sign language deepened her worship experience as she sang and prayed with her hands and voice. Upon request, she demonstrated by praying the Lord's Prayer out loud while using sign language, and all who were present felt the holiness of the moment.

That evening, as I packed for my departure the following day, I was struck by how God had brought four clergy and four divorced women into my life that week and knew this was no coincidence. I was keenly aware there was something He wanted me to learn.

On the long journey home, I had time to reflect on the past week, including a review of my journal. I noted a dream before my trip to Iona in which a church roof was damaged and under repair. A roof is a symbol of safety or security, and one of life's most basic needs is a "roof over our head". We generally only know the roof leaks when faced with a storm. When trials and tribulations come into our lives, can we find shelter from these storms in the church? The Iona Abby's damaged roof was both a physical and spiritual reality. It was not a place of refuge for me during a stormy time, as the worship services failed to provide the spiritual comfort my heart yearned for. God used three humble Catholic women to minister to me. It is a sad reality that for years, the Catholic Church ostracized people who were divorced, denying them an opportunity for community and communion in a time of deep need.

Over 2000 years ago, God chose a humble young unmarried woman to give birth to the Christ child. The experience would have deemed her among the "least of these" by her religious community, which did not understand the divine role she had been given. Her son was born in a stable, and angels announced His arrival to lowly shepherds. God guided Mary and Joseph to safety through dreams, and He continues to do so today if we acknowledge and follow His direction. When Jesus started His ministry, He did not use the existing religious institution and its educated leaders to further His Kingdom. Jesus chose humble fishermen as His disciples. He uses many of those society deems "least of these" to bring about His Kingdom today. I am blessed to experience this firsthand through friendships with wounded men and women who have opened my eyes to see the "spark of God" that is present in every human being, no matter how broken. Life takes on meaning when we are given an opportunity to help bring this spark to the light of day through the gift of friendship, which can lead to healing when we allow ourselves to be vulnerable and share our deep personal stories.

"…I have called you friends…" **(John 15:15, NIV)**

Anonymous ~ Magda

The Lord is Faithful

I was raised in a Christian home, the youngest of four children. We lived on a farm with all kinds of farm animals and yard work to do. It was a busy life. Every Sunday, though it was about twelve miles away, our family made the car trip to church. Initially, we went in the afternoon, allowing us to complete chores at home. However, this was later changed to morning and evening worship services. Sunday was a special day in our family, and most was spent in church. I welcomed the change in the routine.

At a Good Friday service, I went to the altar to accept the Lord for myself. To the measure of my understanding at age eleven, I believed that Christ had died to save me from my sins and reconcile me to His heavenly Father through my faith in Him. On travelling home at night, I thought everything looked brilliant and delightful. The stars were shining. I could hardly wait to get home to read more about Jesus. However, that euphoria didn't last. The old routine set in again, and life changed back to normal. We had family devotions every morning but never discussed what we had read together before we kids rushed out to catch the school bus. And we never talked about my salvation, which was a missed opportunity. Oh yes, I kept attending church with my family as long as I lived at home. I attended youth meetings every Friday with my siblings. Sadly, I was never encouraged to speak about Christianity or what I learned from reading the Bible. I now feel that was a shame.

After graduating from high school after grade 13 and at age 17, I began my nursing school three-year training program at Wellesley Hospital in Toronto. As student nurses, we worked hard and graduated with my registered nurse diploma in my hand at age twenty. However, I had slipped in my walk with Christ and wasn't fully living for the Lord. I tried to be a caring person. But I did not have much of a living relationship with Him in those years. Despite my lack of faithfulness, Jesus has always been faithful to me. One constant has always been that I knew my mother prayed for me. And I'm sure she did it constantly for all her children. When I was twenty-five, I married a young man who graduated from Emmanuel

Bible College in Kitchener and was becoming a pastor in a missionary denomination. I tried to live the Christian life for the thirteen years we pastored together in Presley, Port Elgin, Manitoulin Island and finally, here in Gormly, Ontario, near where I presently live. My efforts were insufficient, as joy in my faith was often missing.

Those were very challenging years, with many moves and our family's expansion. I knew my marriage was far from what it should be. These were often sad and unsettling years for me. In 1992, my husband walked out on me. Neither of us was happy in the marriage, so we divorced shortly after.

Following the divorce, I relied on my faith as never before. It was then I came alive in my spiritual walk. Those years were busy years with home, work, and the girls. Yet, Jesus has always been faithful to me, even when I gave him little of my time or attention. I have lots to learn, yet He has been patient with me as He has changed my life. We have developed a loving, worshipful relationship, which has given my life true meaning. I am older now, and this relationship has grown and become more meaningful each year.

As Hebrews 13:8 says, *"The Lord is the same yesterday, today and forever"* (NIV). My life has proven this to be true. Jesus is alive to me. I have learned to rely on Him more in every situation I face in life. He has guided, sustained, and often forgiven me. I have struggled with questioning whether I, as a divorced person, could genuinely have an impact for good and the extension of His kingdom. Could I change enough to live a Christian life? Could the Lord change me? I asked Him many times to help me, and He has.

Life has been an exciting journey. I have yet to arrive, but I have learned that the answer is yes. God is in the business of lovingly changing us. I can see the way he has done that now in retrospect. Jesus has been faithful as He has transformed me into who I am. Early after the divorce in 1993, I found these verses in Isaiah 42 verses 6, 9 and 16. These verses and others illuminated the light for my life and gave me purpose and fulfillment in my Christian walk.

During our marriage, we were blessed with two lovely daughters. And over the years, they could see a change in their mother. I now had a new trust in the Lord as I walked with him daily. What a blessing for all the ways He has blessed me. Life, at times, has been difficult. I have worked hard. But God has provided for me daily. What a blessing.

In my relationship with Him, by reading His Word and learning along with others in my church, life has become filled with meaning and purpose. What a joy! He also provides and protects me and keeps me safe every day. I am now living independently in a senior's apartment community. The Lord's faithfulness is steadfast. My life has proven Him to be so. And as long as I live, I want to live for Him and serve Him as best I can for the rest of my days.

"I, the LORD, have called you in righteousness.
I will take hold of your hand.
I will keep you and will make you
to be a covenant for the people
and a light for the Gentiles,
to open eyes that are blind,
to free captives from prison
and to release from the dungeon
those who sit in darkness.
"I am the LORD; that is my name!
I will not yield my glory to another,
or my praise to idols.
See, the former things have taken place,
and new things I declare,
before they spring into being
I announce them to you."
I will lead the blind in ways they have not known,
along unfamiliar paths I will guide them.
I will turn the darkness into light before them,
and make the rough places smooth.
These are the things I will do.
I will not forsake them." **Isaiah 42:6-9,16 (NIV)**

Muriel Rosenberger/Suzanne Wilkinson

The Miracle on 141

There is a billboard sign in a grassy field with a powerful message! It sits by a winding, twisting two-lane highway with several blind spots.

Like every other day on the morning of June 30, 2021, as parents, we prayed for the Lord's protection over our family as we read Psalm 91. We said goodbye to our son, who was heading to our cottage along the familiar 141.

He glanced at "the sign" with the powerful words, only 1.5 km from the newly constructed bridge over the Shadow River. Little did he know how meaningful the message on that day's sign would be "PREPARE TO MEET THY GOD".

He passes "the sign" and suddenly hears metal on metal and feels the vehicle taking flight, saying aloud, "Oh boy", now realising he had no control of the car…….one minute, he sees the sky above; the next minute, the pavement below as the car rolls over, more than once, then coming straight back up before hitting the guard rail, flipping over the embankment, rolling over and finally resting on it's crushed roof.

The wheels were still spinning when one of the Ministry of Environment workers at the site did a baseball slide into the passenger seat of our son's car, then quickly moved around to see that the driver couldn't move his arm and his hand was bleeding.

The airbags had deployed, and there was broken glass everywhere, including his glasses, making it difficult for him to see anything. He was not aware that a large, dirty surfboard-sized piece of a trailer with a metal end had impaled his left shoulder and upper arm, where he had previously had two surgeries for hockey injuries.

His seat belt is now suspending him, hanging upside down, supporting himself with his right arm and shoulder to not lean on the 6 ft protruding board from his body. He would be in that position for 1½ hours before he would be extricated from the vehicle using the jaws of life. Thankfully, he never lost consciousness as his foot was stuck under the gas pedal, and the rescue team needed his help freeing him from the wreckage. Our son is not a small guy, and here he is with a 6-foot board through his upper body that could only be removed at a trauma centre because of the high risk of him bleeding out.

Mathematical measurements later showed the location of his hand on the steering wheel had created a 45-degree angle, which cut his fingers but not cutting off his hand or arm. Had the driver's seat not miraculously pushed back at the precise moment, he could have been decapitated.

The board had now been taped to his body by the paramedics to keep it from moving, and he was carried up on a stretcher where the ORANGE helicopter, which had only been reinstated in that area a few days prior, was ready to transfer him to the Sudbury Health Sciences North. He clearly recalls asking the Paramedic if they thought he would lose his arm. She replied that there was more concern that he would lose your life. The ½ hour flight would be very painful because of the wind. The Paramedic told him not to move!

Looking up to the sky and heavens, he recalls an awareness that ministering angels were flying all around. He hummed the Liverpool Football Club Song - You'll Never Walk Alone.

When visiting the wreckers later in his recovery, the shocked tow truck driver said, "I feel like I am seeing a ghost; at the time the paramedics were shaking their heads, not expecting you to live, when they carried you up to the road."

The Paramedic had notified the hospital, making them aware that a significant trauma case would be arriving, the patient having been in an accident after passing an oncoming truck hauling an RV trailer going in the other direction. The vehicles didn't touch, but the empty trailer swaying over the line was just enough to catch the front corner of the driver's side of our son's vehicle, setting this catastrophic event in motion.

The only Orthopaedic Surgeon available in the hospital that afternoon would use a cast saw to cut off the end of the foreign body that was sticking out of the patient's shoulder, not knowing that in it was a sharp, steel rod. Our son was warned he must lie perfectly still, as the slightest movement could cause the board to shift. Had it been mere centimetres to the left, it would have gone straight through his heart and to the right, it would have severed the artery. When successfully removed, he went directly to the Operating Room, where the 1st of two surgeries would clean the wounds of Styrofoam, fibreglass, and shards of wood.

The doctor told us our son's miraculous survival was amazing. If the accident had not been fatal, the impalement could have been. Our son walked out of the hospital ten days later by God's grace. The road to physical recovery has been slow and challenging, with physical limitations moving forward. The impact on the mind and emotions after experiencing trauma of this magnitude has been significant.

Much later, on a visit to the site, our son's business card was seen tucked under a boulder below the bridge. As followers of the Lord Jesus, we believe God was indeed there to protect our precious son at the Shadow River Bridge, clearly showing God's Divine Intervention in this now sacred space.

Janie Brooks

The Power of Prayer

The day is still with me. It was after Hurricane Fiona flew through Nova Scotia. Many trees had fallen or were about to fall on my property. About ten pine trees, at least seventy-five feet tall, were damaged and needed removal. Many trees had hit power lines in our area and we were without power for five days. My heart ached for those trees. I needed to cut the trees leaning toward the ground for safety as well as the fallen trees.

I hired the 19-year-old son of my handyman. He brought a best friend. Both were devoted Catholics and home-schooled on their parents' farms. They are impressive young men and very hard-working. I asked them to cut the trees to about three feet in length, as I wanted to save the time and money preparing them for firewood. I instructed them to stack the wood. The already fallen trees were easy for these young men who wore blue jeans, cowboy boots, and T-shirts but no safety equipment, only earmuffs, gloves, glasses, and baseball caps. As farm boys, they were adept at cutting trees and preparing wood for fencing, fireplaces, or wood stoves. I kept an eye on their progress, and when all the fallen trees were cut, I joined them to determine which leaning trees were the highest risk.

One tree could fall toward the family's front lawn and the young children's play area. What happened as this tree was being cut down was beyond my imagination. One young man stood on a stump, which stood upright (about three feet tall) and reached as high as he could to cut a top section of the tree. Instead of the tree's top section falling with each cut, dropping down next to the cut standing section, the young man walked over and stood on top of it to cut the next section, which also stood in an upright position! What? One time, sure, but two times, unlikely. That would be a fluke. But this happened several times! It was unbelievable! I kept saying, this can't happen again. I looked with amazement after each cut with awe as it also stood upright. I remember telling friends, I had several cords of wood in the field and the story of this one tree. Unbelievable! Time went by before I visited my neighbour. We chatted about the number of trees we each lost. Then she commented that she had seen the two young men cutting the tree. She could not believe they did not have safety gear, like safety helmets and steel-toed boots near her front lawn. My neighbour said all she could do (and did) was stand in the window praying constantly for the safety of these young men. If the tree had fallen like they usually do, it would have caused a severe accident since the boys were working so close to each other. One could have been pinned under the falling section. We chatted about how the tree fell at a safe length and kept falling upright next to the last cut section. Each section stood like fence posts perpendicular to the ground.

We giggled and spoke of how incredible that was. She responded, "My prayers must have worked!" Yes, indeed! Wow!

The power of prayer. I knew it was something I didn't understand that helped that day. My joyful heart imagines several angels playing their part. These young men were kept safe when a terrible accident could have happened. I thanked my neighbour for her prayers and still marvelled at the power of those prayers.

Mary George/Suzanne Wilkinson

The Sovereignty of God

It's a challenge to decide on a specific story to share of God at work in my life. I need to take more time to pause long enough to reflect on the countless ways that I know God has intervened in my life to teach, guide, and protect me over the years as I have followed Him. As a result, I have chosen to reflect on God's sovereignty.

God speaks to me through Scripture to guide, direct, encourage and comfort me whenever I open His Word. He also speaks through people, music, nature, history, love, and uniquely and ultimately through His Son, Jesus Christ.

God has supreme authority and sovereignty and rules over all His creation, and He determines the outcome of all things according to His divine purpose. He shares His sovereignty in perfect unity and cooperation with His Son, Jesus Christ.

In John 6:1-14, Jesus expressed His sovereignty by displaying His power, revealing His deity, and calling people to a saving relationship with Himself in the story of feeding the five thousand. In this passage, I discover that Jesus does not need me to accomplish His sovereign plan, but by His grace, He invites me to join Him in His work so I might experience the blessing of yielding to His good purposes. God's sovereignty gives comfort, peace, and direction and meets my needs despite whatever personal difficulties I may be experiencing.

The great crowd followed Jesus for what He could do for them, not necessarily seeking Him for Himself. This tendency is prevalent among many, including myself, to seek Him for what He alone has the power to do rather than seek after and believe in Him for who He is.

At times, I, too, have responded to life's challenges as Philip did with a sense of hopelessness at what I once considered to be an enormous problem and, as Andrew did, emphasizing an insufficiency of resources and mistakenly surmising that a solution to a given situation is impossible. And yet, I find comfort in knowing that Jesus already knows what He plans to do amid that specific challenge so I can experience His sovereign power and provision.

Though Jesus could have easily multiplied the meagre provisions of the five loaves and two fish Himself to feed the five thousand, He did not. Instead, He seized the opportunity to teach us to come to Him with our needs and trust Him to provide.

Jesus taught that all good things come from God the Father. I am encouraged but also challenged. How do I express thankfulness to God for all His blessings? Do I consistently reflect an attitude of dependency for all He provides for me each day? Jesus answered Andrew's question, "How far will they go among so many?" with something far more than anyone could ask for or imagine. As I offer what I consider meagre offerings of time, talent, and treasure to Jesus, He provides and multiplies the little to accomplish much more significant than I could have thought possible for His glory.

Though I may face circumstances that fail to make sense and challenge me, I trust in my all-sufficient Savior, who has power over the laws of nature and can do something supernatural to provide much more than needed. Eph. 3:20 says, **"*Now to him who is able to do immeasurably more than all we ask or imagine, according to his power that is at work within us.*" (NIV).**

Jesus is my help, enabling and providing for me amidst whatever supposedly impossible things I may face as I trust Him. I come to Jesus for who He is, not just for His miraculous works, and trust in Him for eternal salvation and with all my needs and find He provides abundantly more than I could ever ask or imagine.

Scott Wilkinson

There is Nothing Impossible for God

There is nothing impossible for God says Maureen Coles as she bravely discovers a new world. Here is the story of what happened to Maureen Coles, a Torontonian, back in the 80s. She credits God for her life and the ability to carry on with her home duties and teaching career. Catherine Dunphy wrote an article published in The Toronto Star on August 27, 1987, about this fantastic recovery from a deadly viral brain infection. A few thoughts from that article assist me in telling Maureen's story.

.I have known Maureen for over thirty years and witnessed her exceptional recovery and faith. She has had to re-learn how to function in our world because of her memory impairment, having suffered from encephalitis.

At first, Maureen did not know her husband. She did not know what a husband was. She insisted she had five children and did not know the one and only daughter she had.

She did not know where the basement of her house was, how to get to it, or even why she wanted to go there. "I felt as though I had left one world and gone to another," recalls Maureen. A vibrant, energetic, dedicated teacher, wife, and mother had suffered from this often-debilitating disease of encephalitis, a virus that causes brain inflammation and a condition that can hit hard. It can lead to death or severe neurological impairment, resulting in lifelong limitations.

This neurological severe illness occurred about forty years ago when Maureen Coles was forty-five. Since then, she has lived in a brave new world. New because Maureen suffered some memory impairment and, in the beginning, had to re-learn the difference between soap and detergent, deodorant and radishes, and that teeth needed brushing. She could not drive a car and had to memorize bus routes and learn to walk around the block for some exercise.

Fortunately, Maureen could recognize people, although not places, and often not events, or even if she had read a particular book before. Some people with encephalitis cannot recognize people. She says, "I am lucky, not just lucky but blessed. Recognizing people is an important thing to know."

Even in her weakened state, she prayed, believing that 'nothing is impossible for God', and then she moved forward courageously, step by step. Without faltering, doubting, or complaining, she credits God for His transforming and healing power every inch of the way. Maureen has lived knowing God's power, relying on it, and has felt it at work.

Truthfully, she would prefer to be in our everyday world, but Maureen has accepted that she will never be able to live in that old world again. However, she has discovered ways to live fully in her new world. Her faith deepened as a follower of Christ in ways that would not have happened without this devastating illness. With courage and determination, her journey to wholeness followed as day by day, her physical, emotional, and spiritual well-being has almost entirely returned.

Maureen, a petite woman with sharp features and a kindly manner recalls, "I have great difficulty relating an object to the word for it," Maureen recalls. Visually, the object did not live up to what I imagined. I preferred that imaginary world. The real world was a great disappointment at first. But I could relate better to books because the imagination had free reign. What helped me most, Maureen says, besides the therapy and memory exercises patiently taught by her family, was books.

When she first left the hospital, she remembered her life-long love of books but not those she had already read. At first, reading one paragraph gave her a headache, but with God's help, she persisted, and soon she could read a page in one sitting, then a chapter and then the whole book. She would open a book she thought she had not read only to discover that her memory would come flooding back, and the entire story would appear in her mind. Maureen said, "Eventually, all I needed was the first page to bring it all back. The more I read, the more my confidence returned."

After months of re-learning the nature of the natural world, she eventually returned and was welcomed back into her educational role as a teacher-librarian. Her memory at that point was poor. She had made a slow yet remarkable recovery but had a distance to go.

' Doctors have been amazed that Maureen has returned to good health and resumed many of her former duties. She says that encephalitis has made her a better teacher of children. Maureen had to learn how this world works and how to get around in it, just what children are experiencing as they grow up. She was re-learning and doing it for the second time and at a fast-forward pace. Maureen remembered the wonderful feeling of learning, the same feeling this teacher wanted children to experience when Maureen steered them to books suited to their age. She needed a spark to ignite her memory, not just with books but with her home duties, self-care, and ability to take the bus to school when she returned to work.

Now, more than ever, Maureen has a unique perception of a slow learner. She's been one herself, not as a child, but as an adult. Her encephalitis left her disoriented and almost brain damaged. It forced her to re-learn, like a newborn child, both the denotation and cognition of words from the beginning.

Along with time spent with therapy groups and her supportive family, and with Maureen's perseverance, improvement slowly came. Their husband, Rod, a surveyor, and her daughter, Jenny, then 11, were helpful and patient, never complaining as she worked at re-learning and repeatedly recalled things. They hid their fears the first time she headed out on the bus or left the house to walk around the block. They were afraid she would get lost, and she did a few times, but eventually, she endured it till even those basic things came back to her memory.

She clutched an area map and navigated to a local shopping centre. She was never shy at asking God or a passerby for their help to head her in the right direction. She would methodically write down what streets she would pass on the way and cross off the names of the roads on her 'to-do' list to know where she was and when to get off the bus. Eventually, the big day came when she took the bus and subway to her doctor's office in downtown Toronto. "Yes, it was frightening," Maureen said, but she knew God was with her, and so were her loved ones and some helpful friends.

Years passed, and progress came slowly for Maureen; she got her license back to drive at the appropriate time. She leans heavily on her GPS/Tom-Tom to tell her where to turn. She still lists what she must do and items she must remember, carefully crossing things off her list once completed, feeling a sense of accomplishment after a busy day. She credits God and people who have sparked her memory to ignite and recall something she needs to remember or to learn. Such recalls set off a chain of memories flooding back to an experience she once had. Maureen is ever grateful to God for the memory she now has acquired that was once lost.

As I mentioned, I have known Maureen for some thirty years now. She is a fantastic woman with a dynamic faith, well-read, and enjoyable with whom to share mutual interests. We have prayed together and discussed books, news items, or present-day events. The one thing for sure that she will say at any of our chance meetings is, "There is nothing impossible for God." She gives God the glory for her returning memory, which is almost complete. Maureen is one octogenarian who is a delight to know as she has such a living faith and close relationship with her Saviour, Jesus.

We live in a time when humanity has more potential than ever before. Unfortunately, it is also a time when we risk losing everything that matters. With so many, it appears that integrity is an uncommon quality anymore. We have never had so much information, yet misinformation runs rampant. Lies are commonplace, but not with Maureen. What Maureen, what one sees is what one gets.

For those who believe in Jesus, nothing is impossible with God. For Maureen, this is not just a religious quote; it's powerful and practical. Accepting this truth means we can live without fear and trust that everything will work out for the best in God's will.

We can find peace in any situation with faith, knowing He guides us through whatever may come. What we experience only makes us stronger spiritually. Suffering may only sometimes make sense to us at the time. Yet, with the bigger picture in mind, there is a purpose in God's ways for good for those who believe. Many examples throughout the Bible exist where people do extraordinary things by believing in God.

Humans alone cannot change God's plans. We cannot change our destiny through the power of our will or strength. However, when we pray and let God work in us, God will render beautiful works in keeping with His perfect character and design. During creation, God called all things into being. He continues reconciling fallen humanity to himself through the shed blood of His Jesus, His son, on Calvary's cross.

Even if we think something is impossible, it will become possible as we work towards a goal with God's help, believing that all things are possible in His divine will. What we need is faith! God is the God of the possible. Maureen Coles knows and credits Him as He can do anything if one perseveres, seeks His will and believes.

In Hebrews 11:1, we read, **"*Now faith is confidence in what we hope for and assurance about what we do not see.*" (NIV).** Faith is simply believing in what you can't see and trusting God to work out His will. When you believe in something with all your heart, it shows through your actions. One's effort and courage are evident. The Christian life is a testament to how great God is and how great His power is.

Let us be God's ambassadors, shining a light for others to know Him, as Maureen has done through her difficulties. She has said, "Oh, that they may know our awesome and faithful God". The Bible encourages us to believe and make Him known. The Scriptures teach us that anything is possible when we believe in God's power and trust Him in His ways. Take what seems wrong and turn it around for good with God's help. Let us show our world how loving and powerful God is when we have faith in Him.

The story told by Maureen Coles written by Suzanne Wilkinson

"For nothing will be impossible with God." (Luke 1:37 NIV)

Three Yellow Roses

I had just finished officiating at a funeral at Pine Hill Cemetery, where I had been the on-call clergy for about a dozen years. The family I served had received many floral tributes in honour of the deceased, as it had been a large funeral. After the service, as I was leaving, the deceased's spouse gave me a dozen beautiful yellow roses as a thank-you for the service. I was most grateful for this tangible and kind gesture from this family.

As I drove home, these lovely yellow roses were beside me in the front seat. I thought of who to encourage by sharing them. I needed to pick up a few groceries, so I pulled into the local Plaza, where I usually shopped at the Value Mart grocery store.

As I did, a strange thought kept swirling around in my head. I felt this strong urge - not just a mild suggestion but a directive to take three yellow roses with me into the store. I questioned what I would do with the roses once I got there, but I did as I felt urged.

Once I had obtained my purchases, I headed to the checkout counter. In front of me, an elderly lady was having her order processed by the cashier, whom I had known for several years since I shopped there regularly.

Again, I felt a strong urge that this was the woman I was to give these flowers to. So, as she was about to leave and the cashier had almost finished with my order, I turned and offered these beautiful roses to this stranger.

The woman accepted the yellow roses as her face beamed with delight, and tears entered her eyes. She turned to thank me. I did not know this lady, and the cashier did not seem to know her either.

This lady told me, after we both had left the store, that her husband had died several years earlier, and that very day was her 85th birthday.

Her dear husband had always given her yellow roses on her birthday. Three yellow roses were especially significant to her because they represented his love. They spoke to her, saying, "I love you," extraordinarily and tangibly.

As we parted, she told me she had never shopped at that grocery store. We both marvelled at what had just happened. She thanked me profusely as we put her groceries into her car. God told me to do something unusual by taking three yellow roses into the grocery store that day.

The lady who received the roses said to me that those roses (uniquely yellow ones) were a message from her deceased husband, sending her his love from beyond the veil. She felt it was an assurance that he was safe in God's presence.

Since then, each time I see that cashier, she reminds me of this story. She questioned why I had placed three yellow roses on the checkout grocery belt, and then she saw a little miracle of how a kind gesture brought great happiness through tears of joy to a stranger. It was no credit to us that this touching, unexpected moment came about through a chain of events that God orchestrated.

All three of us were awed by this experience. This is a brief but true story of God's actions in our lives. The thanks go to God. I first appreciated the roses from the first widow and marvelled at how God made sure they blessed another widow that same day. It was a privilege to have been God's messenger of love to a dear lady on her special birthday.

Suzanne Wilkinson

Totally Equipped

With my Bible, study book, pens, and highlighters inside my black purse, I was all set and equipped for our "Experiencing God" Bible study by Blackaby.

Our small group leader warmly welcomed us and gave us an overview of the study. She shared her experience, *"When I did this study a couple of years ago, two of the ladies in our study group* made a huge change in their lives. They both quit their jobs. One even went to move her entire family to a different province."

I was amazed at the testimonials but did not take them to heart.

Within eight months, we went through the seven realities of experiencing God.

1. *God is always at work around you.*
2. *God pursues a continuing relationship with you that is real and personal.*
3. *God invites you to become involved with Him in His work.*
4. *God speaks by the Holy Spirit, prayer, circumstances, and the church to reveal Himself, His purposes, and His ways.*
5. *God's invitation to work with Him will always lead you to a crisis of belief that requires faith and action.*
6. *You must make significant adjustments to join God in what He is doing.*
7. *You come to know God by experience as you obey Him, and He accomplishes His work through you.*

Little did I know that I would truly be experiencing God through this study.

I found myself in a crisis of belief as God was calling me to join Him in His work in helping those who are in great need. Of course, I wanted to join Him, but a major adjustment in my life was needed. There, I faced the reality of leaving my real estate corporate job. I was earning good money, great benefits, travel perks, bonuses, and professional growth in this job. I had a plan: to be a CEO. But now, I had to choose to leave all these comforts to work for a charity that offers a low salary, no benefits, no travel perks, and no bonuses. I didn't even have the professional experience to work in the industry.

Some friends and family members were concerned. We had three high school children who would be going off to university. It did not make sense for me to quit my job to go to something that would pay less. How could we afford to send our kids to university?

Then, I heard God saying, *"Don't you have faith in me, my child?"*

Oh, that's right! My God is Jehovah Jireh!

He says, ***"But seek first His kingdom and His righteousness, and all these things will be given to you as well."*** **Matthew 6:33, (NIV)**

"Okay, Lord. You might provide, but I am not qualified and equipped to pursue work in the nonprofit world." I was waiting for a response from Him while I was lying on my bed. I tilted my head towards my bedside table and saw the sign I got from the Divine Women's Conference I attended a few years back. The word "Equipped" was written in bold letters on it.

I was not the only one who felt unequipped when God called. Moses was called to the daunting task of delivering the Israelites from Egypt. Joshua argued with God's direction, stating he was only a youth and could not speak to the rebellious nation of Israel. Esther feared approaching the king to save an entire nation. But God equipped each one of them.

God sent Aaron to be Moses's spokesperson, using a staff and a cloak to perform miracles. God put forth His hand and touched Jeremiah's mouth. God gave Esther the courage to go before the king.

God promises that if we believe and obey Him, He will reveal what He wants done and equip us to accomplish it. Philippians 2:13 says that God Himself *" is working in you, giving you the desire and the power to do what pleases him."* (NLT).

So, I trusted God and obeyed Him. Just like Moses, I had to come to Him every step of the way. I am goal-oriented, so I had two items on my list to guide me in my job search.

1. It needs to be a Christian organization.

2. The office should be close to home.

And I also wrote * *that it would be great if it's a work-from-home.*

I spent hours, days, and weeks searching through job postings. I narrowed it down to one Christian organization working in West Africa, Ghana. It's a work-from-home job.

Initially, I did not make it on the shortlist of candidates. I got feedback from the Chairman suggesting that I should get more experience in the fundraising field if I hope someday to lead such a function in an organization like theirs. I took his suggestion seriously, but since I had a full-time job, I was only in the position to learn about fundraising through reading books and online resources and attending free webinars. I did not apply for any other job. Still, I kept praying to God for guidance and continued learning whatever I could about fundraising.

A month later, I got an email from the Chairman saying that those on the shortlist are no longer on it for different reasons, and he has decided to consider other potential candidates. He noted that my name keeps coming to mind despite me needing more qualifications.

God led me on a two-month journey of leaning on Him until I was offered to be a part of His work in Ghana.

Since I had no experience at all with fundraising, I knew I had to present something to the Chairman during our in-person interview. God has equipped me to use my talent for marketing. I came to that meeting ready to show a fundraising plan to the Chairman. When I handed it to him, he looked at it and was silent for minutes. Then, he asked me, *"How long did it take you to do this?"* I said that from that day I had the second interview with him, I started doing in-depth research on GRID (Ghana Rural Integrated Development), and during my 'go' train rides, I was working on the plan. He commented that the plan was a good five-year plan. Well, God's hands were guiding me all the way to create that fundraising plan.

Finally, in January of the year after, I met with the founder and his wife for my final interview. Honestly, it did not feel like an interview. They even invited my husband to join in. We had over two hours of what I call fellowship. Over a sumptuous lunch at a Swiss Chalet, God has shown me how this fantastic couple whom

He called to join in His work in Ghana were like me. God called two ordinary people first. They obeyed. Then He equipped them along the way.

I've been with GRID for over five years now. God has shown me the many miracles He was doing in the lives of dear friends in Ghana. God, through GRID's ministry, has rescued thousands of mothers and babies whose lives have been freed from the bondage of poverty and witchcraft; a hospital was built in the middle of COVID-19, and His Good News has spread into the hard-to-reach villages.

As I look back from day one to now, I'm amazed and blessed by how God has equipped me every step of the way as I navigated an unfamiliar and unchartered line of work, as the world calls it. For me, it's a calling! For the first time in my life, I can confidently say that I am good where I am. Why wouldn't I be? God called me to this, and He has equipped me and will continue to do so.

Can you hear God's calling? Answer Him. And don't worry, He will equip you! ***"Now may the God of peace who brought again from the dead our Lord Jesus, the great shepherd of the sheep, by the blood of the eternal covenant, equip you with everything good that you may do His will, working in us that which is pleasing in His sight, through Jesus Christ, to whom be glory forever and ever. Amen."*** **(Hebrews 13:20-21, NIV)**

Ochelle Baller

Transformative Experience – Holds Me Fast

In the fall of 1964, I lived in a rooming house in Banff, Alberta. My "room" was a bed and dresser behind a curtain, separating me from the communal kitchen in the basement, shared by two other men, Nick and Frank, who had their own rooms. The Ukrainian owners lived in the rest of the house. I enrolled in Grade 12 at Banff Composite High School and worked 20 hours a week at Norquay Motors Esso Station on Banff Ave.

I was in high school in Banff because I didn't think I could finish Grade 13 in Ontario while working on the farm, being involved in my local church in the youth group, being a deacon, and dating a new girlfricnd. I was influenced by Rev. Dr Sidney Hillyer of First Baptist Church, Claremont, to finish high school, attend university and become a minister (I told him, "You are crazy!"). Still, after attending a Conference on Christian Leadership at McMaster Divinity College in April 1964, I thought it might be possible.

I wrote a letter addressed to "Principal, Banff High School," asking "how much tuition should I have to pay to attend while boarding in Banff?" and Miss Gratz wrote back, "I have enrolled you in September, and it won't cost you anything." I wrote a letter to my former boss at Norquay Motors Esso, where I had worked in the summer of 1963, asking if I could work part-time during the winter, and he wrote back: "You come and work for me, and choose your hours."

So, on Aug 23, 1964, at age 20, I said goodbye to my girlfriend Margaret and hitch-hiked to the West with my 15-year-old brother Ken. After arriving in Banff, Ken took the train back to Ontario. I found a rooming house on Banff Avenue and enrolled at the High School. But throughout the fall months, I was troubled:

"Have I done the right thing in leaving my family to go to school in Alberta? Do I have the 'smarts' and the 'gifts' to be a minister? Have I really been "called" by God?"

I had many discussions with Nick and Frank, who had their own kind of 'worldly wisdom'. I had letters written to Margaret at that time in which I expressed the emotional and spiritual pain I was going through, and she encouraged me to keep praying and be patient.

Then, on the evening before I turned 21, on my knees at the bed, I was reading through the Psalms as prayers and suddenly came across these words from Psalm 139 (NIV):

1 O Lord, you have searched me and known me.
2 You know when I sit down and when I rise up;
you discern my thoughts from far away.

3 You search out my path and my lying down
and are acquainted with all my ways.

7 Where can I go from your spirit?
Or where can I flee from your presence?
8 If I ascend to heaven, you are there;
if I make my bed in Sheol, you are there.
9 If I take the wings of the morning
and settle at the farthest limits of the sea,
10 even there your hand shall lead me,
and your right hand shall hold me fast.

17 How weighty to me are your thoughts, O God!
How vast is the sum of them!
18 I try to count them—they are more than the sand;
I come to the end—I am still with you.
23 Search me, O God, and know my heart;
test me and know my thoughts.
24 See if there is any wicked way in me,
and lead me in the way everlasting.

It was like a bolt of lightning went through my body – I began shaking. Then, suddenly, I 'understood' – and with it came a peace of mind that has never left me through over 50 years of ministry. Words fail to describe the experience, but the confidence that God is with me no matter the circumstances remain a stabilizing hand to "hold me fast" to this day.

Rev. John Torrance

When God Chooses to Remain Anonymous

August 15, 1953 dawned much like any other sunny summer Saturday. As I prepared to leave that afternoon for Guelph Summer Bible School, where I had been before, I had no idea that my life would begin to change forever by that evening.

I had offered my services to work in the office for the next two weeks, and one of my duties was to enrol new 'students' by assigning them to a specific cabin, giving them blankets, and most importantly, a name tag - a great way to get to know others quickly.

During the afternoon, Ron Adams (who was totally blind from birth) came in with a friend, and since I had met him the previous summer, we greeted one another as acquaintances. After assigning him to Cabin 8, I told him who his cabin leader would be, gave him his name tag and blankets, and he was on his way to the cabin.

I didn't think much about it as I busily enrolled others who came - some for the first time - to this amazing place where young people in their late teens and twenties gathered in August each year to deepen their knowledge of Scripture and meet others who would help them to grow spiritually. Many re-dedicated their lives to the Lord during their time at Guelph. Our teachers were high-calibre and dedicated to helping us on our journey.

That evening, I was sitting at the dinner table near Mr. Horace Lockett (the principal of GBS - Guelph Summer Bible School), and when Ron came in with a friend, he sat nearby. The conversation was animated and enjoyable.

Somehow, we found ourselves sitting together the following day for church. I'm not sure how that happened. I do remember that we also sat together for lunch. As the week evolved, we seemed to be in the same place at the same time, and by the end of the first week, we were seen together often on the grounds.

I vividly remember how impressed I was with his outstanding piano playing, and I later learned that he already had his ARTC diploma from the Toronto Conservatory of Music. He was the accompanist of choice for anyone singing a solo during those two weeks. As the end of the second week approached, I asked him what his plans were for the fall. Having just completed the requirements for a General Arts B.A. at Western University in London, Ontario, he said he'd like to go to Toronto to seek employment. He had a friend in Toronto whom he felt might be able to help him do so. Since he had nowhere to stay when he arrived in Toronto, I asked if he'd like to share a room with my brother. A quick phone call to my mother confirmed that he was welcome to do so. (She had met Ron on a previous occasion.)

It didn't take long for him to connect with his friend, who arranged an interview for him at Heintzman Piano factory, and he was hired as a "fine tuner," meaning he would be the tuner to give all pianos their final tuning before leaving the factory for a piano store. He soon found a boarding place with another friend, which could have ended my seeing him. But it wasn't!

He chose to continue to attend the Gospel Chapel, where my family worshiped and where he had gone with us while he stayed in my parents' home. It didn't take long for him to become the pianist for the services and then a Sunday school teacher for pre-teen boys.

During the fall, we always saw each other on Sundays and sometimes chatted on the phone during the week. Since nothing was seriously progressing, I arranged to visit Vancouver with a friend to see the West Coast and stay for a year if things worked out.

Ron was shocked and more than a little upset when he found out this information. That was at Christmastime, and we were planning to leave in February. There isn't space to give all the details of a whirlwind romance; suffice it to say that by the time Grace and I went to Vancouver in February, he had talked me down to a six-month stay rather than a year! After six weeks, he phoned me to say my mother wasn't well and felt I should come home. Was it a reason or an excuse to get me back? I think a bit of each.

Jumping ahead and leaving out lots of details, I came home on April 19, and we were engaged on May 19. We planned our wedding for September 11, 1954. Many people wondered "if I knew what I was doing." No, I didn't realize how wonderful and fulfilling it would be to live the next several years with the most selfless, considerate, godly, generous, and loving man I had ever met.

By 1957, he was approached and asked if he would be interested in returning to the Ontario School for the Blind in Brantford, where he received his elementary and secondary education, to become the Instructor of Piano Tuning and Music Theory. He accepted and enjoyed a fulfilling career there for the next thirty years.

Ron and I had two wonderful daughters, Marney and Sharon, who adored their father. He was a fantastic role model. After retirement, we moved to Newmarket, Ontario. We had a wide circle of friends in Brantford, and it wasn't easy to leave them. However, we returned frequently to visit, and with the telephone, we kept in touch with others.

After 55 3/4 years together, Ron was ready to "go Home," as he put it, and on June 23, 2010, he went to his Heavenly abode. I thank God every day, forever, for putting him in my life; he made me the person I have become. After thirteen years, I still miss him keenly, but I have so many beautiful memories in my mind and heart. So, I repeat – "Coincidence is when God chooses to remain Anonymous!" Thanks be to God.

The following lines were written by one of my husband's colleagues, who, after she had addressed the graduating class in her moving retirement speech, quoted these lines she had written about her students.

> When **my** eyes close - however soon this be
> And all the world and life are lost to me
> My latest thoughts will turn in love to thee
> Who, lacking sight,
> Yet, it taught **me** how to see.

My sentiments exactly.

Ruth Adams

When Joseph Awoke from a Sleep

I can't remember most of my dreams. Perhaps it is the same with you. And I have never put a lot of stock in what I dream. Swiss psychiatrist and psychotherapist Carl Jung taught that "dreams are a way of communicating and acquainting yourself with the unconscious"[1]. Dreams are a window to your unconscious mind and can solve your problems in your waking life. It seems this way for Joseph, who was wrestling with a problem in his personal life: What to do about Mary?

199

I note that dreams have played a role in the story of the Bible. In addition to Joseph's dream, Jacob had a dream of a ladder to heaven; Jacob's son, Joseph had a dream that was a source of disquiet with his brothers; the Egyptian Pharaoh had a dream that Joseph interpreted; Daniel interpreted the Babylonian King Nebuchadnezzar's dream; the Apostle Peter had a dream of a net with animals let down from heaven; the Apostle Paul had a dream about a Macedonian that helped him change course on his missionary journey.

The thing about these Biblical dreams is that God acts through them to deliver a message to the one dreaming. The other thing I noticed about these Biblical dreams is how memorable they were. The recipient was clear about the dream, which stood out to them as significant. I don't think Joseph, for example, was waiting for a dream to know what to do. Joseph has already decided what he thought was the best action for himself and Mary.

I suspect that Joseph wasn't in the habit of letting his dreams be his guide in the usual course of his life. I am not saying that dreams are of no consequence; I am just saying that I don't rely on them for decision-making. And Joseph doesn't appear to do that either, given that we are told that he was a righteous man and wanted to do what the word of God directed him to do. So, he decided to divorce Mary quietly.

The story indicates that something compelling happened in that dream. It was not of an ordinary sort. Joseph knew that God had addressed him through an angel of the Lord, and he knew what he was being asked to do right down to the name he was to give Mary's child.

Do you ever wake from a dream and are glad to be awake and know it was only a dream? When Joseph woke up, would he think it was only a dream? What will he do? His response tells me that what happened in that dream has stamped itself so indelibly in his heart and mind to render him certain about what he must do.

Matthew 1:24-25, NRSV – "*When Joseph awoke from sleep, he did as the angel of the Lord commanded him; he took Mary as his wife but had no marital relations with her until she had borne a son; and he named him Jesus.*"

As I think of this story, I can't help but imagine Joseph's conversation with Mary shortly after waking from his dream. I can picture him going to see Mary, and Joseph begins to speak, in a place where the two of them are alone, "Mary, I've got a story to tell you." And out tumbles the details of this dream and Joseph's commitment to proceed with the wedding. I can hear Mary finally be able to tell her story and confide in someone who won't think she is crazy.

So, Joseph took Mary's baby into his life and when He was born, named him Jesus.

During worship, perhaps at a Candlelight Service on Christmas Eve, you experience the palpable sense of God's presence— Someone is calling to you, wrapping your heart in the warmth of His presence. It is hard to put the experience in words—it is, well, a dreamlike moment.

If you will, permit me a question: what will you do when you wake from this dreamlike moment? Will we take Jesus into our lives as Joseph did? We, too, have heard the angel's message about this child. He is not only for Joseph but for all of us.

It is in the name. Joseph was to name Him Jesus, for He will save His people from their sins. The name 'Jesus' means' God saves.' As for many Biblical names, the name speaks of the reality of the person's identity or what they will do or become. The gospel writer Matthew doesn't want us to miss the point and cites the prophet, Isaiah, "*Look, the virgin shall conceive and bear a son, and they shall name Him Emmanuel,' which means, 'God is with us.'* (Isa. 7:14, NRSV). Jesus is God's saving.

The story of the Virgin Mary conceiving tells us that the world's Saviour won't come from within the ranks of humanity. Our Saviour must be given to us, and to receive this child into your life is to receive Him as your Saviour. Yes, it means that we each need saving, and for most of us, amid the struggles of life, the need is readily evident. He will save us from our sins.

So, when we awake from the dream, like that of Christmas, will we, like Joseph, take Him into our lives? For Joseph, this meant adopting the child, confessing the child to be his own and being the earthly father to the world's Saviour.

Our response will be to confess Him as our own and serve the Saviour in the places and responsibilities of our lives.

"Christmas is a precious beacon of light entering into a world of darkness, the real world that we inhabit, when we are willing to be aware of it. Even with our comforts, medical miracles, and prosperity, this world remains a vale of tears, as it always has been. Christmas, Easter, Thanksgiving, Communion, and other special times in the Christian calendar challenge us. It is not just a matter of letting go of our pinched spirits and ungenerous hearts, throwing our hats up in the air in joy, and letting our generosity overflow into gifts and feasting. It is God's invasion of our often sad and diminished world. He is performing an intervention."[2]

In the quiet of our hearts, God again is calling, perhaps not through the angel just as He did to Joseph but calling in our lives today. My prayer is that each of us will be able to respond as Joseph. Name Jesus as your own, for He saves us from our sins.

Rev. Dr. James Clubine - Luke 1:26-38, Matthew 1:18-25, Luke 2:1-20, adaptations by Rev. Suzanne Wilkinson, from a sermon given Christmas Eve, Dec. 24th, 2023, with written permission. Adapted from - Wolfred M. McClay, The Challenge of Christmas. [1] Jung, Carl - 2000-2014, Dream Moods

Amazing, Astonishing Grace

Though a three-year-old child can understand it, it is so profound that there are many PhDs, MENSA-gifted people with great intellect who are incapable of grasping it because it scales the drizzliest heights and plumbs the ultimate depths of God's revelation. Our Heavenly Father still reveals His amazing gift to those who accept it.

It is truly incredible. It is, indeed, the very heart of all the Scriptures. I write about something genuinely astounding. It is a word with which everyone is familiar. We have heard it hundreds of times in our lives. It is not a complex theological idea like transcendentalism, esotericism, or supralapsarianism; it is a simple single-syllable Anglo-Saxon word: <u>Grace.</u> But it is profoundly important, for the Bible says we are "saved by grace."

One person said, "Oh, I know what it means." I said, "Well, tell me, what does it mean?" He said, "Well, I knew, but now that you ask me, I.... I don't know." It is truly astounding that many can't easily define it.

You may set your jaw, lean forward and strain, and determine that you will be able to understand it simply because I have thrown down the gauntlet. I have challenged your intellect, but I am telling you that some of you will not get what I am telling you. Unless the Holy Spirit of God sovereignly decides to reveal it to you, you won't understand it. I pray that the sovereign Spirit of God will work in many hearts.

What exactly is "grace"? When our sons were little boys, I read children's books to them. My favorite is by that inimitable author, Dr Seuss, entitled *"If I Ran the Zoo."*

You may remember Dr. Seuss saying, "If I ran the zoo, here's what I'd do." He describes the most incredible, astonishing zoo, with creatures the likes of which nobody had ever seen. It would be unique and different from any zoo before or since.

I thought: "What if Dr. Seuss wrote the Bible?" What if some of us wrote the Bible? Likely, we would write the main message in a straightforward sentence. According to the average person, we would write: "Good people go to Heaven, and bad people go to Hell."

I heard that opinion expressed this past week at a 'Celebration of Life." The message in so many words was, "Good people go to Heaven, and bad people go to Hell." Why, that sounds perfectly proper. That seems fair and just, what most people believe. In fact, after twenty years as a minister and a lifetime of work in a caring profession, that is what most people think.

"No. No. That is not the way it goes." You say Christianity is not fair. Unless you grasp that, you don't know what the Bible is about or what grace is."

203

Justice?

Of course, "fair" can mean different things. Just and equitable can mean other things as well. For example, you give a man a ten-dollar bill and ask for change. If he gives you nine dollars back, we would all agree that that is unfair. But let me ask you this: Suppose you asked him for change for your ten-dollar bill, and he gives you nine million dollars back. Is that fair? You say, "No, but I'll take it."

It is in that sense in which the Gospel is not fair. It is super fair. It is vastly higher than fair. That is what grace is about. It is not fair. Someone said, "Well, what's wrong with the idea that good people go to Heaven and bad people go to Hell?

The problem you must face is that there are no good people. The Bible says, "*There is no one righteous, not even one*" (Romans 3:10). "*...there is no one who does good, not even one.*" (v. 12b). "*Indeed, there is no one on earth who is righteous, no one who does what is right and never sins.*" (Ecclesiastes 7:20, NIV).

When the Bible talks about somebody being good, it is talking about him being good from head to toe, through and through, all together, heart, mind, soul, strength, thought, words, and deed. But there is none who is good. No. Not one, the Bible says.

Let's look at the thesis: "The good people go to Heaven, and the bad people go to Hell." If you are not good, you are bad, and if there is none good, no not one, where will everybody in the world end up? You've got it. In Hell, which is where we belong. It is what we deserve. And that is the problem. That is what we deserve.

Because of that problem, God devised the most unique and wonderful plan the world has ever known. It is called the Gospel of Grace. Grace is not justice. It is not equity. It is not "fair." It is very different from that. It is not a *quid pro quo. So* many hours of work for so much pay: that is not grace at all. A *quid* has no adoration nor a single hallelujah in a *quo.*

I recently spoke with a woman who had gone to church for years, but she quit going. I took a deep breath and asked her about her hope of eternal life. She said, in effect: "Bad people go to Hell, and good people go to Heaven, and I'm basically good." There it is, a *quid pro quo.*

The person who doesn't attend church or never learned of God has never experienced God's grace. That is why they don't go. It has nothing to do with staying home and reading the papers on Sunday. It has nothing to do with "that is my only day off." It concerns God's amazing grace, which has never changed their heart.

Love?

So, grace is not justice. You say, "I'm beginning to see it now. Grace is just another word for love. Right?" Wrong. It is not. There is an element of love in grace, but it is not true that all love has an element of grace. One might say, "You, sir, have fallen in love with the most gorgeous, beautiful girl you have ever met. Not only is she exquisite to look at, but she also has a personality to match. She is lovely inside and out. She is thoughtful and kind, and not only that, but she also even thinks you're exceptional. So, you decide to do something very, very gracious. You marry her. Are you not a marvellous person? "By grace, I am married." That is ridiculous. She is altogether lovable. That is not grace; that is love. Or, if that doesn't convince you, consider this: The Bible tells us, *"Love the LORD your God with all your heart and with all your soul and with all your strength"* (Deuteronomy 6:5, NIV). Therefore, if we love God, that is grace. That has absolutely nothing to do with grace. God infinitely deserves far more love than we could ever give Him. So, you see, love reaches down to the unlovely.

Mercy?

"I've got it," you say, "it is mercy." Well, you are drawing nearer, but you are not there yet. No doubt there is, in grace, a downward reach. But that is still not grace.

This story may illustrate grace: a Russian nobleman travelled from one town to another during winter over ground covered with snow and ice. He and his servant had travelled hundreds of miles in their dogsled. They were drawing closer to home - maybe twenty-five miles away - when the servant looked back and spotted a black patch on the horizon. A shiver goes down his spine because he knows what that means. It is a pack of wolves that have caught their scent and now are closing in on them.

They give the whip to their dogs to urge them on, but little by little, the patch of wolves grows close. They are fifty yards away and now twenty. They can see their red eyes and the saliva dripping from their lips and tongues. The wolves are already savouring their lunch!

There is no hope. They are still miles from home. What can they do? Panic fills their hearts. Then, suddenly, the servant throws himself off the dog sledge. The wolves converge on him to strip away the wrapping so they may get to their lunch while the nobleman makes it safely home. Is that grace? No. It is not grace.

Grace?

Let's change the story some more. This servant is not a faithful servant but an envious man who has stolen from his master. Not only that, but he has also worked with others in a plot to murder the nobleman's son. The nobleman discovers this plot and grieves the loss of his only son. Now, he is next to this treacherous, murderous servant who has killed his only son. It is then that the nobleman throws himself off the sledge to save the life of this deceitful murderer.

Now, *that* is grace. It is not justice. It is not even mercy. It is not love. It is undoubtedly not merely mercy to the unloving, but it is mercy extended to those of ill deserving, to those who are Hell deserving. That is what grace is.

Unless you have come to see yourself as that treacherous servant who has conspired with the rest of humanity to murder the Son of God, who has stolen from your master and unless you have seen yourself as that undeserving, Hell-deserving servant, you can never experience the grace of God.

We often sing "Amazing Grace" at funerals and other celebrations. Do you hear what you sing: "Amazing Grace, how sweet the sound that saved a *wretch* like me." Have you seen yourself as that wretch? That ill-deserving person that we are.

Christ came to seek and save the lost. Until you come to see yourself as a lost, unprofitable servant, a wretch, you cannot experience the grace of God. I hope the Spirit of God has opened your eyes to this truth-" *For it is by grace you have been saved, through faith—and this is not from yourselves, it is the gift of God—not by works so that no one can boast.*" (Ephesians 2:8-9, NIV).

Why?

I wondered why Christ would do that. Then I discovered this verse that says why God would extend that grace: "*In order that in the coming ages he might show the incomparable riches of his grace, expressed in his kindness to us in Christ Jesus.*" (Ephesians 2:7, NIV). God ever seeks to reconcile fallen humanity to Himself.

This world doesn't operate by grace. It works on a *quid pro quo* at best. But God, whose ways and thoughts are far above ours, is a God of grace, and He offers us forgiveness for our sins, many of which we have forgotten.

If you take wet mud and throw it against a picture window, it hardens and stays there. When God looks out at us, He sees the mud of our sin through all the years of our life, through words, deeds, and thoughts, through omission and commission, and yet He loves us enough to send and sacrifice His only Son. If you have not experienced that grace, in Christ's name, I invite you to receive God's perfect, sacrificial son, and receive the gift of God, which leads to eternal life.

Some will say, "Well, there is no such thing as a free lunch," and I say, "You are right. Somebody else paid for the lunch." Is it different in theology? Not at all. Someone paid for that free lunch upon Calvary's Cross. On the Communion Table are emblems representing His broken body and shed blood, the payment for the free gift of eternal life. It is available for all who believe.

The stories shared throughout this book testify to God's love, presence, provision, power, and ultimately to His amazing grace. If you don't know of God's grace, accept it today. Believe in the sacrificial death of Jesus Christ, God's perfect son, given to reconcile us with our Heavenly Father. Christ paid the debt we owe. God's grace is a free gift leading to eternal life for all who will accept this wonderful truth.

Prayer: *Father, speak to our hearts, and if there are any whose minds You have opened, who have understood what an amazingly loving Heavenly Father You are, may readers say, "Lord Jesus, undeserving as I am, I come to You. Teach me Your ways that I may trust and follow You." We thank You for revealing Your presence through the many writers contributing their stories. May each reader feel embraced by Your love and light, and may we glean from their stories how ever-present and loving You are in Jesus. We bring our praises and express our gratitude to You. May this book encourage others to keep the faith and help us to draw closer to Jesus, the Redeemer Saviour, in whose name I pray. Amen.*

Rev. Suzanne Wilkinson

"One thing I ask from the Lord, this only do I seek: that I may dwell in the house of the Lord, days of my life, to gaze on the beauty of the Lord and to seek him in his temple." (Psalm 27:4)

**Thank you for reading this book of treasured stories.**

Consider giving _Embraced by God's Love and Light_ as a gift to someone who is searching for spiritual truths or experiencing life challenges. This book does what a good book should do: it makes you think about life and your relationship with God in a new and fresh way. In our spiritual blindness, we may not recognize God's presence, but He is ever offering us love and light for our journey.

We are not alone. Jacob at Haran proclaimed, _**"Surely the Lord is in this place, and I was not aware of it."**_ **(Genesis 28:16, NIV).**

Treasure life and live in the expectancy of God's presence, and you may experience many heavenly encounters and be _Embraced by God's Love and Light._

Has God been speaking to you or encouraging you? If you are interested in resources to further your faith journey in Christ, speak to a Christian minister or please consider the following https://billygraham.org/grow-your-faith/ or write to me at 2bkind2u2024@gmail.com. I will assist you in your Christin journey of faith in every way I can.

If you have a treasured story of your experience with our triune God, or know of such an experience, please write it out and email it to me. I would be delighted to receive your stories and possibly include them in a sequel to this book.

Be blessed to be a blessing to others!

Suzanne Wilkinson

Embraced by God's Love and Light is a beautiful gift of reassurance, comfort, and encouragement. Over eighty authentic stories tell of enthralling encounters with God. These stories bring hope in unique ways. It is a must-read and a treasured gift.

Be enthralled by this collection of inspiring stories of people who have experienced God in a tangible, memorable and often transformative way. Awaiting you is a reservoir of refreshment, evoking courage, endurance, and unquenchable hope.

Embraced is full of interventions with our triune God, whether through dreams, circumstances, experiences or with others. It is a compelling read.

A trustworthy source of strength awaits you in *Embraced*. This book has uplifting, heartwarming, and thought-provoking stories amid joy or sorrow that need guidance, healing, protection, endurance, refreshment, courage, or comfort. You will treasure this delightful book with value far beyond its covers.

Anticipate within stories that integrate genuine faith with real life. The sovereign God of the universe makes Himself present to the storytellers who share their memorable encounters. These are tender stories of joy and sorrow, poignant reminders of all it means to be alive and loved.

Beneath the smiling faces is the lonely cry for God, whether amid a need for an answer or the touch of a warm embrace. God comes to provide His presence for a wounded heart, the needy, or the fearful. God knows, cares, and comes in unique and unforgettable ways.